AMID THE HAZE

Hazel & Maeve: The Campus Mysteries, Book Two

Jessica Cranberry

A NineStar Press Publication

www.ninestarpress.com

Amid the Haze

© 2023 Jessica Cranberry
Cover Art © 2023 Jaycee DeLorenzo
Edited by Elizabetta McKay

ISBN: 978-1-64890-671-8

First Edition, July, 2023

Also available in eBook, ISBN: 978-1-64890-670-1

CONTENT WARNING:
Depictions of graphic violence via murder, college/sports hazing rituals, beatings, bullying, slurs; smoking/substance abuse, strong language; discussion of trauma: mental and sexual abuse, assault and non-consent, (past, off page), depression, misogyny/misandry, death of a family member (past, off page), suicidal ideation.

"Set at the dawn of the internet age, *In the Trap* is a fast-paced campus mystery complete with one dead body, an anonymous chat room confession, and a burgeoning attraction between two appealing female sleuths, intent on navigating not only campus life but also solving a murder. I enjoyed the subtle indictment of the "boys will be boys" mentality as the university attempts to cover up a series of assault crimes and found myself hoping Jessica Cranberry is already hard at work on the sequel."

—Maggie Smith, author of *Truth and Other Lies*.

"A lonely introvert on an idyllic college campus finds her life upended, first by violence, then by a website where students reveal their darkest secrets, including abuse, assault, and murder. Jessica Cranberry's *In the Trap* grabs readers at the start and doesn't let go until the surprising, tense, and satisfying ending. A definite must read!"

—Merry Jones, award-winning author of *Child's Play* and *What You Don't Know*

In the Trap is a taut, satisfying campus thriller--a throwback to early aughts college days of online diaries, coffee and cigarettes, and "me too" whispers replied to with shouts of "it could be worse" or more commonly "what was she wearing?" Jessica Cranberry isn't afraid to dig deep into the dark aftereffects of trauma, and what happens when we come together to prevent it. Hazel is a compelling heroine whose strength lies in her vulnerability and resolve to do right, and I hope we haven't seen the last of her.

—Lauren Emily Whalen, author of *Take Her Down* and *Two Winters*

"Maybe there is a beast...maybe it's only us."

—William Golding, *Lord of the Flies*

Prologue

Maeve

April 7, 2001

COOL BLASTS OF April air blew her hair around the car, swirling around her head, whipping against my cheek every now and then. It had grown longer, the weight of it suppressing some of her natural wave. We were headed to Indy—just the two of us. Behind us had been hours and hours of nothing but long, straight road, pumping music, those crispy, fried, onion-flavored chips, and countless cigarette butts streaming out the windows as I drove full throttle across I-70. Acres of farmland surrounded us, mounded rows extending beyond the horizon, prepped for corn or soybean seed, until a new city emerged with tall buildings cutting through a span of sky and a falling orange sun. As we navigated through downtown, through the maze of asphalt and concrete, the open fields fell away as if they ceased to exist.

Hazel flicked the radio off and lit another cigarette. She'd started smoking again, and I wasn't going to complain about it. That probably made me a shitty friend, but I was glad to have a smoking buddy.

"I brought you something." I reached into the backseat blindly, keeping my eyes on the road, and felt around in my bag until my fingers grazed the thin pages of the city news-paper. "Check out page three."

Hazel unfolded the *Ledger Dispatch* and found our story, the one Gayle Jackson had interviewed us for, detail-ing last autumn's campus murder of Ryan Newsome (ass-hole and sexual predator, although most media outlets left those bits out) and how we'd pieced it all together...not to-tally unscathed.

"Good for her. She said she wasn't going back to the *Echo* after they canned her last year." Hazel carefully re-folded the paper along the creases as if it contained nothing more than the crossword.

"You're not gonna read it?"

"I know how it ends."

Hazel hadn't gone back to school after Newsome's mur-derer attacked us. She needed time to heal—physically and emotionally. We all did. But I couldn't escape the feeling something else was keeping her away, distant. Before today, I hadn't seen Hazel since October, the morning I'd followed her into the police station to give a statement. We'd been emailing back and forth, but neither of us ever mentioned what had happened all those nights ago—what it had been like seeing her blood soak through her clothes, fear as thick as fog, a death so close you could taste it on the air like the salt and sand of a new shore. No, we'd skirted around all of that.

It didn't stop me from wondering how she felt or what she thought about it. Hazel could be a bit of a mystery to me. Most folks I could see right through, not her. She kept everything wrapped up so tight inside herself, I didn't think I'd ever break through. And maybe that was okay. Maybe even better than okay.

"I haven't been in a real city for months. I forgot how pretty they can be," she said. "All the bustling around. Life, I mean, you can see it happening." Her cigarette bounced with the motion of her lips. She tucked it between her fingers and blew out a long, lingering exhale as though she'd been born knowing how to do that.

"Have you been here before?" I asked.

"As a kid, we hit up the children's museum."

"Really?"

"Yeah, when my parents... We used to live right on the border of Illinois and Indiana."

I still couldn't believe it took her so long to tell me what she'd lived through. But knowing the ways people have been hurt changed relationships—sometimes for the better, sometimes not. So I got it; she didn't want pity anywhere near us.

"You're a regular child of the corn, then, huh?" And this seemed to be how we handled the big traumatic things, poking fun around what caused the most pain. Joking. Deflecting. Sidestepping anything that hurt.

"I told you my middle name, didn't I? It's Malachi."

I laughed and pressed the cigarette lighter. Hazel instinctively reached for the pack in the cup holders and got one out for me. I rolled down my window just as the lighter popped back up, its coils burning orange and hot.

"Do you know where we're headed?" she asked.

"Not really. I printed out a MapQuest for it though. It's in the glovebox."

She took out the directions and spread the folded papers over her lap. "What street are we on?"

"Ohio."

"We're close. If you can find a place to park, do it."

Brake lights glowed red in front of us. I slowed down and watched the last of the sunset, streaking pink and purple behind the high-rise buildings of the Midwestern city. The air smelled of exhaust. I followed the inching traffic into a parking garage.

"You think all these people are going to the same place we are?" Hazel asked.

"Maybe? She has a following."

By the time I parked, night had fallen. Streetlights clicked on and cast the sidewalks in a tangerine glow. Hazel folded the directions and tucked them in her hoodie pocket.

We ended up not needing the map. A decent-sized crowd of mostly women seemed to all be going in the same direction. We just fit in and followed. As we got closer, a line had already formed, and we waited, stuck behind a rowdy group of college-aged kids with dark lipstick and short flowery dresses. They were probably the same age as Hazel and me. They seemed so much younger, though, with all the laughing and the squealing.

Hazel surveyed them; her right eyebrow cocked the way it always did when she tried to puzzle out someone's behavior. I handed her the silver flask I'd slipped in my jacket pocket. Elbowing her, I told her to relax.

"I'm relaxed," she said and took a swig of the peppermint schnapps.

Spring flowers and just...joy scented the air. Yeah, that was it. Joy. After such a dark year, I barely recognized the feeling. The line shuffled forward. Ani DiFranco's name, in black block lettering, stood against the marquee's glow.

"I can't believe you scored tickets," Hazel said.

"I told you we should go."

Hazel's expression lightened whenever I pressed Play on *Living in Clip*, and in the middle of all the shit that had gone down at school last fall, there'd been a notice in the paper about this tour. I figured right then and there I'd pay whatever price to get Hazel to this show if we made it out of that mess.

"I didn't really think it would happen. Especially, in the middle of...everything."

"So, how've you been dealing with all of that?" Asking was a risk, but I wanted to take it. While I gave her a pass on talking about her family, I needed to know about this because the nightmares hadn't stopped for me. I still woke up in a sweaty panic, Shirlee's glowing glasses disappearing and reappearing like pieces of the Cheshire cat.

Hazel shoved her hands into the pockets of her hoodie and stared at her feet. "Honestly, I don't know that I am." Her eyes met mine. "I just ignore it mostly."

"Me too." Time heals all wounds. Unless it didn't.

She fiddled with her hair, braiding the ends absentmindedly. We moved forward a few more steps. At the double doors, security guards shined flashlights in purses and patted down coat pockets.

Hazel pushed her hair back from her face. "I feel kinda frozen in place, ya know?"

"I do."

"Aunt Liddy says not to rush anything. That everything will settle back to normal in time. But what if it doesn't?"

"Maybe this is the new normal."

"Exactly."

"They haven't filled your space in our dorm yet. You could always come back."

"No. I withdrew."

"You did?"

She laughed in that self-mocking way she had sometimes. "You know I'm not meant to be anybody's teacher."

The thought of her surrounded by little kids made me laugh too. "There are other programs."

She shook her head. "I don't belong there. I knew it on day one. The only good thing that happened was meeting you and Doug."

"You guys still talk?"

"Yeah, through email mostly. Like with you."

"That's cool." But my heart said, *Oh*.

At the front of the line, an elderly security guard asked me to turn out my pockets. After she felt sure I wasn't carrying a weapon, I stepped into the theater lobby.

Gilded: that was the best way to describe the old lobby. Thick and lush maroon carpeting added an honest-to-god spring to my steps. Its floral pattern led to three partitioned sets of stairs. I stood under the chandelier, waiting for

Hazel. She came through security smiling her real smile, the one I hadn't seen since we'd sat on the banks of the Skullkey and gotten high.

"This is amazing," she said.

"I know, right?"

Ticket masters stood at the top of each stairwell. We climbed up the center, and I handed our tickets over. The lady tore off an edge and gave me back the stubs, tossing out a set of quick directions I could barely hear.

We followed the crowd past the main theater toward another room. Here, there were no seats, standing room only—the more to dance in. I grabbed Hazel's hand and led her closer to the stage. *This was going to be an experience, damn it.* I looked back to catch her expression as she tucked her hair behind her ears and examined our surroundings. She was probably busy making snap judgements about the people around us and locating the exits.

"Are we going all the way to the front?" she yelled over the din of the crowd.

"You know it," I answered.

I got us as close as possible. I found a spot nearly center stage, next to the girls who'd been in front of us in line. They were still very bouncy and squeaky, but when the lights dimmed, an excited hush ran through everyone. For a second, I'd forgotten I was still holding Hazel's hand, but she squeezed it when the stage lights came on. Faces glowed in the light that remained, but hers most of all.

She let go of my hand to clap as some of the band members came onstage and lifted their instruments into their arms. A stray beat from the bass drum filled the room. The musicians jammed for a few minutes, playing a rhythmic string of notes that weren't quite a song yet, until Ani jogged onto the stage.

Her voice evoked something in me. Something feral and wild. Something that came before the constraints of *this* world. One of my favorite songs floated through the speakers. The whole crowd cheered, then danced. My body, her body, their bodies: we all moved together and apart, like a living, breathing organism. And it went on and on, song after heart-thumping song. Until the band slowed things down, playing a quieter melody.

The audience swayed and sang along. The words of "Untouchable Face" haunted the room.

Hazel's eyes glistened, her cheeks flushed, strands of her hair stuck to the sweaty sheen covering her skin, but she smiled. I touched her arm. And she looked at me, wiping her cheeks.

"Thanks for this," she said, coming in close so I could hear.

"You're welcome." I wanted to suggest something, but I didn't know how she might react. *Who am I?* I never worried about that kind of thing. Most of the time, I relished any reaction. But with her, I hesitated. Worried. I motioned toward the back, where only a few fans loitered along the walls. A crease formed between her eyebrows, but she followed me.

Standing there, with the music still filling up every inch of the room, I brought her closer. The heat radiating off her met the heat radiating off me. I could've kissed her, but I had something else in mind—stupidly.

The song ended, and the band rested for a few beats, riffing with one another through Ani's introductions of each member.

"I think we should fill out those applications Detective Patterson gave us," I said.

"That's what you wanted to tell me?" She scoffed, then trained her eyes back on the stage. "You want to switch schools?"

"The program looks promising, and they have a police academy built in," I explained as if she hadn't read the brochure.

"Do it. There's nothing stopping you from switching programs, Maeve."

She didn't get it. What I knew for sure, after everything we'd been through together, was that the feeling of us working together, fitting the puzzle pieces of a campus murder together, was something I wanted to hold on to.

"I want us to go together, Hazel. I don't know how to...*process* what happened last fall, but I loved working with you. I felt alive for, like, the first time."

She bit her upper lip, exposing the top edges of her bottom teeth. She wasn't making eye contact, which was purposeful. Everything was purposeful when it came to Hazel. "You know how I feel about all of this."

"Actually, I don't because we never talk about it." I felt a little trapped, panicky. I'd gotten myself into this conversation, and now I had to go right through the middle of it, whatever the outcome. Hazel saw through the moments when I manipulated people; she must've seen that was *not* what I was doing now. I wanted this, and I needed her. "We might be able to do good, help people, set things right. Didn't you enjoy working through the mystery of it? I fucking did."

"I did too." She glanced back at me. "It's funny you're bringing this up."

"I don't think it's funny. This is what I want, and I want to do it with you."

"Good." Hazel reached for her back pocket and brought an envelope folded over many times. "Because I got my acceptance letter last week."

"Shut up!" I shoved her playfully.

She stepped back with the momentum, laughing. "I have to pass a physical, then start next fall. If you're going to join me, you better get that application in quick."

"Why didn't you tell me? You said you didn't know what you were gonna do."

"I *still* go back and forth about whether I'm actually going to go. Not totally convinced police work is for me. Plus, I want you to do your own thing, follow your own path— whatever that is. But if you're into this, I think...so am I."

The band picked up the set's pace, starting up another fast song. With the music blaring, we had to keep coming in close to talk, practically screaming in each other's ears.

"I don't want to talk you into anything you don't want to do!" Hazel yelled.

I moved in, near her ear again. Her brown waves, glowing pink in the changing stage lights, brushed my cheek. "So, we're doing this?" I asked. "Together?"

"Yep, together." Her eyes met mine.

What did I see there? Her seriousness, her willingness to just be who she was without really caring what others thought, her sense of humor that no one else knew about. A future.

September 7, 2001

4:22 a.m.

There's a dead body in our basement.

Chapter One

June 20, 2001

I SHIFTED THE car into Park and turned off the engine. Jennifer Lopez's "Love Don't Cost a Thing" stopped mid-chorus. The quiet neighborhood bordered the north side of Oakley University. Trees lined the sidewalk, their leaves swishing in the warm breeze.

"Which one is it?" I asked.

"That one." Hazel indicated a set of row houses across the street. The end unit on the corner had a bright red For Rent sign posted in the front window.

"Looks cute."

"It just has to be livable," she said.

"Well, right. But cute doesn't hurt either."

We'd already been to five different apartments, looking for a place we could move into as soon as possible. Nothing had been perfect, and Hazel provided a detailed list of every flaw as soon as we'd gotten back into the car. Sometimes it seemed that was all she saw—all the ways in which something might not work out. Most of the time, I found it endearing and liked how it put me in the role of disproving her, but not today.

Coordinating apartment hunting had been difficult. With her still living in Lima and me forty minutes outside of the city, we had little way of knowing what was available—most rentals only advertised in the *Echo*'s classified section, and the one's showing up online were way outside our price range. But Hazel had worked it out with Doug. She crashed at his new place—an apartment complex called University Village where a lot of second-years ended up because of its proximity and shuttle service to campus—until we checked finding shelter off our to-do list.

Hazel tucked the newspaper into the passenger door side pocket. The *click-clack* of our seatbelts sounded as we unbuckled and got out of the car. We walked toward the brick row house, and I checked out the front porch, picturing a set of matching lawn chairs, lengthy late-night conversations, cigarettes, and cheap wine coolers being doled out between the two of us on that stoop.

"I like the little porch," she said.

"What?" I nearly stopped in my tracks. "You like something about this place?"

"Shut up."

"No, I do too." I linked my elbow around hers. "This could be the one!"

She gave me a smile and a sideways glance. I let go of her arm, and we climbed the cement steps. I knocked on the screen door, and a woman with an antique beehive hairstyle answered the door.

"Hi, we called about the apartment. Hazel and Maeve." I gestured between the two of us.

"Come in, come in," the woman croaked, and even I could smell the after-smoke clinging to her hair and clothes. "You saw the ad—two-bedroom, one bath, four-fifty a month. Have a look around. I'll wait outside."

Dark hardwood planks lined the floors. Tall windows let in tons of light. The front living room led seamlessly into a back dining room—open-concept style, although historically, it had probably been separated by a set of interior French doors. A closet-like galley kitchen sat off to the side of the dining room. A plain metal sink and yellow Formica countertops ran the length of one wall. Through the window in the back door, I spotted a gravel path, an alleyway stretching behind the row houses, and then another house directly behind us but facing a side street, and another and another, all lined up in a row. Hazel stepped toward an avocado-green refrigerator; next to it was a second cutout, another doorway. A dankness lingered at the threshold.

"Smells like a basement," she said. "Follow me. I don't want to go down there alone."

We carefully plodded down a set of planked stairs, running our hands along the scratchy brick as we progressed. The temperature dropped considerably. A single bulb hung from the ceiling. Hazel pulled the string, and the light didn't do much to alleviate the creepy, damp space. Chipped and peeling white paint covered the walls. Dried-up rivulets marked the floor where water had leaked through in rainier months. Mold pocked one corner.

But there were not only washer/dryer hookups but also

an actual set. On-site laundry that didn't require hoarding every single quarter that came our way? A real bonus, an impossible find.

We left the basement and tracked back through the main floor. In the front living room, another set of stairs led to a second level with two bedrooms and a full bath.

I leaned toward Hazel and murmured, "This is practically perfect."

"I know," she said, inspecting a window seat overlooking the street. "Can I have this room?"

"Fine with me. How should we handle this?" I'd never rented anything before.

"We tell her we're interested and get a copy of the rental agreement. Aunt Liddy said we'd have to put down a deposit."

"Do you want to think about it? Sleep on it?"

"No. This is it. I can feel it."

"Same."

It was a great place listed at a fair price; anyone could nab it. We weren't the only two people apartment hunting for fall quarter.

We walked downstairs and found the landlady on the front porch.

"So? What do you think?" she asked, smoke billowing out of her mouth.

"We want it," I said.

"What's the next step?" Hazel asked.

"Here's the lease application and a copy of the lease. Look 'em over. Fill it out and return it to the address listed. If you're approved, I'll call you and set up a move-in day. You'll get the keys then. First and last month's rent due upfront."

"That's it?" I looked over the paperwork. It seemed to be written in a different language.

"That's it, sweetheart. You two students?" The woman turned away from us and locked up the place.

"Uh, yeah. But not at Oakley. We're going to the community college—the police academy."

She eyed us carefully. "Stay safe, girlies." Then she tossed her cigarette on the sidewalk, ground it out under her sandal, and walked away. "And no smoking!" she yelled before disappearing into a giant green Cadillac.

"Well," I said, watching Hazel survey the neighborhood. "What do you think?"

"Let's do it."

"Cool. Then let's find a place to fill all this out." I handed her the lease application to check over.

We hopped in the car and after a short drive, pulled into the parking lot of a nearby fast-food restaurant. Inside, young people, summer-school students, by the looks of their heavy backpacks, had formed a line. At our turn, we ordered two small chocolate soft serves and french fries, then found a table to fill out the paperwork. Snippets of nearby conversations filled the dining room. I dipped a fry into my ice cream while Hazel scrounged in her purse for a pen.

"This is exciting." After skimming over the legalese, I filled in all the little boxes and signed my name on the line next to Hazel's. Then, I noticed her face. "What? Are you having second thoughts?"

"No, no." She tore open a ketchup packet and squirted it onto the paper mat in the tray. "I'm just thinking about rent and food and stuff. Two hundred twenty-five dollars is a lot each month."

"We decided 450 dollars was in our price range."

"At the top."

"I don't know what you're worried about. You've got the—" I clamped my mouth shut. *Damn it*. Bringing up her inheritance, something I only knew about because I'd overheard her aunt casually mention it, was stupid. That money had come at the cost of her whole family, and my dumbass didn't need to go bringing it up over ice cream. "Sorry."

"It's okay." She waved it off. "It's mostly true." She stared out the window, people-watching. "I still have to be careful. Insurance never paid out. So it's just their savings I'm living on."

"If it's not money, then what are you worried about?"

"Nothing. Everything. The usual." Her gaze came my way, and she smiled.

"Hazel, we turn this baby in"—I fanned myself with the lease—"and we are on our way toward having our very first apartment. It's going to be great."

"You're right. I know you're right."

"You doubt me?"

"No. It's just all new." She bit her lower lip. "I'm not like you. All balls to the wall. It takes me time to, like…calibrate change."

"Take as much time as you need. In the meantime, we need to talk furniture."

"My aunt has a couch she's getting rid of—oh look, there's Doug!" She knocked on the glass and waved, capturing his attention. He waved back and made for the restaurant front door.

Doug. The guy had put his life on the line last year when

Shirlee Hensen had worked out her own little revenge fantasy and taken out a campus predator. She hadn't taken kindly to Doug the night we all confronted her. But it'd been Hazel who ended up in the hospital. She'd been the one to leap into action like a superhero. *Time to calibrate change*, my ass. She knew exactly when to make a move.

Doug stood in front of our table, his cologne overpowering the fryers. "How'd it go? Did you find a place?" he asked.

"We did." I indicated the lease and tried to ignore the way Hazel looked at him. Officially, they'd gone on *a* date last year. After Hazel left Oakley, the two of them had kept in contact through email or instant messaging or whatever. But I didn't know their *status*-status. The past few days, when I'd come to pick her up at his apartment, there'd been times when their body language crushed my rib cage. She could have stayed at my parents' house with me had I had time to ask. But Doug had already suggested his place and she'd already accepted before I could even offer. So for now, I refused to check if she had stars in her eyes.

"Cool. Mind if I..." He slipped his backpack off and put it in the seat next to me before either of us could say anything. Not that we would. He reached for Hazel's fries—which was usually my job—and she swatted his hand, telling him to get his own. I considered it a win until the two of them laughed about it like it was some long-standing inside joke.

I couldn't help but roll my eyes, and then I reached into my bag and pulled out a dollar. "Here." I plunked the cash on the table.

"What's that for?" Doug asked.

"So you can get your own fries."

"Oh, no. That's not really—"

"Take it."

He looked at me, his eyes unsure, brow furrowed, a flush creeping up his neck. It meant I'd overstepped, which had been my goal. Something about my behavior was too much, too direct, too brutally honest, and it threw off his game. I'd gotten that look a million times in my life and loved it most of the time.

"You offered up your place to Hazel so we could do this; it's the least I can do." I tamped my tone down a bit.

"Okay." He drew out the last syllable, showing both annoyance and how much he didn't want a confrontation.

Once he stood in line, Hazel turned to me. "Why'd you have to do that?"

"What?" I shrugged and spooned ice cream into my mouth.

"That *thing* you do. Making people feel uncomfortable. Putting them on edge." She seemed genuinely frustrated.

"I gave the guy a dollar. That's hardly telling him to fuck off."

She laughed, and her features softened. "Just go easy on him. He's a nice guy." Her dark-brown eyes flicked back toward him. He waved at her and smiled.

Once we moved back to campus, their relationship would likely heat up. It was a gut punch of a realization especially with the lease staring up at me from the table. Hazel and I were going to be roommates again, and while last year we'd been randomly assigned to each other, this year had been a choice. And no one chose to live with someone they had unacknowledged and unrequited feelings for...except me.

Day 760

From Within the House

It'd been a long time since I went missing. To all the people who loved me, I'd become nothing more than a ghost. Even to myself, I thought that might be true sometimes. My skin might have gone translucent, my bones no longer taking shape or space. Of course, that was how my whole life had felt with Him anyway. He'd stolen everything from me except this spirit. That, I'd stolen away before He consumed all of me.

But at what cost? Even this meager existence I considered priceless. I'd stayed in the shadows, sneaking throughout the house, stealing bits and pieces of food and clothing, money for the summers when the house became vacant. Living and hiding and thriving within the walls of this old house. And for what? An option. Such a simple word, beautiful on the tongue when I forced myself to say it.

Chapter Two

July 31, 2001

MOM HAD GONE all out, cooking a feast for my last night home. In the kitchen, she filled our plates with grilled chicken, spanakopita, and her rosemary flatbread. She loved cooking and had mastered a lot of Dad's family recipes a long time ago, although my yaya definitely had smart-ass comments about a non-Greek person *mastering* anything Greek.

My immediate family, all loud and laughing, surrounded the dining room table. The room felt heavy and cramped, filled with the seven of us and all my mother's dated furnishings: glossy, lacquered dining table and upholstered chairs, cherry-stained china cabinet, floral-patterned wallpaper, and vertical blinds covering the patio doors. My three older brothers—Nicolas, Patrick, and Evan—talked about some European soccer thing with Dad. We all shared

Dad's dark, thick hair, brown eyes, and at least one dimple located in either a cheek or a chin. Only Evan had inherited Mom's ability to freckle; the light dusting of spots covered his nose and cheeks every summer.

Yaya came in, her steps shuffling, and whacked Dad on the back of the head. "Enough with the sporting talk! I want to hear from Maeve."

Nicolas and Patrick rolled their eyes but shut up. No one ignored Yaya.

Evan, closest to me in age, caught my gaze. They were all worried about the police academy thing. They'd made it clear the moment I brought home the idea. Mom had burst into tears, and Dad got all red in the face. My brothers told me it was dumb, that I'd get my ass handed to me. Really, they'd all handled my coming out as bi better.

I tore my flatbread. "What do you want to know?"

"Where'd this crazy idea come from?"

They all knew what had happened at Oakley last year. My parents had delicately filled Yaya in on the big details, but she wanted to hear my reasoning right here at the dinner table, the night before I moved out forever. Straightforwardness must be an inherited trait.

I swallowed the bread. "Yaya, we've talked about this."

"I want to hear it again. From you. One more time." She pointed her slanted, arthritic index finger my way, then sat in the chair next to me. She smelled like baby powder and hair spray.

I shrugged, a lame attempt at trying to make the explanation seem less dramatic. "My friend and I were involved in an investigation last fall, and I liked it." I always left out the "murder" part of the story when talking to Yaya.

"Gathering information, organizing it. Felt like something I might be good at."

"You know who else does those things?" Nicolas offered up an answer before I could. "Librarians."

I glared at him and scratched my nose with my middle finger. The oldest of my siblings, Nicky had always been really good at reminding me who I was supposed to be. As kids, hanging out with all three of my brothers had been the dream. But by Nicky's rules, it turned out to be impossible. Girls couldn't play Nerf wars or hang out in secret big brother clubhouses. Girls were always left behind, according to him. His poor fiancée... But she wasn't here today; none of the girlfriends had been allowed. Mama had been explicit when she invited my brothers home for this dinner.

"Stop it, Nicolas." My mother, at the head of the table, elbowed his arm. Nicky gave her the *What did I say?* look we had all perfected at an early age. But he stayed quiet. She rarely put up with his bullshit.

"Why police work, dear?" Yaya asked.

"The stakes. The stakes are high." I surprised myself with that answer.

"But a cop?" Evan asked. "It's so dangerous, Maevey." Sweet, caring, more thoughtful than our older siblings, Evan was my favorite brother. He'd tried to include me as we grew up, even if it meant hanging back from what Nicky and Patrick were doing.

"She'll probably spend most of her time handing out parking tickets," Patrick said.

"We don't know that," Evan countered. "You could end up in some really dangerous situations. And god, the academy. Do you know what those guys are like?"

I had an idea.

"That's true," Nicky said. "Patrick, didn't that guy in your class join up?"

"Who?" Patrick asked through a bite of chicken.

"You know, the one that was always beating the shit—"

"Language," Mama interrupted.

"Sorry, Mama. Beating the crap out of kids after church."

"David Kufos? He's messed up, man. Always looking for a fight."

"Well, he's a cop now, right?"

Patrick shrugged. "I guess."

"Point is, a lot of those guys have an axe to grind. On a power trip, most of 'em."

"You mean like you," I said and stabbed a piece of chicken.

"Aw, fuck off—"

"Language!" Mama yelled, her fork clattering against her plate.

"I'm just trying to look out for ya," Nicky huffed.

"No, you're not. You're trying to tell me I shouldn't do something because I'm a woman. That I should be scared of all the big bad men around me."

Nicky rolled his eyes and muttered, "Here we go..."

"David Kufos has always been an asshole and whatever job he ended up doing has nothing to do with my future," I finished.

"It will though," my dad said quietly. He sat at the other end of the table and kept his gaze trained on his meal. Everyone stayed quiet, anticipating more from him. But he didn't offer up anything else. The sound of his knife scraped against his plate. Yaya patted his forearm, and the two shared a long, knowing glance.

"As long as our Maeve is happy, no?" Yaya held up her glass of wine, and everyone followed her lead, sipping until the tension dropped a notch or two.

The wine scorched over my tongue and down my throat, right along with their judgement, its flavor unique and difficult to describe. They all thought cop school wasn't meant for me, but what if Patrick or Nicky had signed up? I'd put money on it not being a big deal. My mother gave me a close-lipped smile and winked.

Then the conversation shifted, and all that was left unsaid stayed that way.

*

AFTER DINNER, I helped clean up the dishes and then excused myself. I had to finish packing and wanted to avoid getting dragged into another conversation about my chosen career path. Because in truth, I had my own doubts. Everything my family felt and said had already crossed my mind at least twenty different times. And at some point, I realized I'd based the whole trajectory of my life on last year's tragedy. Possibly not the best of ideas. But what could I do about it now? The plan had been made. The paperwork turned in. And Hazel...well, she was counting on me to be her partner through all of it.

I zipped the last of my clothes into a suitcase, then grabbed some of my favorite books to take with me: Dad's worn copy of *To Kill a Mockingbird*, one title from my *Sweet Valley High* collection. As I placed them on top of the last box, a soft knock sounded at the door.

"Come in." I knew it would be Mama, and I wasn't wrong. She had a dish towel draped over one shoulder, and she'd kicked her shoes off. Her stockinged feet quietly sank into the carpet.

"All packed up?" she asked.

"Just about." I avoided eye contact because I wasn't sure what I'd find there. My gut said this would be her last stand, a final attempt to talk me out of this.

"Good." She sat on the corner of my bed. "You know the boys, your grandmother, they're just worried about you."

"Dad too?"

She nodded. Her curls, crinkly and stiff, fell forward as her head bobbed.

"What about you?" I asked.

Somehow, she had the ability to frown and smile at the same time. "Terrified."

"Great," I muttered, shoring up my resolve for a big lecture.

"But I trust you, baby. You've been certain about who you are and what you want since day one."

My stomach dropped. I hadn't expected her to say that. Maybe if she'd tried to talk me out of it, I would've told her that I wasn't 100 percent sure about this either—that I might've just upended my whole life, for what? A girl who likely had no interest in me? Or I might've described how every time I considered what the police academy might be like, my throat clenched up. Or how I'd had anxiety-ridden dreams of guys just like David Kufos, or worse, surrounding me, taunting me, harassing me since I'd sent off my ACC application.

She must have picked up on some of my hesitation because she asked, "This is what you want?"

She believed in me. She'd raised me to be strong, to *not* doubt myself. Of course this was what I wanted.

"Yes." And I met her gaze this time.

She stood and wrapped her arms around me. I hugged her back, trying not to lose it, even though a softball-sized lump had lodged in my throat.

"I raised you to be a confident, independent woman," she whispered. She stepped back, her hands still on my shoulders, and looked in my surely red-rimmed and teary eyes. "Which means you can always change your mind."

"I know, Mama."

"I mean it, Maeve Helen." She used both my names, so she was serious. "You don't ever need to give anyone an explanation for who you are or what you decide. You don't need to ask permission to live the life you want."

"Thank you."

"For what? I'm just telling the truth."

"For being a good mom." I hated how this felt like a goodbye. My parents' house wasn't too far from where I'd be living, but in a way, this was it, the big separation. More so than when I left for college last year; this was the greater step, and we both knew it.

"All right, all right. Enough of the sappy stuff. What do you need help with?" She sniffed and wiped her eyes.

"You can roll up those posters."

"You're taking them?"

"Why wouldn't I?" And within seconds, the weight of the moment dissipated with our usual banter.

I thought of Hazel and how she'd been robbed of

moments like this. Because of some psychopath, she'd never experience what it was to be loved, known, and seen as an adult by the woman who'd birthed her. It wasn't fair, and it happened all the time, not just to Hazel. I told myself that was my "why." If, as an officer, I could bring accountability for some of the stolen moments in a person's life, then it was the right thing to do. The only thing to do.

Day 801

From Within the House

He'd brought me here, to His family's oft abandoned city house, many times over the years. The family had paid repairmen to repaint walls, strip and lay new carpet, had cleaners come in, but they never addressed the structural damage. Always choosing to leave the soft and sagging wood for the future, someone else's problem. The house sat vacant for part of each year, becoming a convenient part of my escape plan. When I left behind my life that spring, here I came.

When I first arrived, a team—not His, not yet—still lived within the home. His family, being part of the university's sports legacy and having more money than god, sometimes let teams take up residence, while taking a cut of the room and board stipend, of course. So, in all the glorious stupor of their parties and lifestyle, I became just another girl. I snuck out from my hiding places and disappeared when the clock struck. By then, I was so good at making myself small, making myself nothing more than a phantom.

Yet I hadn't totally planned for this. At some level, I'd known I'd face Him once more, that He'd have his turn here with His team. But time had become a loopy, frivolous ribbon hanging limply among the beams of the attic, woven between the lath and crumbling plaster. And now it seemed we'd all be back together again, under the same roof, for a new school year.

In the front yard, His mother trailed behind Him, her stylish clothes pulling tight against her frame in the hot sun. I looked at my own clothes, dusty and worn from the odd corners and quirks of the house only rodents and insects knew about, and slightly remembered caring about such things.

He laughed at something, His face contorting into the childish expression that had drawn me in all those years ago. How was I to know then that monsters not only existed, but they hid in plain sight? His whole persona was constructed like a gingerbread house, and I'd walked right over and started popping bits of His candy down my throat. Even now, after all He'd done, the unmistakable draw to Him pulled on my neck, my hair, my mouth.

Oh, and yes. My big, dumb brother had tagged along as always. My brother might as well lick His ass, the way he submitted for approval on the front lawn. I'd seen enough, stepping back into the shadows of the attic.

But then another car door slammed, pulling my attention to the shuttered dormer for another peek. The sun blinded, glinting off the shiny gloss of the Porsche's cherry-red paint. A figure stepped forward, and my breath caught in my throat at the sight of my mother.

She caught up to the rest of them, picking at and straightening my brother's collar. She glanced at the house, judging its shoddy outward appearance. She'd kept on, without me. Had Christmases without me. Went on shopping trips. Read VC Andrews. Sipped mimosas. Without me.

She laughed at something He said, stepped toward Him, and touched His arm. She looked over the top of her sunglasses at Him, gaze locked and flirtatious still. Even with me gone. Even with the possibility that He could've had something to do with it. It was always the boyfriend, right? Everyone knew that. Yet, there she stood on the lawn, smiling and winking and playfully slapping his chest until His mother walked between them, breaking up the display.

She'd always done that, even when mysterious bruises appeared on my arms. She'd tsk and hand me a better foundation with instructions on how to cover the marks with makeup. And when He showed up, she'd sidle up to Him, offer Him whatever she drank, a snack, all while finding infinite ways to touch Him as if she hadn't seen me tarnished and marred.

Gradually, I'd realized I never had a home.

Because of Him. Because of Her.

Chapter Three

August 1, 2001

FALL QUARTER DIDN'T start at Acorn Community College for another few weeks, but we moved in on the first of the month. With the new school year impending, a lot of students were doing the same, so our neighborhood sounded different than the quiet day in June when we'd picked out the end unit on Choke Street. A continuous stream of cars drove past the units. Two other guys, carrying crates filled with what looked like computer parts and a collection of records, moved into the apartment a few stoops away. A few people sat on a couch parked on the lawn across the street and passed a bowl between them, the skunky smell wafting our way every now and then.

My family had already returned home, but Hazel's aunt lingered. After realizing we had no curtains downstairs, she'd hightailed it to Target, and they were busy installing them now. She'd also picked up a starter pack of tools and some chain locks for the front and back door, items we hadn't even considered necessities.

I tried not to eavesdrop on their conversation, but every once in a while, I caught Hazel's aunt dispensing advice.

"Make sure you introduce yourself to your neighbors," she said.

"What if they're axe murderers?" Hazel was great at reassuring people.

"Stop it. You know what I mean," said her aunt.

"I will absolutely make sure to meet the neighbors. I'll bake cookies or something."

I stifled a laugh and unrolled one of my favorite art projects from high school—just a copy of a Chagall painting. I couldn't remember what the assignment had been exactly, except maybe "art as imitation." Anyway, I was proud of it, even though it wasn't original. I'd always harbored the idea that maybe I could be an artist. Even took a drawing class last fall at Oakley. But I couldn't hack the critiques. We'd had to present our work each week, and the teacher made a joke at the expense of my self-portrait in front of the class, saying I'd made myself look like Monica from *Friends*. Everyone had laughed; I was so obviously not a "Monica." Another time, they'd grilled me on a random decision—one that was wrong or amateurish or both—I'd made to connect two drawings with strips of white paper. I'd just stood there pouring sweat, biting my lip to keep from calling the professor a bitch. Finally, one afternoon, I sat working on a piece in the courtyard of the dorm when a shadow spanned over the page and a bird leg fell out of the sky, landing on my paper like a withered, craggy, terrible omen. So I let myself flunk versus finishing the thing, and that was the end of my art.

As I pinned my old project to the wall, Hazel told her aunt goodbye. The front door clicked shut, and the apartment—*our* home—grew quiet. Hazel's footsteps came clomping up the stairs, and suddenly, she leaned against my doorframe.

"I thought she'd never leave," she said.

"Your aunt's just worried."

"She's hovering, an overprotective busybody who—"

"I know, right? It's almost as if you were targeted and attacked or something." What happened last fall was still there, a fresh scar, puckered and pink, both literally and figuratively. And I thought about it all the time.

Hazel rolled her eyes and changed the subject. "Your room is coming along." Her gaze slid over my dresser, bed, and posters.

"Thanks."

"Wait, do you have curtains?"

"No, I didn't even think of them."

"You should have told Aunt Liddy. She totally would have picked some up for you too."

I shrugged. "It should be fine."

My brothers had put my bed right under the windowsills of the two windows that faced the front yard of the big house behind us. Hazel went over to the bed.

"No, Aunt Liddy's right. You're gonna need the privacy. At night, whoever's down there can see right up in here."

"I'll hang a sheet or something. It's no biggie."

Hazel and her aunt prioritized things like this because of what had happened to Hazel's mom, Ellen Fischer. Someone the media had recently taken to calling "The

Creeping Cop" had victimized Mrs. Fischer. He stalked women for weeks and then dressed as a police officer to gain access inside their homes. And he'd been the father of Shirlee Hensen, Hazel's attacker last fall. The four of them linked in one hell of a toxic web. Yet *he* was still out there somewhere, flitted into hiding after his daughter's arrest, like a moth whose scales allowed it to slip out of a spider's sticky silk more easily.

"Are you hungry?" Hazel asked.

"Getting there. My mom filled the refrigerator and cupboards. There's gotta be something good down there."

"I'll go check," she said and left.

I still needed to deal with my clothes but felt like smoking instead, so I grabbed my pack and lighter and went out on our little front porch. I sat on the stoop and lit up, watching cars drive by. The neighborhood had quieted some since the afternoon. Lights came on behind windowpanes. The sun blazed orange as it dipped below the black line of trees crowding a ravine. Someone jammed out to the "Real Slim Shady," every word coursing over the street corners. I sat there, inhaling, exhaling, and listening as the songs progressed through the increasingly violent *Marshal Mathers LP*. Something you could really bop your head to.

Eventually, Hazel came out on the porch holding two bowls filled with SpaghettiOs.

"Here you are." She handed me one and sat next to me. Her thigh touched mine, and I tried to ignore the jolt that coursed up my spine.

"Thanks."

We ate quietly, both of us surveying our new environment.

With my bowl nearly emptied, I said, "Weird feeling, right?"

"Completely," she agreed. "I thought it would be like moving into the dorms, but it's not. Feels... It's hard to put into words." She almost always had trouble putting words around what we were going through. I loved her for it because then I got to guess.

"More free? A little dangerous?"

"Yes, both of those."

I stood and asked if she was done eating. "I'll wash since you cooked."

She thanked me and handed off her bowl. I'd barely stepped through the front door when the shattering sound of glass rang out. *What the fuck?* I jumped backward, gripping the tomato-streaked dishes to my chest, realizing the sound had come from inside the house.

"What was that?" Hazel was right behind me. We had each other's backs.

"I don't know," I whispered.

"What should we do? Leave?"

"No." I set the dirty bowls on an end table next to the couch. "Maybe a tree branch or the wind broke something." Although, outside, the tranquil, warm, and humid weather didn't contain a hint of a breeze.

"What are you doing?" Hazel whispered. "Someone could be back there."

I grabbed my purse from the hook next to the door. Quickly, I rifled through it and pulled out my pepper spray, feeling a little silly. What were the chances someone would try to break into our place mere hours after we'd moved in?

Hazel stayed behind me. Her fingers gripped the back

of my shirt. A scenario like this probably dredged up some shitty memories for her. I gave her forearm a squeeze, meaning to be reassuring but the inadequacy of the gesture registered in the pit of my stomach. We stepped past the living room threshold into the dining room, where along the back wall we'd set up a little circular table for two. A desk and computer sat along the side wall. All the windows seemed intact.

As we neared the galley kitchen, bits of glass littered the linoleum floor. *The back door.* My heart beat in my throat. Anyone could be on the other side of that wall, or they could have run down to the basement, setting up an ambush. I adjusted my grip on the pepper spray, and Hazel reached for a broom.

Ready? I mouthed. She nodded. I took a deep breath and stepped closer to the kitchen entryway. *Closer. Closer.* At some point, I noticed the group of guys shouting from outside. But it only heightened my senses as I struggled to focus on what was going on in our apartment. Had there been footsteps? A rattling of the doorknob? I couldn't make out anything with those guys yelling and laughing. I stepped over the threshold into the kitchen. Mace held in front of me, I screamed and sprayed.

The guy standing at the door immediately reacted. His forearm flew up to protect his eyes. "Argh!" He stumbled backward, off the steps that led to our back door. He coughed and hacked, spitting huge globs of foamy spittle onto the grass.

What now? I looked at Hazel. Her eyes were huge, her grip on the broom handle tight and white-knuckled. She shook her head and shrugged, apparently reading my mind.

We hadn't unpacked a phone yet, and installation wasn't scheduled until later that week.

We stood there, stunned, as the guy's friends surrounded him.

"She fucking maced me!" The guy who'd been at the door sat on the grass, his eyes red-rimmed and squinty, a baseball bat in the green near his feet. His friends could barely contain themselves, cracking up, laughing and making jokes. Only one of them ran inside their house, saying he'd grab some milk.

As I stepped toward the door, my toe clipped a baseball. It rolled over the smattering of broken glass.

"Oh, hell," I said and bent to pick up their ball. I showed it to Hazel, whose mouth formed a frown.

"Oops," she said. "Well, guess we better apologize."

"It's not like they didn't bust our window."

"Right, but still." She gestured outside, where a group of guys poured milk over the face of one of their own.

"*Fine*." I grabbed the knob and opened the door slowly; the remaining glass hung perilously in the frame. "Hey, go find a phone and call the landlady. We're gonna need someone to fix this."

"You don't want me to come with you?"

"Nah, I got this."

"You sure?"

"Seriously, I'll be fine. There's probably a payphone at the gas station on the corner."

Hazel retreated among the maze of boxes and left out the front door. I pocketed my cannister of pepper spray and stepped outside, baseball in hand.

Our nonexistent backyard was the front yard of the

huge house behind us. Most people would have called it a Victorian, but since my mom worked in real estate, I knew the truth—Colonial Revival. At least three stories, maybe four, their house loomed over the small patch of green space, boasting its deep emerald color and a big ole buckeye tree. Twinkling Christmas lights spiraled around the columns of a large front porch that sagged off the front of the house.

A couple guys elbowed each other as I drew near. An erratic and hypermasculine energy encompassed the group. Half of them had their shirts off, the ridges and plains of their muscles in clear view.

"Here." I joined the circle of them and held the ball out for someone to take. The whole thing felt weirdly playground-ish, like a latent childhood memory complete with broken glass and burning, stinging eyes.

"Sorry 'bout that," a tall, blond guy said. He took the ball in one hand and stuck his other out for a shake. "I'm Michael. One of your neighbors."

"Maeve." I used my firmest handshake and looked him straight in the eyes. These were the types of guys you showed no fear around—not even a whiff of it. Out here among them, I found myself unwilling to apologize.

"You really took out our boy Ham."

"Ham?" I asked.

"Hamden," he said.

"Well, you really took out our back door." I countered and shrugged.

Michael smiled with an easy cocksureness. His appearance cut a striking and commanding combination: blond hair turned an icy blue in the evening light; his chest, firm and damp; long muscular arms and easy stance; his height, which had me tilting my chin up to look him in the eye. In a different time, maybe I would've acted differently, flirted more. But not after what had happened to me out on the campus trail run last fall, maybe not ever again.

"About that..." Michael said, twirling an oversized ring—class or championship, I couldn't be sure—around his middle finger. "Do you need help boarding it up?"

A couple of his friends got Hamden up off the ground. They staggered toward the house while he sniffled and continued to spit on the lawn. Other neighbors stared at the scene from their windows or front porches as if what had happened were nothing more than free entertainment versus something they should get involved in.

"Maybe. My roommate's on the phone with our landlady now. But yeah, it's getting dark, and we can't really have the back door just wide open like that."

"Let me see what I can find. I'll be right back." He did that thing guys sometimes do because they've seen it a million times on TV and movies—swaggered away backward and bit his lower lip.

I kept my expression neutral, not giving him a hint of encouragement. Then I went back inside, grabbed our broom, and swept up the glass.

"I got ahold of the landlady," Hazel called out, her voice coming from somewhere near the front of the apartment. She walked to the kitchen and leaned against the wall. "And she is not happy."

"I bet. It's our first night here."

"I got the sense she thinks *we* did it."

"*Great.*"

"What did they say?" She tilted her head toward the yard, indicating the guys.

"One offered to board it up. The rest kind of ignored me, which is fine."

"What're they like?"

"Bunch of jocks, seems like."

"How many are over there?" Hazel sat at the dining table with her chin cupped in her palm.

From the sound of it, some of the guys had restarted their game.

"No idea. A house like that? Could have five or six good-sized bedrooms, and that doesn't include rooms that just got turned into a bedroom. I bet they have basement and attic space too. Could be five people, could be twenty." I dumped the dustbin contents into the trash, the glass shards tumbling and tinkling all the way, like wind chimes. "When did the landlady say she could get someone here to put new glass in?"

Hazel sighed. "She didn't. Said she'd get back to us on the details." She worried her lower lip. "Hope it doesn't cost us anything." She crossed to the computer desk and flicked on the monitor.

Hazel's aunt had installed several hooks in the stairwell that led to the basement, and I hung the broom and dustpan in place. As I turned around, another person's silhouette caught the corner of my eye. I jumped, then annoyance filled my core. Michael stood at the threshold, holding up a board and toolbox.

"Can any of you guys knock like a normal person?" I said.

"What? Oh. My hands are kinda full. I found a scrap

from a cornhole set we made. I think it'll fit almost perfectly." He held up the particle board, and it covered the broken glass insert. He set it aside. "You okay with me nailing this into the door?"

"Kinda have to be, don't we?" I countered.

"We?" he asked.

"If our landlord charges us, we're bringing you guys the bill," Hazel said from the desk, AOL instant messenger's creaking door sounding.

Michael peeked into the dining room, introduced himself to Hazel, then added, "You do that. I mean it; we'll chip in and cover the cost for sure."

"Yeah, right." I crossed my arms.

"You don't believe me?" His eyebrow cocked. I got the feeling he wasn't used to people openly questioning him or his intentions.

"Why should I?" Although, his running shoes were an expensive brand, so maybe they did have the means to follow through with payment.

"I make it a point to be a good neighbor," Michael said, then turned and got back to work. "One of you wanna hold this for me?"

I sighed and gave Hazel an exasperated look. She shook her head and mouthed, *no*. So I played handyman's assistant.

The Oakley Book of Lacrosse

You are one of the few—the chosen. You deserve this. You've worked hard. You've spent your free time honing your skills, eliminating weakness, becoming perfect specimens. Perfect players. You've done it all for this game: the sweat, the pain. All for our team.

We will test you. We will break you. Because it's our time to conquer. To win. No one can take that away from us. So, we must make sure you really belong here.

Signed,

Your Forefathers in Game, 1972

Day 803

From Within the House

I watched from the secret passage as He hunched forward over the desk in the room He'd claimed as the captain's office, the single bulb spotlighting his work. He thought highly of Himself, understandable as He was always team captain, always with my chump brother and the others propping him up, crowning Him king. A devious consternation overtook His facial features. I knew that look, had seen it many times. It sent involuntary shivers and goosebumps throughout my body. And I rubbed at my wrists, where His knotted ropes used to tighten and squeeze, touched the puckered skin of the scars He'd left behind. Then He locked His little book—His little diary, all His big and little lies—away in a drawer and placed the key in a loose floorboard under His chair.

What did He have planned? What new and old crimes had He written about? Was my name among the pages? Did I want it to be? He pulled the string on the light, and the room went black. His footsteps knocked over the hardwood as He left. I waited a good long time, for what was time, before coming forth from my hiding spot. Quietly and slowly, because that was how I did everything, I retrieved the key and pulled His book from its place in the desk.

The pages...well, it wasn't what I'd expected. Who were the "forefathers in game"? Something He'd made up, a fictional narrative? It read like a manual—instructions of some kind for the team. I didn't really understand it. But I knew if this became anything like what He'd planned for me throughout the course of all our years together, they'd all be so sorry they ever kissed His ring.

Chapter Four

August 10, 2001

THE FIRST LINE of Kid Rock's "Bawitdaba" blared for the third time. I lay in bed, lights out, watching partygoers stumble around on the lawn below my window. Their awful taste in music filled the late night/early morning air alongside hoarse laughter, drunk monologues, and "I love you, bro" shrieks and screams. Somebody bent over and puked at the base of the big buckeye tree in their yard. Michael, the guy who "fixed" the back door, had said they were having a "get-together" and warned us it would probably be rowdy—an anniversary or memorial for a friend or some shit. He'd even invited us. But now I realized there really hadn't been a choice. When this group of guys partied, they made sure everyone was involved in one way or another.

"Shouldn't they be winding down soon?" Hazel stood in my doorway leaning against the frame. The moonlight highlighted her bare legs. Her oversized T-shirt billowed midthigh.

"Doesn't seem like it. Wanna see?"

She crept around my lingering mess from unpacking and knelt beside my bed. "Do you think they can see up here?"

"Not when it's dark." I'd made the mistake of turning the lights on earlier in the evening, which resulted with a bunch of half-drunk guys catcalling at me. I'd flipped them off, and they hurled insults up at me for forty-five minutes until they tired or grew bored.

Hazel leaned forward and rested her chin in her hands. "It's like an episode of *The Real World* down there."

I snorted. "Bunch of drunk people and all their bad decisions."

"How is this going to work?" she asked.

I shrugged and bit my lower lip. After my alarm clock flashed 2:00 a.m., I'd spent the last hour wondering something similar. Parties were to be expected, especially right before the quarter started, but how were we supposed to function if this became a consistent thing?

"What's that?" she asked. "What are those guys wearing?"

Two guys ran around the lawn with athletic gear on: helmets, chest plates, and shoulder pads. Then I saw the stick with the little basket on the end—the crosse.

"They're lacrosse players." Everything I knew about lacrosse players came from my high school team, which had been full of pompous, entitled assholes.

"That one's got an Oakley jersey on. You think they're the university team?"

"I guess? Lacrosse guys were always such dicks in high

school."

Hazel looked at me, her irises a shining pool of black in the dark. "We didn't have a team. I don't know anything about that sport."

"Picture football players who don't get enough attention."

She crinkled her nose. "So they have something to prove."

"To the world, definitely."

"And the rest of us just have to deal with it."

"Pretty much."

"Ugh," she mumbled.

"Indeed," I said.

"Guess we should add ear plugs to the list of shit we need to buy."

I nodded, not really loving the idea. The only thing worse than being up all night because of shit neighbors was sleeping through their shit unawares.

"You can sleep in my room if you want," she offered.

My heart skipped, lodging itself at the base of my throat. I couldn't swallow, let alone answer.

"'Course the hardwood floors are liable to be pretty uncomfortable," she added, lassoing my heart with her words and wrenching it back to its proper place in my chest.

"I'll be fine," I managed.

"'Kay."

My bed creaked as she stood to leave, a murmur compared to the din outside.

"Good night," she said.

"Night." I watched her leave, feeling like nothing more than a fool.

*

SUNLIGHT STREAMED THROUGH my windows, and the birds outside tweeted and chirped wildly. I turned over and pulled the blankets over my head. It was too early, no matter the time, especially after last night. The music hadn't stopped pounding until the sky turned gray with dawn.

Surprisingly, the cops hadn't been called. But maybe everyone in the neighborhood had been waiting for someone else to do it. Or maybe they'd all joined the party, leaving Hazel and me as the only two people stuck watching and listening all night.

My brain had already started churning thoughts, making the attempt at sleeping in pointless. Though my eyes were half swollen and sensitive to the sun, I threw off the blanket and stomped downstairs to make coffee.

Hazel always set up the coffee the night before, so all I had to do was flip a switch. Then I went and sat at our kitchen table, waited for the beep, and surveyed the damage outside. Solo cups, beer cans, sporting equipment, and clothes littered the neighboring yard. A robin hopped around in the grass, casually pecking here and there, before flying to the branches above. A peaceful scene, minus the trash.

The brewing coffee filled the house with a fresh, cozy morning smell. I looked around at our own mess, then went back to the kitchen and removed the half-filled trash bag from the can. I collected crumpled newspaper that had been used to secure our set of glasses and plates, picked up the plastic and cardboard packaging from all the other new stuff we'd needed for the apartment, and tied the bag. As I opened the back door to take the trash to the dumpster at the end of the alley, a flash of red caught my eye. I turned and saw it. The bag toppled out of my grip, landing on the stoop and rolling down the stairs as I stood frozen. The wind knocked out of me, I stared at the thin, dripping letters of the word "cunts" spray-painted across the wood where our window should be.

Words can never hurt me—bullshit. Who would do this? Why would they do this? The answer sat before me: the house, the guys. The slur had been one of the words they'd hurled up at me after I'd flipped them off and turned out my bedroom light. Had that small act inspired this?

So... Fuck them. I regathered the trash bag, marched through the wet, dewy grass, then up their porch stairs. The robin cheeped a warning—traitor. Their house stood dark and quiet. In one open window a stereo speaker had been propped up behind the screen where it had blared their shit music all night long. I scrounged through the trash bag and found a used coffee filter, the pouch still full of grinds, and winged it at the speaker. A rush of revenge spiked through me. It felt good, really good. I upturned the bag and dumped the rest of our trash in front of their door. Cardboard, plastic wrap, the remnants of chopped broccoli, leftover noodles and sauce, wadded up tissues and paper towels, toilet paper rolls: all of it littered their nonexistent welcome mat.

I stepped back into the yard and picked up an empty beer bottle. Rolling it from hand to hand, I imagined what it would feel like to toss it, hear the glass break, and watch it spray against the siding of their house. It could wake someone up. Was I ready for a confrontation? Sure. Why not? I pitched the bottle at the door. It shattered upon impact, and

I felt smug as hell about it.

"What the—" a voice from inside called out.

I found another one and did it again, and again, and when I walked back to my place, the thrill of what I'd just done set my whole body aflame. Let them come. Let them even fucking try. The slur they'd left on our door greeted me as I entered our kitchen.

The coffee percolated its finish, and I grabbed a mug from a still-packed box, rinsed it out in the sink, and filled it to the brim. Steam wafted and rose above my cup as I took several deep cleansing breaths. I sat at the dining table, right in front of the windows that looked out over their yard. I wanted to sip my coffee and watch them clean up the mess I'd made.

A couple of guys stumbled onto the porch. The first one yelped and hobbled toward the railing. There he sat, examining his foot. Surely, he'd stepped on glass. I smiled to myself, then unlocked the window and pushed it up so I could hear better.

They looked my way, but I didn't flinch. Instead, I focused all my energy on maintaining the direction of my gaze—on them. I watched *them*, judged *them*, held *them* accountable. Not breaking eye contact, I took another sip of my coffee and gave a little wave.

"Fucking bitch," said the one who'd sliced his foot. He hopped to their stoop, sat, and held a dirty-looking towel over his wound.

"Cunt," I yelled. They all looked at me as if I had lost my mind. "Not a fucking bitch. A fucking cunt." I pointed toward the kitchen door, and their eyes followed.

Some of the guys cracked up laughing. The guy with the

injured foot didn't think anything was funny. Then Michael came out on the porch, an attractive and hungover-looking woman on his arm. The others explained what was going on, and his gaze landed on our door. He exuded nothing but "leading man" energy. *O Captain! My Captain!* or some shit. They looked at him to decide what to do next. He peeled the woman off his arm, maneuvered her to one of the couches on their porch, where she lay down, then walked over.

As he got closer, I said, "What are you gonna do? Break this one too?"

My comment ran off him like water. He was smooth, easy. Probably used to getting his way in nearly every situation. He knew enough not to bristle; he could fix anything with a crooked smile and an ounce of Midwestern nice. And damn if he wasn't attractive. Watching him assess and begin to handle this situation, it—that quality of command—radiated off him and stirred anyone's urge to follow.

Knock knock knock. He rapped against the graffiti-filled door panel, even though he knew I was right there watching him. I took a breath, realized I wasn't wearing a bra, but answered the door anyway. If they were already calling me names, why bother keeping up with their expectations?

Michael stood there with a sorry expression on his face, the sickening-sweet smell of booze wafting off him. But I wasn't about to give in and be the first to speak. I stood with my hand on my hip and waited.

"Sorry 'bout "—he gestured at the drooping red letters— "this."

"Did you do it?"

His brow wrinkled, probably used to the bare minimum—an ounce of regret, puppy dog eyes, a touch—being enough. "Uh, no."

"Then your apology means nothing." I adjusted my stance, never breaking eye contact, never showing weakness. Having three older brothers did that to a girl. "Do you know who did?"

"I, um…" He looked away. His gaze darted to his front porch, his friends behind him, and then back to me. He scratched the back of his head. "Might have an idea."

"Then you deal with them and save your sorries for when they actually mean something."

"O-okay," he stammered, like a child. Meaning I currently played the role of mother, scolding him and his friends. *Ugh.* That old binary. *This* or *that*: cunt or mother, slut or saint, reduced to a caricature, not a person.

"We'll fix it."

"That's literally the least you could do."

He rolled his teeth over his lower lip. "You gotta understand something about last night."

"Actually, I really don't." I moved to close the door.

He put his hand on the door to stop it. "See, it's Stef—" He gestured back to the guy who'd cut himself on the broken glass, now hobbling back inside. "His sister. She's missing."

That got my attention. He must've noticed because he continued.

"Been missing for a while now. We don't have a lot of hope about what's happened to her. And yesterday was her birthday, their birthday; they were twins. So I thought a party might help. Obviously, it didn't."

"Right, look— I'm sorry about your friend's sister, but

we have to live next to each other. And this shit," I said, pointing at the spray paint, "is not okay."

"You're right. It's not. We'll paint over it." He tucked his hands in his back pockets and looked away. "If it makes you feel any better, Stef'll probably need stitches. He won't be able to practice with that cut on his foot, which means he'll miss a game. Maybe two."

"Why would that make me feel better?" I asked, even though it did.

"I don't know." He shrugged. "Revenge, right? Tastes good." His eyes sparkled with the thought.

His comment pinged on a truth I understood and had been told to suppress my whole life. Categorized among all the other things that weren't *ladylike*—don't be too bold, don't look for confrontation, don't make people pay for what they did to you. I let several beats pass between us, our eyes locked. What he kept there, behind the quiet, cool, even-keel demeanor, was a mystery, but a hint of recognition, *something* he instinctively knew about me, shined through. Being seen by him brought a strange, unsettling comfort.

"Maybe," I said. And because I wasn't interested in being viewed as anyone's mother, I lightened and cracked a joke. "You should apologize for your taste in music too."

He grimaced. "That bad, huh?"

"My ears bled after the fourth 'Nookie.'" I shouldn't be giving him a pass; the red paint of the slur hung right over my shoulder. "I don't forgive you by the way."

"I would never do that." He pointed at the ruined plank.

"Doesn't matter, because one of *your* friends did."

Michael looked as if he might rebut, but I stepped back and closed the door before he could.

Excerpt from *The Oakley Book of Lacrosse*

Item #1: Train hard, party harder.

You've done the work: the relays, box drills, the maze, gauntlet, rock and roll, death drill...on and on. Your body is a machine on the field. It's automatic now. An elite, performance vehicle in peak condition. Everything you do on the field has been made part of a memory, something your muscles can never forget; you are your learned response. And when it's over, when that whistle blows, we drink. Let loose. Rock out with your cock out. Balls to the wall. You deserve it.

Chapter Five

August 22, 2001

THE BUSY HIGHWAY spanned ahead of us, dotted with speeding vehicles of all types as we headed to the community college. I rolled down my window, and the hot August wind overpowered the AC. I pressed the cigarette lighter, then searched through my purse for a pack without taking my eyes off the road. I pulled out a pen, some tissues, and a small notebook until Hazel took over my pursuit. Her fingertips grazed my forearm, an accident, but the soft, light touch packed enough punch to leave me breathless.

"I got this," she said. "Nervous?"

"I don't know." And I didn't.

Hazel pulled out two and handed me one. The lighter popped up, and she touched the hot coils to the end of hers, inhaling as she did so. The car's interior filled with the smoky tang of a burning cigarette, and it put me at ease.

"I've never had to take a drug test before," Hazel admitted, blowing her first puff out the passenger side window, then handing me the lighter.

"Me neither." I lit my cigarette and pressed hard on the brakes as rear lights glared angrily in front of us.

Today, we would complete the drug test and background check for the police academy program, and next week, we had to meet the physical requirements. It wasn't much, but it marked a start, the beginning.

"Have you talked with your mom?" Hazel knew how my family felt about cop school.

I nodded. "She's pretending it's not happening. Thinks I'll come to my senses eventually." That hadn't been *exactly* what she'd said—not even close—but that was how I thought she felt.

"And?"

"And what?"

"*And*? Will you come to your senses?"

Hazel had done this a couple times, checking on me and my motives.

"All my senses are right where they should be."

She shrugged, turned on the radio, and adjusted the dial to the indie channel. A Modest Mouse song lilted through the speakers. She turned up the volume until the noise of the rushing traffic faded in comparison.

Unlike Oakley, huge and sprawling and claiming a large portion of the city, Acorn Community College came nestled between a handful of high rises and the rivers that converged downtown. I turned into the parking lot, paid for a day pass, and found an empty spot.

We passed under a slightly crooked banner strung

between a brick multistory building and a lamppost: *Welcome to Acorn Community College!* The architecture was plain, straightforward, and unembellished, especially compared to what we'd grown used to at Oakley. Clusters of '70s-style rectangular-shaped buildings, obviously containing offices and more classrooms, sprawled across the grounds. It was quaint.

Hazel pulled a packet of paperwork from her backpack. She flipped to a map she'd printed out, and we navigated through campus until a one-story, monotone building of umber bricks and matching dark-brown mortar came into view. Davis Hall had rows of tinted windows that reflected our images as we made our way toward the entrance. About two dozen men—most of them young, most of them white— milled around the front of the building. They shook hands in enthusiastic, nearly aggressive ways, and held their acceptance packets in rolled up little batons which they occasionally used to swat one another. Some of them were loud and boisterous, and others held themselves back a step or two outside the circle's radius. Everyone surveyed one another, quietly deciding important things about pecking order and laughing when it seemed appropriate.

"Bet we're all going to the same place," I said under my breath. Hazel nodded and slowed her stride, stopping on the outskirts of the group. We were the only two women among them, which I'd expected, but the reality carried a weighty intimidation. "How're you doing?"

"I'm fine," she said.

Hazel's posture straightened, and while she *seemed* distracted and aloof, she'd actually become overly alert and a little jumpy. Maybe not the best qualities for a cop, but I hadn't said *that* out loud yet either.

A Black woman in a pair of khaki pants and a forest-green polo shirt opened the front door. "Welcome." Her eyes flicked up from the clipboard. "I'll be your advisor throughout the ACC peace officer program—"

"You mean the police academy." A stocky white guy near the center of the group interrupted her.

"I say what I mean, cadet. My name is Beth Thomas, and my job is to make sure you meet all the necessary requirements of this program at certain intervals. The first of which is a criminal background check and drug test. So if you all will follow me…"

She turned and reentered Davis Hall, not checking if anyone trailed her. The group formed a quick line, and everyone went inside. Beige painted cinder blocks and potted plants decorated the dim hallway. Every so often, we passed a closed door with a placard announcing the room number. Through the glass lites, I could see rows of empty desks or tables. At the end of the hall, Beth opened a door and held it for us. As we walked in, she directed us toward the seating area. Three rows of chairs sat in front of a sectioned-off space, like the waiting area at the DMV. Not at all like the auditorium-style classrooms at Oakley.

We all stayed quiet, anticipating further instruction. Nobody wanted to mess up the first day. Beth took her place behind the counter and did a quick roll call. One by one, we walked up to the counter, and she led us to the back, where we placed our fingertips in ink and rolled them along a piece of paper. We filled out forms asking us if we'd ever committed a crime and signed next to the *X*.

Eventually, two male employees appeared and took the

men to complete their drug testing while Hazel and I stayed with Beth. She had us follow her to the ladies' restroom and handed us cups to pee in.

"Keep the doors open," Beth added as we approached the stalls.

"Seriously?" I asked.

"Why would I joke?"

Okay. So maybe this was what my family had been trying to warn me about—not that I couldn't do the job because I was a woman, but rather how hard the culture would be for me. To just follow orders? No questions asked? Me?

"Because I said so" never worked for me. I needed explanations, an understanding of why things were done a certain way. "Convention dictates, we…" Screw that. And when reasoning wasn't made available, I never shut up about it.

Or at least, I hadn't in the past.

This time, I kept my mouth shut and pissed in the damn cup.

Beth took the samples in her gloved hands, and I glanced at Hazel in the mirror as we washed our hands. I must've had *a look* on my face because she smiled and just shook her head.

And then it was over. We were dismissed. Told our results would be mailed to us, and if anyone hadn't passed, we'd be automatically removed from the roster. Beth explained the peace officer academy procedure: you fail, you're out. Classes started in two weeks.

Before we drove back to our apartment, Hazel and I decided to grab a coffee from a kiosk and explore.

"So that was weird," I said once we paid for our drinks and a giant chocolate chip cookie to split. We walked along a paved path that snaked through and around campus.

She gave a little laugh. "I was waiting for you to go off in the bathroom."

"I almost did!"

"That would have been a mistake." Hazel split the cookie in half and handed me my share.

"You don't think there are other ways to administer a drug test? Ways that don't include a stranger watching you pee?"

"I have no idea," she admitted. "She was just doing her job. Maybe they want us to experience what we might have to ask others to do some day. Maybe it builds empathy; I don't know."

"That's some gracious thinking on your part." I took a bite of cookie and thought about what she said. She had a point, but I remained skeptical. "Seems to me to be more of a humiliation tactic, a power move."

"Oh, well. It's done and over," she said.

"Except for the physical." We came upon a track; the burnt sienna oval rounded a bright, green soccer field. Rows of bleachers enclosed each straightaway.

"Right."

"We gotta run a mile and a half in under twenty minutes, which I don't think will be a problem." I wasn't in bad shape, but the smoking probably wouldn't help. "You wanna practice or something? Maybe this evening when it's cooler outside?"

"Can't tonight. I'm meeting Doug."

"Oh, right." I took a sip of my iced coffee, savoring how it blended with the sugar and chocolate taste lingering on my tongue, even as her news soured my stomach. There had been a night last fall when I thought something might happen between Hazel and me. I could have sworn there'd been chemistry in the air by the river. But then, the moment was interrupted. Someone got themselves brutally murdered, and Hazel was implicated, then stabbed, and I'd spent the summer giving her the space she needed to heal. Apparently, Doug had not.

"So are you guys, like, a thing?" There. I'd said it, asked one of the big questions. Sometimes, Hazel turned me into someone who tiptoed around what they were too afraid to hear. I didn't love that version of me.

"Oh." Hazel's brow wrinkled in the middle, a vertical bar right above her nose. I loved that spot—could've pressed my lips to the little line that always showed when she was thinking hard about something. "No."

She didn't elaborate.

So whatever Doug and Hazel had nourished throughout the summer was officially none of my business. And I shouldn't let it affect what she and I had—some kind of boundless, undefined connection that drew me in and sometimes made me change aspects of myself.

Which I knew to be a red flag.

But then she'd smile or laugh, and the red flag fluttered away in the same breeze that whipped her wavy hair around her face.

We wandered through the campus, occasionally checking a directory. Every once in a while, my arm would brush against hers, or she'd press in behind me to let someone pass by on the sidewalk, and I'd ride the electric shockwave piercing my heart. It was exhilarating, intoxicating, frustrating...sure to be a disaster.

Day 820

From Within the House

Most nights, the house quieted between 3:00 and 10:00 a.m. Yet I waited for stragglers—drunks refusing to sleep, forcing conversations or sex—to peter themselves out before I emerged in the still dark of the early morning. The secret passageways mazed throughout the home, and I could go anywhere I pleased.

I'd spotted Him with another girl at the party earlier. And though I recognized how sick it made me, I headed for the bedroom He shared with my brother to see what happened between them.

I tried not to think His name as the walls pressed in so close the newspaper insulation crinkled against my arm. Without His name on my lips or in the folds of my brain, I could still cling to the idea of being free of Him, but it wasn't enough. The whole idea of Him still sent tremors down all the parts of me that struggled so hard to survive. And while I loathed to admit it, I'd grown used to us being in this house together; a kind of possession over Him had emerged within me. My whole life, I was His, and now I caught only glimpses of His power exerted in small doses, scattered over many people instead of wholly focused on me.

The passage door opened into their closet. They'd only hung a few dress shirts on the rung, but a mess of shoes and sports equipment and god-knows-what tangled around my ankles. From my vantage, I watched them sleep. Their chests rose and fell; their jaws hung open, slackened and loose with nothing to clench about. The bedroom reeked of sweaty, spoiling clothes and hangover.

I stepped out from the closet and toward His bed. The woman slept next to Him, but she didn't nestle or drape herself across His chest in the lazy, open way one might with a new love. Instead, she'd turned her back to Him, practically pressing the whole front of herself against the wall, positioning herself as far away from Him as possible. Smart. I wished I'd done that sooner. But he had her pinned there; she couldn't leave without waking Him. Though difficult to make out in the lower light, bruises bloomed across her backside. I could practically hear the smacking sound of His paddle against flesh, my flesh. No, her flesh. My breath caught in my throat, and I stumbled backward. Full of wanting. Full of hatred. For Him. For me.

I slowly stepped toward a low bookshelf, curious about what kinds of classes a monster took. Nestled among titles like Essentials in Social and Cultural Anthropology and Probability and Statistics, I found our old yearbook. I opened it, quietly turning pages until I reached my memorial page. The photo was not one I would've picked for myself, but I gave up the right to choose that kind of thing when I fled, letting them all think the worst.

My brother turned suddenly, bed rails creaking with the heavy shift of body weight. He smacked his lips. I watched, too afraid to move and yet knowing even if he opened his eyes, he'd only see me as a ghost, a fever dream, nothing real. To him, I was already gone. Exactly what I'd wanted them to think, exactly what they all deserved. I felt no guilt for how my disappearance may have affected him because he'd done nothing to stop Him from inflicting all kinds of pain on me. Stef knew exactly who He was, what He was capable of, how He'd treated me. So fuck him. Fuck all of them.

A coffee mug on top of the bookshelf held a collection of pens, and I grabbed one, cursing the tink of plastic against glass. I flipped to the back of the yearbook, where friends left memories and well wishes and "don't ever change" notes.

I quietly scratched my own message between all the others. Something I'd been thinking about for a long time. What happened to people like Him? I'd given up everything just to preserve some part of myself, and He lived on, viewed as a great guy. A leader, even. It wasn't fair. But who was willing to do anything about it? Not a soul alive. A deep sigh escaped me as I capped the pen, closed the book, and slipped it back into its place on the shelf.

"Stonie?" The question, my name, quietly whispered into the blue dark of the room sent a cold spike through my heart. I turned and saw my twin brother's wide-open eyes.

His irises, nearly silver in the shine of the moon coming through the window, same as mine, stared right at me. He blinked, rubbed at his eyes, and let out a groan. Then he turned over and fell back asleep, his breathing rhythmic and regular. All I could think of was how long it'd been since someone actually saw me.

Chapter Six

August 24, 2001

I WAS NOTHING but a lump on the couch, flipping through hundreds of channels, searching for something, anything, to take my mind off the fact that Hazel had left with Doug again. I landed on something mindless, MTV's *Jackass*, ready to laugh and cringe at whatever ridiculous thing these guys might try next.

Music started blaring from the neighbors' house again—loud, screaming, jarring, entitled, hypermasculine. I turned up the TV volume. No use. Everything, all their noise, just became unbearable.

Shmack! Something struck the dining room window, something squished and wet from the sound of it. Fear, anger, and then annoyance billowed through me, a fire that never really went out. They were fucking with me. *Splat*! Again. They'd broken our window, spray-painted a slur across our door, and now, this: I couldn't have ignored them if I tried.

"Hey!" I stomped through the house, then swung open the back door, the night air still swampy with humidity. "I called the cops!" I lied, but maybe it was time for that.

"Good," muttered someone walking up the alley. They turned into the row house a few doors down.

A group of shadowy figures ran off—laughing and whooping and smacking one another's asses—some down the street and some back into the house party. I counted five of them. Below our dining room windows, split tomatoes and squished balls of raw hamburger lay in the dirt. Even if I called the police, they wouldn't do anything. They'd view this as a college prank, nothing more. They had more serious things to deal with. Still, someone had to clean this up, or it would draw rats and raccoons.

Well, it wasn't going to be me.

I marched up their porch steps, buoyed by indignance, and didn't bother knocking. Guests came in and out of their house all night long. No one would notice I hadn't formally been invited. Most of these people didn't even know who I was or that I existed.

Inside felt like a scene from every stereotypical college movie...only the vibes were different. In Hollywood, this was all fun and games. Kids being kids, but especially boys being boys. Yet in real life, something—malice, spite, belligerence—lurked in the corners and behind the drunken masks. I could taste it, yeasty and overripe, something right on the verge of spoiling.

In the living room's dim lamplight, a couch seemed fit to burst with one too many people. They passed a bong among themselves. Another kid cut lines of white powder on a textbook in his lap. At some point, I realized I was looking for Michael. He'd helped us before; he'd do it again. The living room's end split into a choice—stairwell or dim hallway. I stuck to the hall; ground level felt like the safer option.

In another room off the hallway, people crowded around a green rectangular table and played beer pong. The group erupted with cheers. As I passed through the house, guys nodded and smiled at me. Their eyes roamed all over my body, but they were shaky on their feet, stumbling and shuffling over the matted carpet. And the girls? They looked right through me as if I weren't among them. As if I weren't one of them. I kept moving, unsure of my plan now.

The hall led to a bright kitchen. Two long and sputtering fluorescent tubes illuminated the space. Their kitchen was triple the size of our tiny galley but still not huge, especially given the size of the house. A slick brown sludge covered the tile floor. Puddles of melting ice formed around the kegs and spilled beer. A line of people waited for drinks. I checked for an exit. To get out, I'd have to maneuver around the line and between two guys hefting the legs of a thin blond into the air for a keg stand. One of the guys in front of me looked vaguely familiar—the guy with the missing sister. The one who'd spray-painted our door and then cut his foot on the broken glass. Steve or something. No, Stef.

"Have you seen Michael?" I asked over the music pumping through all areas of the house, like a heartbeat.

The guy didn't seem to recognize me as he shook his head and smiled. His arm snaked around my waist, and he pulled me toward him. Pressed up against me, his chest was thick and hard. A slab of rock. A cliff face. A crag. He reeked of liquor and could barely keep his eyes open.

I set my palms against his pecs and pushed, but that only made his grip tighten. My breath felt trapped in my lungs as if he really might squeeze the life out of me. He didn't say anything, and his eyes seemed blind, searching for or seeing something that wasn't there. A flash of what had happened to me on the trail last fall pressed into my memory, its mouth reopening, fangs flashing a bright red warning. The phantom feeling of being groped bit into my consciousness once more, again and again.

"I gotta go." I gasped out the words and began to fight against him, wiggling and pushing for any free space I could reclaim.

Someone retched behind us. A thick, stewy, splashing sounded from the other side of the kitchen. The room erupted into sloppy jeers: "Ohhhh!" and "Dude!" and "Come on, man!"

I struggled still.

"Fucking lightweight!" another guy yelled.

Stef's hold on me slithered loose, distracted. I grasped at the opportunity, breaking free and pushing my way past more drunk and messy bodies. I had nothing against getting wasted at the right time in the right place; this was neither of those things. I checked behind me. Stef slumped against the wall, laughing and gesturing at the kitchen scene as if he'd never cornered me. Like I wasn't even real.

At the end of the hall, I stood at the bottom of the stair-well. The open door and fresh night air were a mere ten steps away. I just had to cross back through the living room, and I'd be free—out of this chaos.

But then the music stopped, and any lingering chatter

dropped off too. A trumpeting sound blared, and four guys, stripped to their underwear with pillowcases draped over their heads, paraded through the front door. People scrambled up off the couches. I shrank against the wall, getting out of the way, stuck and unable to leave. As they passed by me on their way upstairs, I made out words written on their bare chests in what looked like red lipstick: pussy, whore, bitch, slut.

How they hated us.

Nobody seemed as drunk as they were minutes ago. As if the lights coming on and the sound going off had sobered them all. Or maybe the sense of public humiliation kept everyone quiet. Somber even. The agreed-upon strategy being silence. But these poor guys—what was about to happen to them? If we spoke up, would bad things happen to us? If we said nothing, were we even here?

From somewhere, Michael emerged. Lamplight shined over a long, silky cape draped across his shoulders. A patchwork of messy stitching and torn jerseys made up the cloak, the color vaguely like bloodied, raw steaks. In one hand, he carried a lacrosse stick as if it were a royal scepter, in the other, a leather padfolio. He trailed the procession through the house. And others, likely teammates, set down their beers, wiped their hands on their jeans, and broke away from the groups they were in, following Michael to the upper floors of the house.

Once they'd gone, someone cranked the music back up. Someone flicked off all the lights, and the room glowed in neon blues and greens from a black light and the occasional fluorescent orange. Every once in a while, a smile shined with a malevolent brightness. The party reconvened as if nothing strange had just happened.

But where had the team gone? What the hell were they doing? I had to know.

I crept upstairs, the music's beat still pounding but muffled as it traveled through layers of wood and insulation. I peeked over the banister, into the bowels of the party below—a kind of vertical crossroads. I could've gone back downstairs and left, locked myself away in my row house apartment, like a princess who forgot all she'd witnessed. But that had never really been my style.

The stairwell led to a hallway lined with an array of doors. Most of the doors were closed except the bathroom. Its tiled and plastered walls glowed pale lavender in the moonlight streaming through a window above the toilet. At the end of the hall, one door had been left slightly ajar, yellow light shining bright from within. My heart pounded in my ears as I crept forward and looked through the crack into the room beyond.

The guys stood lined up before Michael, pillowcases still covering their heads, backs to me. Other team members stood behind Michael, looking on solemnly. I prayed the lot of them were too drunk to notice the sliver of my silhouette at the door.

"Turn away from me," Michael said, an air of commandment tinging his tone. The line of four turned toward me now. A tremble quivered through the fingers of one of them. Another gripped the hem of his boxers.

"We call upon our ancestral teammates, the Oakley lacrosse teams of decades past, to be present with us tonight as we partake in a ritual that binds us."

The young men around the room shouted, "Here!

Here!"

Michael opened the leather portfolio and flipped through the first few pages of a yellow notepad. "Pain builds trust," he read, then pounded the handle of a lacrosse stick against the floor. He tapped out a measured, slow rhythm. A palpable sense that the house might be alive, over-whelmed me, that he was knocking into a pulsing, living evil. I couldn't swallow, couldn't speak, couldn't move.

"Grab your knees," Michael commanded.

All but one bent over until a bigger, older-looking team-mate slapped the holdout on the back of the head. Only then did the guy do as he'd been told, placing his hands on his knees. Michael cracked a beer, and at this, the whole crowd of men behind him came alive. He chugged, and as he swal-lowed, the guys egged him on. When he held up the empty can and crushed it in his fist, the room erupted with praise and applause.

What came next? Did I really need to see? Again, I thought of leaving. I could back away, escape now. But I stopped myself. They lived next to me; I should know what they were capable of.

"Bring forth Ramrod!" Michael bellowed.

I bit my bottom lip, catching and tearing a piece of dried skin between my teeth. This could go a lot of different ways, and none of them were great. I'd seen news reports about how bad hazing could be at frats and sororities, with a hand-ful of young people ending up dead every year. Was it hap-pening with sports teams too? Obviously.

Two guys, one of them Stef, carried a thick stick, a broom handle, decorated in the university colors. They passed the rod to Michael, who, in turn, held it above his head and chanted, "Pain. Trust. Pain. Trust. Pain! Trust!"

His teammates caught on, then echoed the words back to him as he assumed a batting position and swung. Ramrod slammed into the backside of one of the recruits, who grunted with pain and stumbled forward. I flinched at the hit, stepping back, not wanting to see, not being able to fully look away.

"Get back in line, pussy," grumbled someone.

Michael swung again. And again. The younger guys didn't scream, but sometimes, a low moan came out from under the pillowcases. I imagined they clenched their teeth, bit the inside of their cheeks, their tongues, anything to keep from making a sound. Some fell to their knees, but they kept getting back up. The gathered group roared, calling for another shot, another strike. They were bloodthirsty and callous; the scene pitched toward frenzy. How long could this go on? I could barely catch my breath, let alone my voice.

One guy stumbled, his head drooped, and the sack over his head slipped off. He looked greasy with sweat, maybe tears, red with emotion and strain. He pulled the fabric back over himself, covering up once more. Maybe if he stayed anonymous, he could pretend he wasn't being assaulted. In his mind and throughout his life, he could just be one of them. One of the guys. Teammates.

At the perimeter of the room, a guy stalked, dressed in a team jersey, his face painted with stripes of black. He double-fisted beers, but his eyes scanned the scene—seemingly sober as hell. His darting pupils passed my way, and excitement twitched under his face paint. Had he seen me? No. He kept tracking the actions of the room, surveying. Watching for the instant he could insert himself into the fray. I'd known guys like him, friends or acquaintances of my brothers, the worst kind of people.

The stalker put an arm around Michael, handing him another beer. Michael took it and drank deeply, his Adam's apple bobbing with each swallow. Then the stalker made his move, pantsing the recruit closest to him. The room erupted with laughter at the display of the poor dude's bare, very pink, and welted ass. Michael spit the remainder of his beer out with a laugh. Foam exploded from his mouth, all over the exposed guy.

Laughing. This was fun? A comedy?

The stalker reached for Ramrod. No. A tragedy.

I pushed the door open and screamed, "Stop!" And for some reason, they listened, at least for a moment. All their eyes trained on me. "What the hell is wrong with all of you?"

The guys looked to Michael to gauge how they should react.

His gaze met mine. His jaw ticked, and a flush crept up his neck. I wasn't supposed to witness this. No one was supposed to see him this way.

"The lady doth protest?" he asked, mocking my concern as if this were normal.

"This is *fucked* up and you know it," I spat.

"Give it here." Michael yanked Ramrod from the stalker, who slunk back into the crowd, dematerializing. Michael shook his head and noticed the guys in front of him, asses in the air, one of them bare. "Get up. Get dressed!" He swiped his hand through his hair. "Jesus, fuck," he whispered. It was as if a spell had been broken—the prince awakened not by a kiss but a protest.

I left, storming back down the stairs, through the

hallway toward the kitchen, pushing through to get to the other side of the kegs. The screen door clattered behind me.

The night air steamed with moisture, and crickets screamed. I stood on their back porch. Nobody was out here, and I stopped for a breath—just a second to think, to process. The wooden planks felt soft and nearly rotten under my feet, as if I might sink through them.

Footsteps clomped behind me. Through the screen, I watched as two guys from the weird little torture room scrambled into the kitchen, then slipped and fell in the dirty puddles all over the floor. Michael, his cape fluttering, filled the door frame behind them. We made eye contact once more before I turned and fled.

"Wait!" he called.

I kept going, welcoming the darkened alley between the row houses and his home. But he kept coming too.

"Maeve?" He hopped over the porch railing. "Wait, please!"

My breath sounded heavy and rasping in the night. Running seemed futile. He knew exactly where I lived— could look up into my bedroom window at any time, could break down our flimsy doors with their flimsy chain locks whenever he felt like it.

So I slowed my pace. *Face the monster.* And I turned to meet him.

He stopped short, maybe not expecting me to confront him. In the darkness, the brightest light shined from the windows of his house. I swallowed and waited for him to talk.

"You—you weren't supposed to see that."

I snorted. "What? That you're a psychopath?"

His face was a ghastly yellow-green. And yet, he had the nerve to smile. "You know I'm not crazy."

"I have no idea what you are." I turned to leave, but he grabbed my arm.

"That stuff back there. It's just tradition. It doesn't *mean* anything about me."

"You're wrong," I said. His grip was firm, biting. I pried my arm loose.

"I'm a good guy," he pleaded. "Look." He held up his portfolio and flipped back to that first page. "See, this is from 1972. It's not me; it's the way it has always been."

But for once, I was speechless. I looked at him for another beat or two, searching his eyes for the lie. But it was absent. He believed himself. I'd seen what I'd seen and stopped what I'd stopped, and *he* was somehow still able to maintain his decency? What a world. There was nothing left to say.

I turned and walked away, not looking back until I reached my place. But the alley stood empty. Michael had gone, and the night was filled with nothing but hazy ghosts.

Excerpt from *The Oakley Book of Lacrosse*

Item #2: Pain begets trust.

Pain. Your brothers will test you in ways you never thought you could endure, but do not fear; your body will rise up stronger. To dominate the game as a team, you must submit to your brothers. In all things. Never spare the rod. Trust.

Chapter Seven

August 25, 2001

"WHAT HAPPENED LAST night?" Hazel sat at the dining table. She spooned a bite of frosted cereal into her mouth and indicated our windows, streaked with dried tomato guts.

"Just what it looks like. They had a party, and somebody thought it would be real funny to trash our place again." Amid everything that had happened, no one had cleaned up the tomatoes or hamburger smeared across the screens of our back windows.

"They're such a nightmare." Her spoon clanged against the bowl. "I hope they chill soon."

Images from last night replayed in my mind. "Doubtful."

She smirked, then drank the milk out of her bowl. I went to the kitchen and poured myself a cup of coffee and added a generous amount of vanilla-flavored creamer, then checked the expiration date before putting it away.

Date. I hadn't gone on one of those in a while. But Hazel had.

"How was your date with Doug?" I asked, trying to sound nonchalant, as if the idea of her being with Doug didn't sting.

"Well, for one thing, it wasn't a date."

"Is Doug aware of that?" I picked up my coffee from the counter and leaned against the doorframe separating the kitchen from the dining room.

Her lips tightened into a line, eyes piercing as if to say: *Stop being an asshole; it's none of your business; I know what I'm doing.*

"Sorry, sorry," I said.

"He's a friend. That's it."

"How do you know when someone's just meant to be a friend?" I asked, more for myself, checking if Hazel put me in the same category as Doug. If so, I needed to do the same with her—to bury these feelings along with the garbage outside our window.

She sipped her coffee and shrugged. "Doug's attractive, but when we spend time together, the chemistry just isn't right. There's nothing...electric going on there. Sorry. I'm talking in clichés."

She was, but that didn't make what she said any less understandable or clear. Every time we stood in the same room, I felt a jolt. My body sparked when hers was near, even first thing in the morning when her hair looked a mess and a toothpaste splotch painted her chin. When we first started hanging out last year, she hated me. Then something clicked over time. I could feel her eyes on my body when I danced in the laundry room or when she'd watch me smoke. I liked being the object of her gaze, even though I wasn't sure she was aware of herself, of her preferences. But before we could even explore options, we'd gotten all tangled up in an assault and then a murder. And maybe those feelings were too mixed up now. Maybe that guy, Ryan, had ruined our chance of ever being together. We couldn't possibly carry the weight of what had happened *to us* alongside a real shot *at us*.

"Wanna hit the track this morning? Practice for next week?" she asked, changing the subject and knocking me right out of my reverie.

"Sure. Let me finish my coffee."

About a half hour later, we stood on the front porch as I locked the door. We strode down the steps and over a little mound of grass before catching the sidewalk. Lots of people were out already, setting up kiddy pools in their tiny yards, sunning themselves, generally soaking up the good morning weather before the humidity became unbearable. I'd parked on the side street, so we had to pass the lacrosse house. As we did, Michael stood on the lawn, hands at his waist, obviously directing some of the others. A few of the guys had a hose and were aiming it at our stained and streaked windows.

"Thanks!" Hazel called to him.

He waved magnanimously, then held up a paint can and roller. "For the door panel!"

Hazel gave him a thumbs-up.

I stayed skeptical and disapproving. Dude was not a hero, no matter how desperately he needed to see himself that way. "Don't encourage him."

"Why?" Her brow formed that sweet line in the middle of her forehead. "They're doing us a favor."

"After *they* wrecked our house. Those guys are not nice."

"They can't control everyone who comes to their parties."

After what I'd witnessed last night, I didn't want to see anything from those guys' perspective. What was wrong was wrong, and no amount of backstory made it right. And I would've argued that point had my brother not been walking toward me carrying two heavy-looking grocery bags.

"Evan?"

"Hey, Maevey. Looks like I got here just in time."

"Barely. We're on our way out, headed to ACC for a run."

"Right." Evan tried to hide his smirk, but I saw it pulling at the edge of his usual breezy demeanor.

"What? I can run." Although I hadn't lately. "What are you doing here anyway?"

"Why do you think?" He gestured, holding the bags. "Yaya's convinced herself you're not eating. She asked me to bring all this to you."

The bags were filled with cookie tins and Tupperware.

"Nice," I said, imagining all of Yaya's best recipes. "Let me help you."

"I've got it. Just unlock the door for me."

I walked my brother back up the sidewalk while Hazel stayed at the car.

Barely a few paces away, Evan stage-whispered, "Is that the *roommate*?" He emphasized that last word, giving it so much more meaning.

"Shut up."

"You didn't even introduce me!"

"Shit, yeah. I will on your way out. But do *not* embarrass me."

"How would I even? I mean, the only thing that comes to mind is that one time you sharted on the Magnum at Cedar Point. And then there was—"

"Evan, I swear to god, I will punch you in the fucking..." I trailed off as Evan had stopped walking, his face gone pale, eyes wide with shock. "Evan? What is it?"

He blinked, seeming to notice me again. "Huh? Oh, nothing."

"Dude, don't even lie. What's wrong with you?"

"I just...thought I saw someone I used to know."

"One of them?" I asked as we passed the lacrosse house. They were still working on our place, cleaning it up.

"Uh, yeah. Thought I recognized one of them. Keep walking." He sped up his pace.

"I *am*." I jogged a few steps to catch up with him. "Why are you being so weird?"

He didn't answer, but his jaw flexed, his teeth being ground to bits.

On the other side of our building, I unlocked the front door, and he pushed past me into the living room. He dropped the bags in front of the couch. A sheen of sweat covered his forehead.

"Are you all right?" I asked. "What's going on?"

"I don't know. I don't know." He struggled to catch his breath. He'd had panic attacks before. I reached out, grabbed his shoulders, and squeezed. Pressure helped sometimes.

"Hey, hey," I said in my softest voice. "You're okay. I'm here with you. Evan?"

His breath caught, and his eyes met mine. He licked his lips. "That guy, Maevey. You gotta be careful."

"I know, Evan. They're nuts."

"I mean it, Maeve."

"Do you want to sit down? I'll get you some water."

He didn't sit; instead, he paced the room. I grabbed the grocery bags, thinking some of this stuff should probably be kept cool. The guys outside were finishing up the windows, spraying the suds off the glass and screens. I stuffed both bags in the nearly empty fridge, not even bothering to pull out the containers, then grabbed a cup of water for my brother. *What had triggered him? Or who?*

When I came back out, he stood in the center of the living room, staring at the guys cleaning off our windows. I handed him the glass, and he looked at it as if I'd just handed him a dead kitten.

"Are they messing with you?" he asked quietly.

I frowned. "A little."

He set the water on the end table without drinking and turned to the front door. "I gotta go."

"Wait, Evan!" I rushed after him. The screen door banged shut behind us. "You gotta tell me what's—"

But he was already jogging back to his car, halfway up the street. I turned back and locked the front door again. *What the fuck?*

As I approached my car, Hazel said, "Your brother just sped outta here. I tried to introduce myself but..."

"Yeah, I don't know what's up with him. He was fine,

and then he wasn't. He said he recognized one of the guys that lives behind us, but that's all I could get out of him. He does that sometimes—panics. Started a few years back."

"Been there," Hazel said.

I let the conversation drop as we both got in the car. Of course Hazel would understand. She'd been through more trauma than most. But had my brother? Not that I was aware of. But would he tell me? I remembered the guys from last night being beaten. Would they tell anyone? Had I?

Day 826

From Within the House

He tried to clean up all his messes, but the girl next door, a cliché and a half, had caught a glimpse of His true nature. And now...well, He'd either gaslight her into believing she hadn't seen what she saw, or she was in real danger. Only time would tell.

I watched from the attic as the whole scene played out below me: a clear, sunny day, the team in the yard, some of them painting while others fooled around. What it must feel like to toil freely under the late summer sun. Then someone marched up the sidewalk, grocery bags in both hands. He stopped to talk to the girl next door, and I caught a clear glimpse of his face. Oh. My breath hitched at the sight of him. Evan.

Dear, sweet Evan.

Seeing him, and all the possibilities that had once hovered about him, the attic never felt so small and stale, filled with must and mites. I breathed them in, letting them take residence in my lungs, the scratch of dust and mold a constant in the back of my throat.

I could've had it all with Evan—real, actual love. But He'd destroyed it. He called me obsessively at work, threatened to hurt Evan if I talked to him too much during my shift. When I wouldn't stop seeing Evan, He, Michael, threatened to punish me in a way that would leave me permanently disfigured. He wanted to ruin my face, more specifically, my eyes. He promised that if He took them, He'd keep them preserved and hidden in a dark place, never to look upon another man again. Then He turned around and asked me why I looked so scared. Told me I was crazy if I actually thought He'd hurt me. And He'd wrapped his big muscular arms around me and held me for a long time until the trembling stopped and my heartbeat slowed and I doubted what I knew to be true.

Chapter Eight

August 25 (continued)

ACORN COMMUNITY COLLEGE had a gym and track open to all students, so that was where we headed. We had a few more days to train for the physical element of the academy, and the brochures had painted a fairly intense picture regarding fitness. Images of recruits lifting weights, climbing obstacles, decked out in full body tactical gear graced the pages. My mom hadn't said a word as she read through the material, but her mouth had clenched up like a butthole. I knew what she was thinking: *My baby girl wants to do this*? I'd be lying if I said I hadn't thought something similar.

"Have you ever trained for anything before?" Hazel asked, putting actual physical scare quotes around "trained."

"I mean, I was in dance since I was five. That's a kind of training." I put the car in reverse, then swung my arm over the back of her seat to maneuver into a parking spot.

"I hate running."

"Same," I agreed. But that hadn't always been true. I used to run a couple times a week. The city had a well-maintained trail system alongside the Skullkey River, and I'd used it frequently until... Well, I didn't like being alone in the woods now.

I put the car in park and shut off the engine. We meandered over the pavement that led to the track. Well-manicured greenspaces and maple trees, whose leaves were sure to burn with orange and red this fall, dotted the sidewalks. The track came into view, and the burnt-sienna gravel seemed to attract the sun with blurry waves of heat radiating off the ground. Lots of folks had the same idea. Unlike the sweltering moist heat of most summer days in Ohio, the humidity had stayed low, and a perfect seventy-degree breeze wafted over my bare legs.

Our footsteps crunched over the sandy pebbles, and we picked a spot alongside the bench to put Hazel's backpack and our water bottles. She checked the brand-new Nokia cell phone Doug had helped her pick out at the mall.

"We've got to do a mile and a half as fast as we can. You good?"

"I can handle it."

We took off, keeping a quick, steady pace with each other and not talking. After a lap, some people I recognized from the initial drug test jogged down the bleacher steps and joined us.

"Hey, you guys are part of our class, right?"

I managed to nod, feeling myself getting breathy with each step.

"Cool." This was the short, stocky guy who had interrupted the instructor the other day. He introduced himself as Todd and had a knack for being able to run and chatter. The guys stayed together, in general. But they ticked it up a notch every few feet, each of them trying to be the lead. We kept going faster and faster until even Todd had to shut up.

Hazel had fallen off pace, so I veered toward the edge of the track and waited as she caught up.

"You don't have to slow down for me," she said.

I fell in line beside her. "They're sprinting hardcore."

"I noticed." She laughed. "That ain't me."

And I was reminded again of how endearing I found her to be. She followed her own instinct and was wholly unswayed by the people around her. The exact opposite type of person than Michael and his friends from the party last night. Those folks had been ready to go along with however the tide turned. Not Hazel. Not me. We were alike in that way.

"How we doing?" I asked with one lap to go.

Hazel checked her phone. "We'll make it." And we did with minutes to spare within the recommended limit.

Todd and the others, who'd started later than us, jammed the track, crossing the finish line at a fast clip. They slowed up, hands behind their heads, faces flushed and sweaty, chests heaving. They opened water bottles and poured them over their heads, ripped off shirts and used them as towels.

Hazel and I stood nearby, sipping our water and watching the display.

"Quite a little show they're putting on," she said.

"Right? Think it's for us or themselves?"

She snorted. "Both, probably."

Todd jogged toward us. Obviously, he had established himself as leader. A couple of the other guys joined him, and before I knew it, we were surrounded.

They all introduced themselves. David, Scott, Tim... names I'd forgotten as soon as they said them. They were nice enough, seemingly easygoing and supportive. We were in this police academy thing together, they said. They wanted to exchange phone numbers. Okay. We did that, and then they left. Off to do...whatever.

"They seem different than our neighbors," I said. "Like, the vibe they give off is...less threatening?"

"I guess." Hazel zipped up her backpack. "The neighbors are just a bunch of drunk assholes."

"No, it's more than that." I drank from my water bottle.

"What do you mean? That one guy had them cleaning everything up today." Hazel had not witnessed the straight-up sadistic side of that team and their captain.

"Yeah, and last night, he was beating the shit out of four nearly naked guys with a stick."

"*What?*" Surprise painted all her features with an excitement that every person on earth agreed we were supposed to hide. I loved it. The thrill of telling something at the exact right time, to get the exact right reaction, fluttered in my stomach.

"I'm not lying. They had hoods on their heads and everything."

"Jesus." Hazel's upper lip curled as if she smelled something foul.

"It was a whole *thing*. Like, ritualistic and shit."

"I thought that only happened in fraternities."

"Apparently not," I said as we headed back toward the bleachers, bypassing and weaving around other groups of students using the track. "Apparently, it's everywhere."

"Well, that's not true. One university sports team doesn't equal *everywhere*."

She could be so specific about language. I rolled my eyes. "Fine, whatever. What should we do about it?"

"What do you mean?" She reached the top of the steps and turned around to face me. I almost stumbled into her, and she grabbed my arm, stopping me from tumbling backward. "Be careful."

"Thanks." I steadied myself, and as she let go of me, the absence of her simple, saving touch weighed heavy. I walked past her, pushing my crush down and away. "I mean, should we, like, call someone? Report it? The university would want to know, right?"

"I don't know." She jogged a few steps to keep up with me. "It's happening off campus. What could they even do about it?"

I shrugged. "I'm not sure. But there has to be someone that handles this kind of thing. Hazing isn't just something that happens once. It's ongoing, a kind of system. We wouldn't be the first to report it, I'm sure."

"We can try." She didn't sound convinced, and that was confusing to me.

"Why are you being so nonchalant about this?" I asked.

"What? I'm agreeing with you." The line between her eyebrows reformed, not so sweet this time.

"This is some legitimate abuse. It changes who people are, and you're acting like it's no big deal."

"I just agreed; we *should* report it."

"I don't know. You just seem...kind of flippant."

"Look, I don't think the university will do anything." She stopped walking, so I did too. We stood in the middle of the campus, where a bunch of walkways converged. "If there's already a file on the team, then it's something Oakley's swept under the rug. If there isn't, then what are they gonna do about a first report, Maeve? Especially from two rando neighbors. We don't even go there."

"So what? You think since there won't be any consequences, we should just ignore it? Let it happen. Don't get involved."

"That's...not exactly what I'm trying to say." She'd wavered though. "I'm just not going to get all riled up about what's happening to a bunch of guys who chose to put themselves in that situation."

"Do you even hear yourself right now?" I tried to keep my voice level, but it didn't work. "You sound like every campus cop that asked me if I'd been drinking that day I got groped on the trail. Like every admin who asks what a woman wore the minute she comes forward." People passed by as we argued, side-eyeing us. "Those younger guys signed on to a *sports team*. Period. Probably got a scholarship, which means their education is at stake. Their futures. They didn't ask to be humiliated or fucking caned, Hazel. This is a big deal. And it's happening in *our* backyard."

Hazel pressed her lips into a line and looked past me, toward the people streaming by us on the sidewalk. "You're right; you're right. I get it." Her shoulders dipped with a sigh. "Okay, let's start the ball rolling."

"Yeah?" I asked, unsure if she really agreed or was just trying to placate me.

"Yes."

I did a mini fist pump.

"Don't look so excited."

"Don't even act like you don't love it when we partner up to fix something," I teased, right on the edge of flirtation.

Day 826 (continued)

From Within the House

I made a mistake. I couldn't help it. Seeing Evan had caught me so off guard.

Ultimately, Evan had been the catalyst for my disappearance, the person who'd made me realize I didn't have to fit into the mold Michael made for me. I was a whole person who deserved more. So I left. The house became my cocoon. And when I felt ready, I'd emerge anew. Even if it took thousands of days.

But spotting Evan had made me reckless. I stepped too close to the dormer, let the light shine on me, pressed my palm to the glass as Evan hurried away from the girl next door's row house. And when I cast my glance back to the yard, I saw Him looking up at me.

He'd seen me. Plain as day, He looked up at just the right moment and knew I was here. I should leave. Run! My insides screamed. Get out of this house and out of His grasp forever.

I looked down at myself, wearing the borrowed and ill-fitting clothes I'd pilfered during and after their parties.

Two years of living off pantry scraps and stale leftovers. Stealing change and rummaging through castaway purses. I only risked going outside in the summertime when the house was left vacant, so now, my veins were easily traceable along the underside of my wrists. It would only take something sharp to pop through those wiry blue strands, ending this limbo-like phase once and for all. The glass of a window or mirror would do.

But another thought stopped me; a seed of an idea metastasized and pulsed alongside my blood cells within those very surface-level veins I gazed upon. What happened to the boys who'd gone feral in the end? As far as I'd seen, nothing. But that was only because everyone else was too afraid. And fear? If there was one thing He had taught me, it was that fear wasn't what hurt the most. It was just what stopped you from doing anything useful.

So instead of withering away, lurking among shadows, what if I did something else? What if I stopped Him for good, never allowing him to hurt another person? No one would suspect someone who didn't exist. So, what if I wrote a new ending? An invisible narrator knew no bounds. The seed of revenge cracked open and grew and sprouted inside me. Bloomed. Nurtured in the cold, dark spaces of the house, it said, Stay.

And that was when I figured out how to play this my way, when I claimed some of the power that came with living this way for so long. He couldn't be sure if what He'd seen was a real, live person. I'd been out of His life too long. He'd surely convince himself that what He'd seen in the window wasn't actually me, but a vision. Or His conscience. Maybe a ghost.

One that could actually haunt Him...him. Him him him him him. He was only a him.

Chapter Nine

August 29, 2001

A SOFT KNOCK sounded at my bedroom door. I'd told Hazel to wake me up this morning because it was still summer, and I resented setting an alarm. But today was the physical exam for the academy.

Hazel handed me a cup of coffee and sat on the edge of my bed. I lit the day's first cigarette, then blew the smoke toward the open window. She held out her two fingers, index and middle like a pair of open scissors, and I handed it to her. She took a hit.

"So after today, we'll be official cadets," I said.

"Seems so." She nodded, blowing out smoke. "How was last night?" She indicated the littered yard below my window.

"Unusually quiet."

"That's good."

"Yeah, I finally got some sleep."

"Why do you think it happens?"

"Hazing, you mean?" I sipped my coffee, thankful for its heat and bitter wash over my tongue. Our conversation about what I'd witnessed next door had continued, but we'd yet to do anything about it.

"Yeah, like, how did degrading people evolve into some kind of social requirement? In order to be accepted into a group you have to debase yourself? That makes no sense. And why are parents okay with it? It's not like they don't know it's happening."

"I would think they know to expect some of it. They've probably convinced themselves it's just the way it is, that it isn't *that* bad." I shrugged.

"But it always is just—so bad. And it always escalates, right?" Hazel said, finger-combing her hair into a ponytail. Obviously, she'd put some more thought into this, especially after our disagreement at the track the other day.

"Totally. If you're willing to cane someone in your own home, I don't know what stops you from doing *anything* else."

"Makes me think of that scene from *The Breakfast Club*, where the one guy tapes another guy's ass cheeks together. Like, I remember watching as a kid and thinking, *Big deal*. But that is a very huge deal, and why the fuck wasn't I horrified by that when I heard it as a kid?"

I shrugged. "I remember thinking the same thing." I paused, then added, "The world is definitely fucked."

She took my mug and sipped, then handed it and my cigarette back to me. "Get dressed. We gotta leave in twenty minutes."

"That's your segue?" But I said it with a smile.

"We're not gonna solve the world being fucked right now. But I'm positive there'll be consequences if we're late for the physical."

"You're so motivated this morning, especially for someone who wouldn't even speak to an officer a year ago." I cringed. Why had *that* come out of my mouth? Hazel hadn't been able to talk to a cop because the man who'd killed her mom had dressed up as one. That was how he gained access into homes—trust. And then the real officers had gaslit her mother right off a bridge. What a dumbass thing for me to bring up. I was an idiot.

She scratched her forehead. "Yeah." She sniffed, then stood up and headed for the door. "We'll figure out what to do about the hazing when we get back, okay?" She called from the bathroom. The sink turned on, and I heard the *squish-swish* of her toothbrush against her teeth.

I pulled on clean clothes, slipped on my running shoes, and ran some water through my short hair, which needed a cut.

Hazel waited for me downstairs. She sat on the couch, her feet tucked underneath her as she flipped through one of the nerdy science magazines she always grabbed at the gas station.

"Hey, remind me to call my brother later?" I asked, hoping to smooth over my earlier misstep. "I need to check on him about the other day."

"Sure," she said flatly. Emotionless. "You ready?" She stood and zipped up her hoodie. "Let's go."

Twenty minutes later, after a very quiet drive, we pulled into the community college parking lot.

We were scheduled to meet at the track, so we headed in that direction. A couple instructors in polo shirts and reflective sunglasses already stood around the starting line holding clipboards. We waved at a few of the guys we'd already met. They were nice, inclusive, and made sure to let us join in the circle they were casually forming. When it was time, one of the instructors barked out the directions and time requirements. We were to run in packs of eight and in alphabetical order, which meant Hazel and I were in the first heat.

The other instructor, a man with a crew cut and round belly, introduced himself as Training Officer Gillespie and indicated us with a dismissive wave. "You two have extra time." He said it with a sneer, and it wasn't even like he was talking to us but rather, to the other guys, letting them know we were being treated differently. The desired effect, snorts and side-eyes, came from a few members of our cohort.

TO Gillespie pulled out a stopwatch and counted down. We all took off at "Go!" Of course, a few cadets sprinted while Hazel and I started our own consistent pace. It had worked for us in practice; it should work now. The guys who needed to lead always petered out eventually.

Before too long, I had to focus on keeping my breath under control and the feel of pebbles crunching under my feet. No room for any other thoughts except a laser-like focus on my body. And I couldn't say I didn't like it. It was what I'd always loved about running, only thinking about how my body worked and needed to move versus the million other distractions that flitted through my head.

We started the final two laps, and that was when we'd agreed to pick up the pace. We passed a couple of dudes who had spent themselves too soon and crossed the finish line with most of our soon-to-be classmates.

After our heat, another instructor led us to the gymnasium, where we were to complete the other two components of the test: sit-ups and push-ups. It took very little time, and before we knew it, we were done, real anticlimactic-like. As we sat on the bleachers waiting for the other groups to finish, Hazel handed me a water from her backpack.

"So that's it."

"That's it."

I took a drink, then handed her back the water bottle, and she gulped from it. When the others finished the testing, they joined us on the bleachers. We waited for further instruction. The two instructors came in, and the three of them huddled over the results.

Two guys were called forward, and their hushed voices filled the room. They were being released. They hadn't made the cut and would have to try again for the winter semester if that was what they chose to do. One of them took the news with grace, accepting his papers and waving to those of us in the stands.

"See ya later!" he said. And I had a feeling he meant it. He was a huge guy, bearlike, and had a smiling face with deep dimples.

The other guy practically had a tantrum, crumpling his paper in his fist. His neck flushed beet-red, and his gaze never left the floor. He seemed like the kind of person who would carry this around with him forever. A constant slight that never eased up. Maybe not the kind of person who should be a cop anyway.

After that, the instructors handed out packets with class

information. Things like "tactical training" and "defensive driving" glared up at me from the page; nerves like acid crept up my esophagus.

Hazel glanced over the pages with a slight smile. She was in her element. I had loved tracking down the "bad guy" with her; it had been exciting. But when we'd found ourselves in actual, physical danger, when Shirlee Hensen came after us, when there was nowhere to run and no way out...well, that had been terrifying. My best friend had been stabbed. I watched it. I saw what was inside her seep and pool into cheap berber carpet. And now...now, I second-guessed whether I could put myself in that kind of situation again.

Except that seemed to be how our relationship kept unfolding. A certain amount of danger had spattered our bond throughout. First Ryan, then Shirlee. Now cop school. Until finally, the real world—whatever that meant.

When everyone around me started packing up, I snapped to attention.

"You okay?" Hazel asked.

"Yeah." My voice sounded weak, inside a bubble of its own making, even to my ears. I cleared my throat and tried again. "Hell yeah. We made it."

Hazel smiled. "Damn right we did."

As we gathered our things and congratulated some of the other cadets, I noticed movement out of the corner of my eye. On the other side of the gym, someone else stood in the doorway, their silhouette filling the open space. For a second, I worried about the guy who'd been dismissed. Maybe he'd come back, snapped in the parking lot, and grabbed a gun or something, like all those postal workers. But as the person stepped into the light, my breath caught in my throat for another reason. It was Michael.

I tugged on the loose fabric of Hazel's T-shirt. "Hey," I whispered, and she turned. "Our neighbor's here."

"What?" She looked around inconspicuously and spotted him on the other side of the room.

He didn't see us. Instead, he homed in on one of the instructors, making a beeline across the gym.

"What's he doing here?" she wondered.

"Let's find out."

"How are we going to do that?"

"Follow me."

A short line of cadets waited in front of the instructors, so I pulled out my class packet and started toward them. I stopped at the edge of the crowd, as close to Michael as I could get without being obvious. I didn't want him to spot and recognize me. He was engaged in an urgent-seeming conversation with our instructor, the slightly overweight one who'd singled Hazel and me out on the track. Deep in dialogue, Michael seemed...flustered. His cheeks flushed pink, and a sheen of sweat covered his handsome features, so unlike the breezy, confident leader he usually projected.

"I thought you'd help."

"Help with what? It's not my jurisdiction anymore, Mike."

I eavesdropped. Trying to be nonchalant and blend in with my class, I kept my gaze focused on the two instructors who were answering questions from the group, when one of them called on me.

"You. What's your question?"

"Uh...me?" Hazel's arm pressed against mine. "I was

just gonna ask..." I had nothing. My mind went blank. Everyone stared at me, and now, I could feel Michael's eyes on me too. *Think. Think of something.*

"Yes..." the instructor encouraged.

"About tuition. Financial aid."

"You'll need to go to the bursar's office for that stuff, hon. I don't know anything 'bout all that."

"Okay, sir. Thank you, sir." I forced myself *not* to look at Michael as Hazel and I made our way toward the double doors.

Outside, the day had progressed into a squelcher of a late summer day. Even the birds seemed affected by the heat with their usual upbeat whistles and squawks sounding muffled and desperate. The campus still had that vacant feel every school had for three months out of the year. Yet that would all change in a couple days. For now, it felt laid-back. Stress-free. Lazy. Except, what the hell was Michael doing here?

"Did you hear anything?" Hazel asked as we paced through the grounds and toward the parking lot.

"Yeah. Seemed like Michael thought that instructor could help him with something."

"Training Officer Gillespie."

"So what would our neighbor need someone with police training for?"

"Nothing good."

"Agreed."

"Hey! Hey you guys!" a voice called. We turned to see Michael running toward us. "Wait up!" He jogged in that obvious-athletic way, every move seeming effortless and full of grace, animalistic.

"Do we wait?" I asked Hazel out of the side of my mouth.

"Leaving would be the rude thing. He's totally seen us."

"Right." I nodded. "Who cares about being rude again?"

But before we could make a different move, he stood in front of us, not even panting. "What were you guys doing back there?"

"We're in the peace officer training program," Hazel said.

"That's cool. My uncle runs some of the trainings."

"Oh." I nodded my head. "What are *you* doing here?"

"Uh…" He scratched the back of his neck. "It's nothing. Ancient history."

"Like?" I asked. He wasn't getting off that easy.

"Someone's…come forward." He twirled the ring on his middle finger; the big, ruby-red stone glinted in the sunlight.

"Issued a complaint against you guys? Good. They should," I said.

Michael's expression flashed indignant—of course—before his cool, confident demeanor regained control of his features. "Whatever."

"Yeah, whatever. Having a whole group of people watch while you beat four people is just totally normal, right? A regular Friday night," I countered.

His smile became a mask. "You don't understand. This is something different. Not about the team."

"Well…" I waited. "We're listening."

His eyes shifted to Hazel as if she'd help him. The only lifeline she gave him was to cross her arms and adjust her posture, waiting just like me.

"Too scared to talk?" I asked, letting the challenge drip over my words.

"I don't know what you mean." His tone was sharp and gritty; it rattled like bones and chains and a whole lifetime of being told to be a man. "You couldn't possible know…"

"Enlighten us," Hazel added.

Michael looked around, his eyes nervously darting around the quad.

"There's, like, no one here, dude." But then I realized… Fear. This legitimate big man on campus seemed scared. "Are you okay?"

"Yeah. No. I don't know." He looked toward the clouds; his eyebrows creased with worry. "Someone I used to—" He stopped, glanced away, checking the horizon. "Look, I-I want to talk about it." He blew out a puffy breath. "But I don't know. I can't."

"Here. Sit down." I indicated the bench just off the path and guided him toward it.

"It's okay, Michael," Hazel added and sat next to him.

I wondered whether we were being manipulated. The moment Michael was confronted, he crumbled like a dried-out autumn leaf? It didn't exactly match up with the swaggering bro who'd insisted he wasn't a bad guy in our back alley. Sure, people contained multitudes. And who knew what he faced? Real-world consequences could be a bitch that way. But I wasn't completely convinced of the authenticity of this moment, yet I tucked my doubt away. Because either way, watching him, listening to him, questioning him gave me more information, and that was what I craved.

He bent forward, resting his elbows on his knees. He wove his fingers together and brought them up toward his lips as if to pray, staring only at the grass.

We waited. Hazel and I made eye contact, and I tried to communicate wordlessly. I opened my eyes wide and gestured with my hands, meaning to suggest *What now*? She shrugged. Her mouth turned down at the corners.

"You guys need to be more careful," he said.

"What? Why?" I asked.

"There's a lot you think you might know about...the team. And me. But...there's more to it than you realize."

"Well, yeah..." I said, hoping he'd continue. Of course there'd be more. I'd witnessed one night out of countless others. He couldn't think we'd be so naïve as to think that was as bad as it got. "No shit."

For an instant, his gaze met mine. But I couldn't read what he stored behind his eyes. All I had was his cryptic behavior and a mealymouthed warning. Still, the moment had the feel of something more, something deeper, something else passing between us. I thought of an angler fish, how they attracted prey with a little dangling light in the deep, dark ocean. Our neighbors wouldn't be ignored; they were both the light and the monster with all the teeth.

Before Michael said anything else, he stood and walked away.

"Wait!" I called after him now. Why had he stopped us only to reveal nothing? "You can't just leave! What's going on?" I started after him, but then he picked up his pace, and I knew I'd never catch him. Slowing down, my knees jarred with each halting step. Hazel came up beside me.

"Well. That was weird," she said.

I laughed, then added, "Seriously."

"Those guys are nothing but drama." Hazel casually

gripped the straps of her backpack.

I nodded. "Especially when they're abusing each other all the damn time." We continued our trek to the parking lot. "We should probably at least *consider* what he meant. That warning... I don't think he was putting on a show."

"I don't either." She paused, but I knew her brain was working overtime. "He said, 'Someone's come forward.' Do they think we have?"

"Maybe."

"Who all saw you at that party the other night?"

"I don't know." I'd caused a scene, so a lot of them, but I didn't tell her that. She shouldn't be made to feel scared in our own home because of something I'd instigated.

"Kinda makes our living situation less than ideal." She bit at a hangnail on her thumb, then cursed when the skin ripped away and started to bleed. I pulled a tissue from my bag and handed it to her. She wrapped it around her bleeding thumb, and we made our way back to the car, my brain replaying the two warnings I'd received. One from Evan, one from Michael: Be careful.

Chapter Ten

August 29 (continued)

I GRABBED A bag of potato chips and pulled up a chair next to Hazel who sat at the computer desk. We were trying to find out exactly who we were up against, and what—if any-thing—we could do about what was happening next door.

Our knees brushed against each other, and I ignored the volt of electric-shock coursing through my body.

Hazel clicked on a link that took us to the university's website. She asked, "Do you know Michael's last name?"

I crunched down on the chip I'd already placed on my tongue. *Did I?* I couldn't remember if he'd ever given me his last name, and I shook my head.

"Okay then. Let's start with the team." Hazel went to the athletics section and selected lacrosse. She scrolled until she found this year's team. A couple of articles from the *Echo*, the campus newspaper, popped up.

She scanned the articles. Her glasses, which she hardly ever wore, preferring contacts, slipped down her nose. "We need a team picture. Or a roster."

Pictures loaded onto the screen along with the articles, but none mentioned Michael's name. No full team photos, just action shots.

"Click on that tab. Stats," I said.

She did, and a document filled the screen. It included information about wins/losses, shot statistics, something called "man-up opportunities," goal breakdowns—a bunch of stuff I didn't understand. The second page, though, had the team ranked by all their individual statistics, and it included full names.

Michael Gillespie was at the top of the list, a high performer.

"Same as our Training Officer..." Hazel said. "We should've thought of that."

"Yeah, his uncle. But why is he calling in a favor from a training officer at the community college campus?" I frowned. "That seems...I don't know, kind of desperate?"

"Agreed." Hazel pinched her lower lip and then her upper arm. "What kind of power would he have?"

"None apparently. He said he didn't have any jurisdiction anymore."

"But maybe he did?"

"That might fit with what Michael said about ancient history. Can you look it up?"

"Where's he from?" Hazel asked. "I might be able to find a police website listing him as an employee, but I'd need to know what district he worked in."

A dead end. "I don't know where they're from. Could be

anywhere."

For a minute, the only sound between us was the crinkling bag of chips and the traffic whooshing by outside. The curtains swayed with the afternoon breeze. Hazel sipped from a can of lemon-lime pop.

"Not if your brother knew him," she said.

"What?"

"If Michael was the guy he recognized the other day, then he must have lived near you guys."

"It's...possible? Evan didn't say who got him all worked up."

"Well, can you ask? You wanted to check on him anyway."

"Yeah, hand me the phone."

I dialed Evan's cell phone number, but he didn't pick up. The call went to voicemail. I left him a message and told him to call me back; it was about the guys next door.

"That should get his attention," I said, hitting End. But Evan hadn't been all that predictable lately. Sometimes he stayed at an apartment he'd rented with a friend, and other times, he was at our parents' home for weeks at a time. The only thing consistent about him was that he worked at the little indie coffee shop near campus. "If he doesn't call, I'll go see him at work."

"Well, we can't really go any farther with the TO Gillespie angle until we know where he might have worked."

"What about reporting what I saw?"

"I searched the university website. But what you witnessed isn't a neat fit for any department. I got the feeling you needed to be the victim to make a report, not witness people being victimized. And it's questionable what you saw fits under sexual assault, right? So Title IX is out."

"Okay, but Michael said 'someone came forward.' They had to go somewhere."

"Sure. If someone went to the actual police, or maybe a lawyer, they might look into any past complaints against the team. Filing a report *somewhere* would corroborate the original complaint. Make it more likely that something changes."

"So maybe the athletic department?"

"Probably a good place to start."

It didn't feel like enough though. Campus security had made me feel responsible for getting groped last year. They'd kept quiet about there being a pattern of attacks happening on campus. What on earth might the university's athletic department say about the guys next door abusing the shit out of one another?

Hazel clicked something, and the printer whirred to life. She handed me the paper, warm with fresh ink, and a pen.

"Think it'll do any good?" I asked as I filled it out.

She shrugged. We both understood systems kept secrets. Certain organizations wholly functioned in the murky perimeters where everyone knew atrocities existed yet pretended otherwise.

"So I just put this in the mail?" I scanned my report, then folded it into thirds. "That seems... I don't know." Whatever it was left a sour taste in my mouth. Like I could just drop a few papers in a bright and shiny blue box and my responsibility absolved itself. Nothing risked, nothing gained, nothing changed.

"Like a cop-out?" Hazel asked.

"Something like that."

"You wanna hand deliver it?"

For whatever reason, that did feel like a more proactive choice. "They open today?"

"Till four."

"I'm ready." I brushed chip crumbs from my lap. "Let's go."

"Let me message Doug first," she said.

My shoulders slumped. Nothing risked, nothing gained, nothing changed. *Fuck it. I'm asking.* "What *is* up with you two?"

She side-eyed me. "Nothing." Her fingers clipped over the keyboard as she typed.

"You sure about that?" I grabbed my keys and purse. "You guys are together all the time."

"He's helping me with something."

"What?"

She could be like this sometimes. For someone so specific about language, she had the ability to answer questions without really giving away anything.

She scratched her neck. Avoided eye contact. Logged out of the computer. "Just a project."

"Got it."

She wasn't going to tell me. Whatever she and Doug had going on, she wanted to keep it separate from me, which gave me every answer I needed about her possibly harboring feelings for me.

The door slammed behind me, something I hadn't actually meant to do, but whatever. I was sick of this. I knew exactly where I stood with every other person in the world. I could piece out where they were coming from and how I could manipulate them. But not Hazel. She kept me guessing all the damn time, and I'd thought that meant something. How could I be so dumb? I lit a cigarette and let the first inhalation of smoke soothe me. I sat on the stoop, realizing I'd been pining away for nothing. I should just move on. Maybe move out.

Hazel came outside and locked the apartment. She sat next to me and stole the cigarette from between my fingers, then took a hit. After a beat, she asked, "Why don't you want me spending time with Doug?"

I swallowed. "It's...nothing."

"You're always asking about him and me. Are you into him?"

"Ha! No." The last thing I needed was for her to be mistaking my interest in Doug as a crush on him. "Not him."

"Then why are you're sulking about me spending time with him? I can have more than one friend, Maeve."

That hit a mark. Instead of answering, I took my cigarette back. Should I just come out with it? Was this the moment? I didn't want her thinking I was a shit friend who got all possessive and weird every time she went to the mall with someone who wasn't me.

I looked around, avoiding eye contact. The neighborhood sounded like a neighborhood: cars swooshed by us; the occasional blurb of music filled the air around the sidewalk; screen doors slammed; AC units hummed. Nature faded. There were birds chirping, but I had to strain to hear them. Squirrels probably chittered and their nails likely clacked against the bark of the trees they scampered up, but the sounds of their lives were muffled by all this human shit. There was no babbling brook or pink and orange smears of the sunset. In a word, unromantic. But I was the girl who took hold of the moments I was given. Always have. Always will. Fuck the setting.

"I'm not interested in Doug, Hazel." We stood, and both walked toward my car. She carried my report in a manila envelope.

"Well, I'm not either. So if you wanna hook up or whatever…it's cool with me."

"That's so *not* what I want." I stopped at the driver side door, Hazel at the passenger. Our gaze met over the rooftop. "I'm into—"

"Good because he's helping me piece some shit together. You know what happened to my mom. We're trying to find other victims."

You was how I would've finished the sentence she'd interrupted, but what she had just said quickly registered alongside a swell of confusion. "Wait, what? Doug's helping you find more victims of the Creeping Cop?"

"He is." A smile crept into her eyes.

"And you didn't want me in on it?" A prickle of hurt formed right in the center of my stomach. This was going so wrong. I was supposed to be confessing my feelings, and she was supposed to be admitting hers, and then we'd kiss—all happily-ever-after-like.

"Oh, no. It's not that I didn't want your help. Doug started it. He sent me some articles he'd found over the summer, and we've just been collecting them, piecing them together. It's just now starting to come together." She wrapped a strand of hair around her finger, turning it pink and then purple. "Are you mad?"

"Uh…no. I don't know. No." I fumbled both my words and my emotions. I'd changed the whole course of my life to work in crime next to someone who didn't even think to include me on an investigation involving their own mother. I looked down at the car keys in my hands until I finally managed to unlock the doors.

"I don't think you get it."

"Oh, I do! Totally understand." I got in the car, shoved the key in the ignition, and turned. The engine roared to life, but Hazel stayed outside. I pressed the button and the passenger side window rolled down. "You coming?" I asked, knowing she wouldn't. Knowing I'd lost her. Knowing I'd blown it by acting jealous or angry or whatever the fuck it was I was feeling at the moment.

She bent over and leaned into the car, her long, wavy hair nearly dusting the seat. "Uh...I've got some other things—"

"Yeah, okay. See you later." I swept my hand through my short hair and nodded, barely having the courage to look at her. When I did, she handed me the envelope. I took it. Our hands lingered over both ends, our eyes meeting until she let go and walked away. All I could do was swallow and keep breathing. I watched in my rearview as she made her way back to our apartment. She didn't turn around, didn't give me another look. She chose him.

*

I HADN'T BEEN on campus since last spring, but nothing had changed except which roads were under construction. Traffic pulsed along until I arrived at the nearest public lot and parked. Unsure how I'd even gotten there, I'd spent the whole drive thinking about what had just happened between

Hazel and me. Friendship strained. Living arrangement—awkward. All because of a project she had going with Doug? Why had they excluded me? When shit went down last year, I'd been right there with her, helping any way I could. But that didn't count for anything anymore because I'd been tossed aside for computer boy.

As I walked through campus, it came alive, a warm hub pulsating with life and learning. I caught snippets of conversations as students, all moved in and ready to start classes next week, joked and laughed and made new friends. Oakley was its own organism, a living thing, breathing and breeding as people passed through its halls and learned. I...liked it here. I...missed being here. *Great.*

"Maeve?" someone called from behind. "Maeve!"

I turned and saw Bridgette, my smoking buddy in the dorms from last year, coming toward me.

"It is you," she said as she got closer. Her style had smoothed itself out. She'd ping-ponged between goth and prep last year and finally settled somewhere between the two, wearing a pair of loose-fitting khaki pants and her signature combat boots. Her long blond hair sat in two buns, one tucked behind each ear.

"Bridgette, hi!" I tried to garner some enthusiasm, but really, my head was still wrapped around being left out of Hazel's project.

"What have you been up to?" she asked.

"Uh, you know. Moving into an apartment, getting ready for the academy."

"That's right! You left Oakley."

Judgement left a little ring around her words, but I ignored it. "How're you? Sticking with..." My mind drew a blank. I knew it had something to do with death.

"Mortuary science," she filled in for me.

"That's right."

"I am, yeah. Family business, remember? I'm working freshman orientation today though."

"That's cool." I nodded as behind her, a wave of young students swelled.

"What are you doing here?" she asked.

"Oh," I showed her the folded piece of paper. "Just some paperwork." And suddenly we were surrounded, the sidewalk flooded with young people, the looks on their faces seemingly alternating between exuberance and anxiety. "I better let you get back to it," I said.

"It's good to see you. We should grab a coffee or something," she added just before a freshman started peppering her with questions about dorm policy.

"Yeah, okay," I said, but she hadn't heard. She'd already been swallowed up by her responsibilities. I walked away feeling a little...hollowed out. Nothing made sense anymore.

I'd thought leaving Oakley had been the right call. It wasn't as if I had any other career options screaming at me. I hadn't known or chosen a major last year because I liked the freedom of just learning for learning's sake. But people had asked me about it constantly. Then the peace officer program presented itself, and I'd made a move. Hazel had been an influence, but she wasn't the only reason I'd made that choice. It had been everyone else, too, hounding me about what I wanted to do with the rest of my life. How could I make a decision so huge without trying new things? Without living alone. Without any experience outside my

Greek/Irish family and suburban life.

As I paced the perimeter of the Trap and neared the building that housed the athletic admin office, gray clouds blotted out the sun and filled the sky. The temperature dropped, and the air smelled of ozone and imminent rain.

I opened the door to the building and stepped into a hallway. A big frame affixed to the wall contained directional information behind the glass. I found the department I needed and started walking.

The building worked like a maze, turning and turning in on itself. Every few feet, there'd be a door with a numbered placard near it, a list of names followed by their titles—an abbreviation of degrees—underneath.

Finally, feeling as if I'd wander forever, I found the athletic department office. When I grabbed the handle and turned, it didn't budge—locked. There were no hours posted, but Hazel had said they'd be open until four. I didn't have a watch or phone, but I should have had about twenty more minutes. Faced with a slab of solid wood, a lock, and a mail slot, I slipped the paperwork into the slot and hoped my report got into the hands of someone who would do something, which felt more like a fairy wish than anything real.

I turned to leave, more deflated and anxious than ever, and followed the maze back outside, into a fierce afternoon storm. The building had been like a bunker. From inside its halls, there'd been no indication of the rain falling in sheets and the leaden sky illuminated sporadically by cracks of lightning. I stood under the portico. Rain splashed onto my shoes and ankles while I sat on the stoop and waited for the storm to pass.

A team, their practice outpaced by the weather, ran by in matching university-colored shorts and sleeveless T-shirts. Their strong, muscular bodies sprang and splashed through the rain. In the middle of the pack, blond hair plastered to his head, raced Michael.

The lacrosse team.

I looked down, hiding my face. He'd warned me. And my brother had warned me. What would these guys think if they saw me outside the athletic administration offices? Michael knew I went to ACC, not here. My heart beat faster, and a new wave of anxiety coursed through my veins. They'd know. They'd blame me for getting them into trouble. And they'd... I couldn't even fathom what they'd do. I exhaled to the count of five, struggling to push out air on the last two beats, and then I inhaled. *Count. Relax.* Surely, he hadn't seen me through the blurry rain and chaos of trying to finish their practice in the storm.

A blinding whipcrack of lightning highlighted the Trap in a silvery flash. Goosebumps broke out all over my body, and a strangely metallic-burning taste filled my mouth. Then came the growl of thunder, roaring as if the whole world had broken open. The tree, the historic oak in the middle of the Trap, smoked and burned. Flames were quickly extinguished by the rain, but the oak split, and a sizeable chunk crashed to the ground.

The team had stopped running. They stood in front of the steps and reacted as I did—amazed and cursing, unbelieving that something so random, so powerful, and frankly beautiful had struck from the heavens. But as we snapped out of our reverie, laughing and blowing out held breaths, I realized Michael and Stef weren't looking at the destroyed hundred-year-old tree at all. Instead, their eyes were fixed on me.

I flipped them both off.

Day 830

From Within the House

Haunting was a practice, especially in this house. There were so many people in and out it was difficult to do a proper job of it. Turning the lights on or hiding things just didn't do anything because he blamed issues with electricity on faulty wiring; missing stuff was just lost. So I scratched at the lath and tore up the insulation in every room he spent time in. But then I overheard him talking about needing to call a pest removal company, which put me at risk of being found out, so I paused that tactic.

My methods had to become more drastic, more specific. I'd carved both our names over and over again into the wood, the ribs of the house, creating my own magic, a spell he could not escape or explain away, and got back to work.

I followed his movements whenever he was home and stood nearby, only the wall separating us, whispering my name like a heartbeat. Two days ago, I wrote "Liar" on the handle of his crosse with permanent marker. While they were at class today, I took a pair of scissors to his bedclothes, then stabbed the mattress until only fluff and springs appeared.

Through a knothole in the door of their closet, I watched

how my brother slept in fits and starts on the floor, an old sleeping bag covering him and a rolled-up towel for a pillow. Michael lay in my brother's bed, muttering to himself and biting his nails, and stared at the ceiling, his own ruined mattress out on the curb. He was more dangerous this way, the lack of sleep driving him to the brink as he lashed out at his teammates not just in his little ceremonies but all the time now.

It was working.

Chapter Eleven

September 1, 2001

"EVAN, CALL ME back. I just want to check on how you're doing, okay?" I spoke into the phone. After a beat of silence, I pressed End on my recording.

"No word?" Hazel asked as she stuffed a few water bottles and granola bars into a backpack.

We'd been avoiding each other, or rather, I'd been avoiding her. I shouldn't be offended she chose to work with Doug. Shouldn't try to hold on to her and keep this as mine. Shouldn't have betrayed my own self just to be here with her. That was codependency—the red flag that'd been waving itself around me and this relationship since I'd stolen her fries last fall.

"No. He's like that though. Freaks out and then falls off the face of the earth for a while. Big plans?" I asked, attempting to break the bad spell I'd cast around us.

"Just a hike."

"Where?"

"The wetlands nature trail that runs behind Oakley." She added, "With Doug."

"Oh."

"Wanna come?"

What the hell else was I going to do with my afternoon? I needed to set my feelings for Hazel aside for good and be happy for any progress she and Doug were making on her mom's case. I needed to move on.

"Like now?"

"Yeah. He'll be here in a few minutes."

"How long is it?"

"I don't know. Couple miles."

"Okay, yeah. I'll go."

She smiled, seemingly happy for the return to normal. A car horn sounded outside. I already had on a pair of swishy athletic pants and a T-shirt, so I quickly pulled on my sneakers and locked the door behind us.

Doug sat behind the steering wheel of his emerald-green Honda. Hazel climbed into the front seat, explaining about me joining them. To Doug's credit, he didn't seem to mind and greeted me kindly and casually.

"How ya doin', Maeve?"

"Good. You?"

"Just waiting tables, mostly. Ready for classes to start."

"Yeah."

"Hey, when do you guys start?"

"Couple days. Same as you," Hazel offered. "ACC mirrors Oakley's schedule."

The neighborhood blurred as we drove away. The small

talk died. Doug cranked up the local indie radio station and Smashing Pumpkins "1979" blared through the speakers. I rolled down my window to let the breeze blow through my short hair. We stalled at stoplights, then accelerated over the Skullkey bridge. A comfortable vibe filled the space between us. We'd been through some real shit together and survived. Now here we were, thriving even.

Not for the first time since we'd moved back near campus, I thought of Shirlee—the fourth wheel in last year's trauma. Actually, she'd been more like the driver. For months after, I'd obsessed over what was happening with her until my mom took me aside and put an end to it. She'd warned me about being unhealthily obsessed, took my computer out of my room, and prescreened the newspaper. When I walked into the living room, she made sure the channel was never tuned to the news.

"I know you guys are working on the Creeping Cop stuff. Have you kept up with Shirlee's case at all?" I blurted. Hazel's face went pale in the sideview mirror. She shook her head. I guess I shouldn't have brought it up, but why not? Why shouldn't we talk about what had happened? Especially around each other.

Doug took a breath and straightened his posture. He gripped the steering wheel with both hands now, his knuckles flexing a pale yellow. "A little," he said and gave Hazel a sideways glance. His hand reached for her shoulder and gave a supportive squeeze.

I admitted to them how my mom had limited my access to the case over the summer.

"I know she had her arraignment," Doug said. "She pleaded not guilty. Her bail was set pretty high, and I don't think she's out or anything." His gaze flicked to mine in the rearview mirror. "If you're worried about that."

"Oh." I wasn't worried about Shirlee not being in jail. That she'd still be there seemed obvious to me, but maybe it shouldn't have been. Maybe I'd let too much space and time and scar tissue build up around the whole ordeal. It did feel distinctly distant now, as if the whole thing had happened to another person, and really, it had. I'd changed a lot, morphed into a person I didn't always recognize. Or like.

"Can we talk about something else, please?" Hazel asked. She'd been the one in grave danger; her life had hung in the balance due to Shirlee Hensen. Not to mention how Shirlee's dad posed a threat now too. A fact that lingered, like a phantom stuck in her peripheral. He was an even bigger monster—a Kronos-like figure.

Doug parked on a slab of asphalt, pocked with a public restroom and a ranger station. I'd rather pee in the woods than go near one of those glorified whole-in-the-ground restrooms, so I skipped it and followed him toward the station.

The park ranger sat behind a window and slid it open as we approached.

"Howdy," they said as if we'd crossed the Mason-Dixon line. "Nice day for a walk."

"Sure is," Doug answered.

"You can put your wallet away, son. It's free."

"Really?"

"You bet." The ranger handed him a slip, like a receipt, with a strip of masking tape attached to it. "Put this up in your windshield. And have a nice day!"

"Thanks," we said in unison.

Doug picked up a brochure with a map and unfolded it,

showing me the trail he'd picked.

A field of tall grasses, marshland, spread out before us, but not too far off, a dark line of trees loomed. A tremor of recognition ran through me. I hadn't started from here, but this trail led all the way back to the university. It was where I'd been running last year when I'd been assaulted.

"That'll lead us to a little pond, and if we keep going, it follows the edge of the Skullkey for a while."

"I know." I liked nature. Sure, I did. Most trails were fine. This one had not been.

Hazel came up behind us. "You okay?" she asked.

She knew what I was remembering. Had she known all along? When she'd invited me, did she realize exactly what this might do to me?

No. No way had she purposefully brought me back to the place of my attack last fall. It was a coincidence. If anything, *I* should have known. The trail system was all interconnected and it wasn't huge.

"I'll be fine. Can't spend my whole life indoors." I parroted my parents, who'd noticed how, all of a sudden, I preferred exercising at home. They chalked it up to the whole Shirlee-thing. To this day, I'm not sure why I didn't tell them, except it probably had a lot to do with shame and not wanting to upset them. I got a kick out of drama, but not every kind. Not the kind that would make my mom cry. It had been minor. Some guy pushed me down and copped a feel? Hell, lots of women had the same story, if not worse. I was lucky. Lucky. *Lucky.*

"What's up?" Doug asked.

"Nothing," Hazel and I said in unison.

"Okay, then." Doug turned and led us past the asphalt

patch onto a gravel trail leading around the meadow and toward the woods.

Brown-eyed Susans dotted the field with bright yellow. A robin, its breast a matte orange, took off as we approached and flew right over our heads. I homed in on the surrounding sights, sounds, and smells and felt reassured.

We neared a line of trees and entered the forest. The three of us were quiet, plodding along the path without feeling the need to fill the air with chatter. And I had to hand it to Doug; his whole aura oozed calm. It wasn't awful being around him. Every once in a while, he'd stop and point out different trees: bald cypresses and swamp white oaks, the occasional red maple and ash.

I hadn't seen Hazel this chill since...never. Even when I'd first met her, she'd been tense. Out here in the wild, and maybe because of Doug, she let herself open up. Her forehead stayed unwrinkled, and her shoulders lowered from their usual perch near her ears.

The gurgling splash of the river lured us toward it, off the beaten path. It came into view, a slick brown and white rush of fresh water, containing so much. Shirlee had washed Ryan's blood off her hands in the Skullkey and wrote of a hag who lived among its murky depths. Hazel had let it swallow her mother's necklace. Carried downstream, it'd probably made it to the ocean by now. Nothing more than stories, memories, to us, stored in the earth for some unfathomable number of years.

I found half a boulder sticking out of the ground and sat down. I took off my shoes and socks and dipped my toes in the cool water.

"Need a break?" Doug had already taken off his

backpack and unwrapped a granola bar.

"This is nice, Doug," I said. If he was good for Hazel, if she wanted him around, then I needed to at least *try*. "Thanks for letting me crash today."

"More the merrier," he said, and I knew he was being genuine. The opposite of me, the dude could be earnest as hell.

Hazel stepped between us and sat on the bank, a little section of damp, tightly packed sediment and rocks. Calling it a beach would have been an overstatement. She lay back and crossed her arms behind her head, closing her eyes against the dappled sunrays. I watched her relax as her chest rose and fell and then caught Doug doing the same thing. For a brief moment, he and I made eye contact. We held each other's stare, which contained multitudes of unspoken understanding, until a scream jolted all three of us.

"What was that?" Hazel sprang up, her fight or flight instinct activated.

"An animal?" I said, adding a tinge of hope to my tone. And yet, I knew full well only people made sounds like that.

"Uhh…" Doug's eyes were wide, but he couldn't decide where to set his gaze, letting it wander around the clearing.

The sound came again. This time longer. A high-pitched keening. A low growl.

At that, I jammed my feet back in my shoes and set off in the direction of the cries, Doug and Hazel following. He asked what we planned on doing. I had no idea. The only thing leading me on was the sense that someone was hurting. I'd been there—a lonely voice in the woods, and no one had come. Then, when I finally found someone to help, they'd blamed me. I wouldn't let that happen to someone else.

"Stop! Stop." A person choked out. As we got closer, the voice registered as low, bass in tone.

The trees thinned a bit, and the river still gulped and rushed beside us. I saw a flash of color—red—and stopped. Hazel and Doug followed my lead and stayed right behind me. I crouched, and they did too.

"Can you see anything?" Hazel whispered.

Instead of answering, I crept forward, staying in the brush for cover. On a shoal in the middle of the river, several figures milled about. Three guys were on their knees, blindfolded, hands bound behind their backs. The Oakley University standard draped around their shoulders. From the bank, I couldn't see expressions or features really, except their skin gleamed wet, and they were shivering, which didn't make sense. The temperature had steadied around seventy degrees, a gorgeous sunny day.

Behind the three men on their knees, more men stalked. They paced like wild animals, occasionally stopping to scream insults.

"You pussy! You fucking disgust me!"

"Little bitch-ass punk!"

"Is that a smile on your face?" The question came with a backhand, sending the man on his knees sideways, splashing into the water. With his hands bound, he grappled to get himself back up again.

"Let him struggle," the guy who hit him said.

"He could drown, dumbass." A few of the others helped the guy flailing in the water back up onto his knees. They didn't untie him though.

"What the fuck?" I spoke softly, no more than a hush

over the water.

"How long do you think this has been going on?" Doug whispered.

Hours. Decades. Centuries. I shrugged.

"It's gotta hurt like hell to be kneeling on the rocks like that," he said quietly.

I hadn't thought of that, but yeah, it probably was a kind of agony. All their body weight pressed into one spot, balanced on jagged rocks. Hell, even a smooth pebble could be misery with two hundred pounds loaded on top of it. Those guys were in pain, and we had to stop it.

I turned back to Hazel and Doug. "How do you want to handle this?"

"Don't look at me; those guys are massive," Doug said.

He wasn't wrong. A couple of the men screaming insults had their shirts off, and their muscles rippled.

"Kinda seems like it could be an initiation or something," Doug added.

"We heard one of them screaming," Hazel said, "begging them to stop. Even if this is some kind of group thing, somebody's backing out now. And we should make sure they're able to."

"Agreed," I said. Our eyes met over the patch of grass and clover where we crouched. I tried to read her thoughts, puzzle out exactly how she wanted to handle this without using words. But I couldn't.

"I think the best bet is to just walk by. Like we would have," she said.

"Everyday hikers," I added. "We aren't too far off the public trail. They're taking a big risk, doing whatever it is they're doing here."

"Okay," Doug said, drawing out the second syllable. "And what happens when they turn on us? You think they're just gonna pack up and leave because three people *happened* upon them?"

"True. What weapons do you have?" I asked.

"Weapons? None!" he said.

"Shh." I paused, waiting to see if the men on the shoal had noticed. "You didn't even bring a knife?" Doug confused me.

"Why would I bring a knife?"

"Jesus, Doug. Because—I don't know, wilderness preparedness."

"I was never a Boy Scout."

"You don't have to be. It's common sense." I swung my backpack around in front of me and pulled out the knife I'd bought for myself after last fall—a foldable blade. Nothing too fancy, except for the handle that I'd picked out because of the Orion constellation carved into it.

The color drained from Doug's face when he saw it. "What are you doing with that?"

I looked at him as if he were a moron. "We don't *all* get to sit behind the safety of a computer screen, Doug. Some of us have to make arrangements to move around in the world." Maybe I shouldn't have scolded him, but whatever. The moment didn't call for his pearl-clutching. Hazel brought out a similar blade with an ivory-looking handle.

"Why do you guys have these?" Doug asked again.

"Doug," I started, "nearly every woman you know has had a moment she thought she might not live through. So, yeah, we carry knives. Or Mace. Or position our keys between the fingers of our fists."

Splashing sounded behind us, and we turned to see one of the blindfolded guys emerge from the river. His hands were free, the rope still twisted and dangling from one wrist.

"Get the fuck off me, man!" He staggered toward the bank of the gravel island. "You guys are fucked up! This is so fucked up!" He tore the university flag away from his shoulders and threw it. It landed with a splat. His chest heaved, and his face flushed a dark pink. A man dressed all in black rose out of the water behind him. Another man in black stood in front of him on the shore. He held a cold pack in his hands, the kind used for injuries. For a second, I thought he was going to help him.

"Stop being such a little bitch, recruit!" the man on the beach said.

"I'm not your fuckin' recruit. I earned my spot, just like the rest of you. This shit is crazy."

"Drop your pants."

"Just do it, Ham," one of the blindfolded guys said. "Then we can all get out of here sooner."

Ham? I'd heard that name before. How many "Hams" could there actually be on or around campus?

"I'm not doing this." Ham spat, the glob landing on the river rocks.

The man coming out of the water jumped on Ham's back. With lightning speed, he wove his arms under Ham's and locked them in place behind his neck. They all laughed then. Except for this Ham person. He kept struggling, kicking, and wiggling like a worm on a hook. The man with the ice pack stuck it down the front of Ham's shorts.

I glanced at Hazel. Together we stood. I grabbed her hand and squeezed, then dropped it and moved through the woods as if we were nothing but innocent hikers enjoying a beautiful day—which we had been until stumbling onto this psychotic mess.

"Hey!" Doug called out before we came into the clearing, before the group of guys knew we were there. "What kind of bird is that?" A smart move. Doug's question gave the group time to cover for themselves. Still, this could go a lot of different ways. There were at least ten guys on the shoal, not counting the ones with ice packs strapped to their dicks.

"I don't know anything about birds," Hazel answered. And the three of us made as much noise as possible on the trail, shuffling feet and snapping twigs until the trees thinned and we stood directly across from the group.

Here, a totally different scene presented itself than the one we'd watched hidden in the underbrush. There were only about half the guys on the bank now. Most of them had taken off their black shirts and lounged, dressed in only the stripes and plaids of their boxer shorts, their legs outstretched toward the water. A couple were submerged and swimming, their clothes discarded on the banks. But where were the rest? Where were the blindfolded ones? The one screaming for help?

They must have retreated. I imagined a few from the group holding them back, like hostages, just outside our view on the other side of the river, where the trees grew thick again. We'd given them too much warning. Too much time. And now we couldn't help the one who needed to get away. But maybe if we stalled...

"Hi!" I waved. "Do you guys know where this trail leads?" It was a dumb question, but it bought us time.

Maybe that guy, the one who'd been protesting, would be able to escape, or come forward and leave with us.

"Nah, think you're off the trail a bit now," a guy with shaggy chestnut hair said. He sat on the beach, bare-chested, pretending to be doing nothing more than enjoying a lazy Sunday with his boys. He opened a cooler next to him and pulled out a beer, cracked the tab and gulped.

"Toss me one, man," said one of his friends who stood in the waist-deep water and held up his hands for a drink.

"Mind if we join you?" Hazel asked. She positioned herself beside me and bent to unlace her shoes.

"I could use a break," I added. "The water looks nice."

"Think you better head on out, actually."

I wasn't sure who'd said this. I'd been too busy noticing how the temperature seemed to drop, the birds had gone silent, and the mosquitos stilled in the air. A rustling on the other side of the river broke through the unnatural quiet.

"Hey." The distinct voice sounded familiar.

No, it couldn't be him.

Yet, Michael walked among the understory on the other side of the river. This was his team. "It's you." He smiled and came closer, nearly reaching demigod status in my mind with his ability to just be...omnipresent. Not minding the water, he waded in and was soon submerged up to his waist, his black jeans and bare feet disappearing under the surface. His bare chest glowed white and an alarming shade of pink in the midday sun.

He's burning. A random thought. *A son of Hephaestus then.*

"Yeah, it's me." I stepped toward him. I remembered the night he'd insisted he wasn't a bad guy, that he was just another human wrapped up in a warped system, one too powerful to control. How very ungodlike. I recalled him crumpling like a leaf when we saw him at ACC, his sense of fear had seemed somewhat sincere. I projected those men to the one standing before me. Did he yearn to be someone else, a different type of person in a different type of scenario? Did he need saving too?

Just before I reached the water, Hazel grabbed my arm. She shook her head. A warning. Michael was not a good guy. I knew it. I'd seen it. But if anyone could stop all this, it was him. But when I looked back at him, the moment—that glimpse of any possible vulnerability—passed. Swagger fell over him like a cloak, and he performed as scripted.

"What are two pretty ladies doing all alone in the wilderness?" he asked.

"Ladies *can* hike," I said.

"Sure, sure. My bad." He acted apologetic, holding his hands up as if he hadn't meant any offense.

"What are *you* doing here?" I figured he'd lie.

"Guy's day on the river."

"That all?" Hazel asked.

Michael's lazy, leering gaze made its way toward Hazel. He took in her features, licking his lips and rubbing his hands together.

"'Cause it didn't sound like it," I said, hoping to grab his attention, steal it away from how he leered at Hazel. My comment worked. His eyes met mine again and a nonplussed, pleading look lingered there.

"Why would you say that?" he asked, a hush creeping over his tone.

"We heard someone yelling," Hazel said, keeping her

voice low, too, not wanting to spark notice from the others.

"We're just fooling around," he said.

"Sounded like someone needed help," said Doug, finally treading into the situation.

Michael stepped closer; we stepped backward. One of his buddies called out to him. Michael assured them everything was fine. He practically stood on the shore with us now. Each of his steps kicked up clouds of silt. He checked over his shoulder, and when he looked back at us an urgency flashed in his eyes. This guy pulled masks on and off in seconds.

"You should go," he said.

"We heard the screaming," I said. "This is more than what you're letting on. Someone needs help. Because of you."

His shoulders slumped, confusion churning through his features: a tic and tightening at his jawline, his blue eyes searching, he squeezed his own shoulder. "It's over now," he said. "They won't want to keep it up now that you guys have come along."

"And if you're wrong?" Hazel asked.

"I can talk them into ending it." He checked over his shoulder again; obviously his time with us had limits. Someone from his group would be running over here soon if Michael couldn't wrap this up.

"Come with us," I blurted, surprising myself. "Grab the guy that wants to get out of here and walk out of these woods with us.

"I don't—"

"You want a beer, Mike?" one of his friends asked, and without waiting for an answer, they'd already popped the can open and carried it toward him.

Uncertainty teetered across Michael's features.

"Just do the right thing," I urged.

"You don't understand." He wavered. "These guys...if they catch even a hint of weakness, they'll—"

"What?" Doug interrupted. "Shove an ice pack down your pants?"

A wave of surprise swept over Michael's face, and then his friend was upon him. He shoved a beer into Michael's hands and surveyed the three of us with suspicion.

"'Sup?" he said.

"It's our neighbors, dude."

"Oh, hey." The guy, unfamiliar to me, nodded at us in an unwelcoming way. Ranks closing, the expectation for Michael to go back to the others and act as if we hadn't interrupted hung in the air. Instead, he slurped at the beer, then tipped it back and finished the whole thing in a couple swallows. He belched, and his friend clapped him on the back.

"That's it. Come on, dude."

Michael hesitated. We stared at each other. He rolled his teeth over his lower lip. "You go on ahead, Stef," he said. "I'm going with them."

Stef again; I hadn't recognized him from a distance with his hair slicked back, but the memory of the subterranean pull of his arms slithering around me in their disgusting kitchen caught my breath in my throat.

Stef's eyebrows raised high on his forehead. "What? We're in the middle—"

Michael grabbed Stef's shoulder before he finished that sentence and took him aside. They communicated the way some bros do, not really saying what they mean but being overtly obvious about their intentions.

Stef clapped him on the back and said, "Both? Go get 'em, my man." They engaged in some kind of secret handshake.

I bit my lip, realizing all I knew about Michael, all I'd witnessed with my own eyes, meant walking away with him *could* put Hazel and me in real danger. I slipped my hand back into my pocket and gripped my knife handle. Could I hurt him if I needed to? A flurry of memories bombarded me, flashes of images from last year. No doubt.

Excerpt from *The Oakley Book of Lacrosse*

Item #3: Ice begets fire.

You must burn on the field. Your passion for the game is an inferno in your gut, flames roasting your entrails and licking your chest cavity. It must always blaze bright and full, even when it feels like you can't go on. When the cold creeps over your skin and threatens a sweet sleep, you must overcome. Overpower even the elements, and the whole world is yours.

Chapter Twelve

September 1 (continued)

"WHAT NOW?" MICHAEL led the way—I didn't want him behind us—asking the question that banged around my head too. We'd left his group behind but could still hear them. Michael said they'd probably leave, pack up, and go home after they'd almost been caught assaulting guys out here in the woods. But that hadn't happened yet. Instead, they'd cracked open more beers and relaxed into the sunshine of the afternoon as if they didn't have a care in the world. As if nothing could ever phase them.

"Well...?" he reiterated.

"Shh!" I needed to plan, but all I could think of were the screams we'd heard earlier. We had to help that guy; I just didn't know how. We plodded forward until the din of the group faded. "Stop."

The forest grew thicker here, crowding us along the

path. Hazel handed me a water bottle, and I gulped from it, then gave it back to her. We were quiet, all four of us eying one another. Hazel's cheeks puffed out, filled with water, before she swallowed. Doug swatted at a couple mosquitos, the claps against his skin the only sound. Michael's mood seemed to flicker between relief and rage, a battle playing out inside him.

"Why are we going this way?" Doug asked. "Let's just head back to the car."

"We can't," Hazel and I said in unison.

"Why not?"

"Honestly, I'm not sure what those guys are capable of," Michael said.

"Your *friends*"—Doug used scare quotes—"you mean."

"Yeah." Michael deadpanned against Doug's sarcasm. "If they think they're in trouble or 'bout to get caught doing something they shouldn't, all bets are off. All's fair."

"Seems like they just went back to partying," Hazel countered.

"Sure. The ones you can see. But I left a few of them guarding the new guys on the other side of the river." Michael paused and pushed his blond hair off his brow. He clasped his hands behind his neck and looked toward the middle distance. "Tommy and Shane are okay. But Stef... He's been pretty unpredictable since his sister went missing. I could definitely see him taking out some serious steam on those new guys."

"What's that even mean?" Doug asked. "'Take out some steam'?"

Michael unclasped his hands and shrugged. "Knock them around a bit. Like I said, he's hard to predict."

"Beat them, you mean," I said.

He nodded but didn't look me in the eye. He stared at the ground with his hands gripping his waist. Red scratches painted Michael's abs. Places where the branches had reached out and grabbed him as we'd trudged away from his friends. I handed him the rest of my water. He thanked me and finished it.

"So, let's say we keep going upriver until we find a place to cross. Backtrack to the group and free those guys," I said.

"Easier said than done," said Doug.

"We have to try," Hazel said.

Doug looked as though he'd rather eat shit. "Why?" he blurted. "Those guys... You can trust that those guys aren't innocent of anything." He pressed his lips together, seemingly trying to decide what to say next. "I've known a lot of people just like them. They are not worth the risk."

He probably wasn't wrong, and I said as much. I just disagreed with that being a viable reason not to help them.

"It's not about whether or not they've done terrible things, Doug. No one deserves to be left in the middle of the woods calling for help." Hazel's eyes met mine after she spoke up. She understood. I was lucky to have her as an ally and a friend, even if that was all it ever turned out to be.

Doug stayed quiet. He worried his bottom lip.

"I can distract them," Michael offered. "But do you have anything to cut through duct tape?"

Hazel and I brought out our knives, open and glinting.

Michael stepped back. "Okay, then." He smiled and gave a laugh tinged with what sounded like nerves. "Let's do this." He turned and started back down the path. Hazel and I followed.

"I'm out."

The words came from behind us. All three of us turned to see Doug standing in place.

"I'm not doing this," he reiterated.

Bewilderment and then incredulousness crossed Hazel's brow. "How—how?" She couldn't even finish the question, and I kept out of it. But I couldn't stop my eyebrows from raising high up on my forehead. I looked at Michael, who had an equally surprised expression, and stepped toward him, leaving those two to hash this out.

Birds and frogs trilled. The city itself had all but drained away, except for the distant call of sirens. When Michael and I got a few paces away from them, he leaned in and whispered, "What's with that guy?"

I shrugged. I had no idea what was up Doug's ass. My gut said he'd had several trauma-inducing life experiences with guys like Michael and the rest of his team, but I didn't know that. And while I liked calling people out sometimes, I wasn't a gossip. Plus, this exact thing had happened last year when Ryan Newsome's body was found in the Trap. It could be that Doug just wasn't cut out for this kind of thing, and good for him for knowing where his boundaries lay.

"Well, he's never gonna get the girl if he acts like such a pussy."

"That's a shit thing to say." Not to mention how it stung. Even Michael, after mere minutes, picked up on what I'd been trying to clue Hazel in on for weeks. Doug was into her.

He huffed and rolled his eyes.

"What? You think you have to be some manly-man to get a woman to like you?"

"I have to act that way for lots of reasons." He was quiet

for a beat. "Not just to get girls to fuck me."

He was either trying to shock me or make me feel sorry for him. Maybe both. I could feel him tinkering with the way he wanted me to perceive him.

"Well, that's stupid," I said.

"Yeah, it is."

Hazel came toward us. However she felt about Doug taking off, she'd hidden it behind her wall. I knew enough not to ask. Michael didn't.

"He's really not coming?"

She parroted his question back to him as a statement and took over leading us down the trail.

*

AFTER WHAT SEEMED like an impossibly long time, we returned to where they held the four guys we'd seen earlier, trussed and literally freezing their balls off, lying on their sides on the ground near the river. They'd been gagged with gray duct tape and their ankles were bound together too.

Sweat poured down my neck and forehead as we crouched in the brush while Michael approached his friends. My stomach felt as if it might flip itself up my esophagus and out my mouth. Throwing up my own guts—all sticky and pink and speckled with dirt on the forest floor—not really the action of a true hero.

Michael seemed to be doing a good job luring the guards away.

He'd had me slap him and scratch his face. And his eyes sparked with enjoyment as he caught my wrist midair. Then he'd let go and smiled, concocting some story about how he'd made a move, but I'd struggled and run off with Hazel. He hyped them up now, making the group feel his embarrassment. How could I have rejected him? What was wrong with me?

"That bitch!" one of them yelled.

"She's probably a dyke. Living with that other one."

Stef leaned up against a tree, intermittingly nudging a nearby newb with his shoe throughout the whole spectacle. Michael had pointed him out before he rejoined them and said he was the one to convince.

"And you *let* her go?" Stef asked. "She overpowered you?"

"I like willing participants, Stef," Michael said.

"Since when?" Stef rolled his eyes. "You've gone all honorable now, huh?" The comment dripped with history, a deeper knowing of Michael, something that went beyond what I'd been allowed to see.

"Drop it, man," Michael said.

"You go soft? This is what we do. What we're called to do, right?" Stef stepped up, bumping his chest against Michael's. "You never had a problem controlling my sister," he said, his voice somewhere between a whisper and a growl.

Silence pulsed between the two men, their gaze communicating information neither Hazel nor I had full access to.

"Help me find that girl," Michael said.

Stef blinked, seemingly breaking whatever he and Michael shared in the silence. Then understanding filled his expression. "Okay." He straightened his shirt and stepped away from Michael. "Okay, yeah, man. You wanna teach her a lesson." Stef manically jabbed at his temple. "I know how you think, bro. Let's do this." Stef gestured at the other guys. "Come on. Let's go teach this bitch who's boss. For our boy!"

My heartbeat pounded in my ears. I struggled to keep my breathing even. I'd never felt more like an animal because, no doubt about it, they'd all just agreed to a hunt.

We waited for several minutes after they left. I realized, too late, how much trust this plan put in Michael *not* being a psychopath, especially after all I'd witnessed within their house. His personality shone like a golden boy most the time, seemingly harmless until he stood behind you with a broom handle. No, something underneath the veneer had spoiled. And we shouldn't have trusted him, but we were in the thick of it now. We needed to move fast and get the hell out of here before anyone caught us.

After enough time had passed, I gestured to Hazel. I touched my index finger to my lips; we did this quietly or not at all. Hazel nodded and held up two fingers, then pointed at herself. I agreed, mimicking her gesture. Before we made our move, I took a deep breath, and she took my hand. Our fingers tangled together, finding their places within the palm and crevices of another, until they locked in place. We stood and moved forward, letting go when we had to. As we came out of the woods, some of the bound guys wriggled on the ground, trying to break free. One lay still, resigned but breathing.

We could make out the rest of the team, those who hadn't run off with Michael, on the riverbank. From our hiding spot, I'd thought they were farther away, but standing here, it was clear they were much closer. At any moment, one of them could emerge on this side of the clearing and— then what? I didn't really want to find out. I crept toward one of the guys struggling on the ground, fearing any commotion might bring the attention of the group near the water.

"Hold still," I whispered close to his ear. Dirt and flecks of grass stuck to his skin via a film of sweat. "I got you. Just hold on."

He nodded. My knife made quick work of cutting through the tape around his wrists. As soon as he was free, he flipped himself into a sitting position, ripped off his blindfold, and removed the cold pack from his shorts. When he started scrambling with the tape around his ankles, I motioned for him to stop. He did and let me cut through the rest. Once he was free, he was gone. He took off through the woods in the opposite direction of Michael and that crew.

Next, I crept over to the guy who lay still and whispered the same thing to him. But there was no indication that he heard me. He only slouched there, wet and stinking of river water. I cut through the tape on both his wrists and ankles before anything even seemed to register with him. He slowly sat up. I touched the blindfold to pull it down, but he stopped me.

"What's your name?" I asked, but I already knew this was Ham. The guy we'd watched from the bushes, probably the one who'd been screaming in the first place.

He let the blindfold slip. His eyes were red, still watery with tears. "I didn't—" His voice cracked, and he stopped. He cleared his throat. "I didn't know it was going to be like this." The bridge of his nose looked cracked and crooked. Blood coated the lower half of his face.

"It shouldn't be." I leaned in to untie the blindfold from around his neck. He took it and swiped at the blood. The fact that the rest of the team was still right there, just on the other side of the trees, took lead in my mind. But this guy seemed so obviously damaged, like full-on disassociated, that he needed a little more time to gather himself before getting the hell out of here. "What's your name?" I asked again.

"Hamden."

What hell had they put him through in the last thirty minutes? It didn't matter. Not now. What mattered was getting him out.

"Those guys are right over there, Hamden," I said.

Hazel crouched beside me to help, having freed the other two guys who'd also run off into the woods. "We're gonna get you outta here. Okay?"

He nodded but didn't move.

"Can you walk?" I asked.

"I-I..." He blinked, then shook his head. "Dizzy," he muttered. "C-can you call my brother? C-call Felix; he can come get me."

Hazel and I stood and stepped a few paces away from him.

"I think we're gonna have to help him out of here," I whispered. "He seems pretty out of it."

"Sure, sure." She looked over her shoulder, beyond our immediate circumstances and on, to the possibility of any one of Hamden's teammates coming into the clearing. "Now though."

Hamden and I made eye contact, his blank expression dripping with shock.

"Can I help you up?" I asked. He nodded, and I scooted alongside him and put his arm around my shoulders. "Lean on me, okay?"

"Yeah." His voice sounded as tremulous as his legs, but together, all three of us got him up and moving.

"You're gonna be okay. We're getting you out of here."

We stepped from the clearing and onto the path leading back to the parking lot. It then occurred to me. Doug had left; we had no car. We could get Hamden out of the woods, but then what? Every once in a while, my gaze met Hazel's. I tried to communicate *What next?* via those looks, but I could only see worry in her eyes.

Hamden grimaced with each step, the pace slow going. His ankles looked fine: not swollen, normal coloring. Maybe a twisted knee? A trickling of blood ran down his thigh.

"You're bleeding," I said without thinking.

"Yeah—"

I wasn't sure he'd say anything else; it looked like it hurt him to talk.

"It was—" he tried again.

"You don't have to talk about it," Hazel interrupted. And I wished she hadn't.

Step by step, we plodded forward. The blood nearly reached his wet socks now, sure to color the fabric a deep, dark maroon. Hamden would be dealing with what happened to him in these woods for a long time, the rest of his life, maybe. We all would. We all did. Forever and always, this shit never stopped.

"No." Fury inflicted his statement, seeming to flip a switch in Hamden. His cheeks flushed, and he stood taller. He stopped limping as much. "Dude fucking carved his initials in my leg." His nostrils flared. "I'm gonna fucking kill him. Me and my brother are gonna fucking kill him."

Excerpt from *The Oakley Book of Lacrosse*

Item # 4: Fight or flight.

Brothers, will you run? Or will you be men and hold fast against what's in front of you? Face it. Fight it. Win at all costs, even if the price is all you have to give. That's what a man is. That's what a brother does for his team. You freely give of yourself, sacrifice everything for the guy next to you, and you are one of us. The chosen. The righteous. The victors.

Chapter Thirteen

September 5, 2001

HAZEL AND I sat at the dining table, crunching through some sugar-sweet cereal. Everything had been eerily quiet next door. No parties since we'd helped Hamden limp out of the woods. Luckily, Doug had waited for us in the parking lot. Hazel and I wanted to take Hamden to the hospital or a police station, anywhere where people would help him file official reports, but he'd refused, preferring to just go home. So we'd used Hazel's cell phone to call Hamden's brother and then dropped him off at the Oakley stadium parking lot, like he'd asked. We'd tried to do more, offered to get him food or at least wait for his brother to get there, but he'd yelled at us. "Just go!" His scream still echoed in my ears. The look on his face as students hurried past him, not wanting to linger in front of someone so obviously wounded, haunted me.

We'd come back to the row houses. And I hadn't seen anyone go in or out of the lacrosse house in days. I stared out the window, watching a pair of squirrels hop through the dewy grass. Two girls dressed in matching velour track suits walked past the neighbors' yard, casting evil looks at the old home.

"What do you think's going on over there?" I asked.

Hazel shrugged, her gaze intent on the soggy flakes floating in the leftover milk.

"You think Hamden reported what happened to the university? Told his parents, maybe?"

Her spoon clattered against the side of her bowl. She leaned forward, resting her cheek against her fist. "He should report them. Get the authorities involved. But you never know what people are gonna do. Or what they're able to stand up to."

I nodded, spooning another bite into my mouth. "He'd be up against a lot."

"For sure. A group like that? Who knows how long stuff like this has been going on? What kind of secrets they have..."

I looked at the house with its chipped paint and sagging porch. Rotten. "The house knows. It's in the walls."

"What?"

"Oh. It's just something my yaya says sometimes. 'Keep your house in order, or the walls will tell on you.'"

"What's it mean? I've never heard that."

"Just, like, part of what happens inside a home will show through eventually." I took a sip of coffee. "One of her many ways of keeping people in check."

"I'd like to meet her." Hazel smiled as she ran her hands

through her hair, detangling some of the knots. The long waves fell about her shoulders and framed her face, lovely in the morning light, like a portrait from the renaissance. Then, her eyebrows scrunched together—her thinking face.

"What is it?" I asked.

Her teeth grazed her lower lip. "What if she's right?"

"Who?"

"Your grandma."

"Hazel." A smirking, little laugh made its way up and out of my throat. "My yaya won't hand anyone a knife because she thinks it'll end a friendship. No one should take advice from her superstitious ass."

Hazel's eyes glowed with a light I hadn't seen since we were putting the pieces together from Ryan's murder last fall. I loved that light.

"But what if there *is* something in the house..." she said. "Something that shows what they've been doing..." Her voice trailed off as she thought this through.

"Like what? Pictures or something?"

"Maybe!"

"Why would they keep something like that?"

"Tradition?" She practically vibrated.

I knew what she wanted. "And you wanna go check it out?"

I hadn't told her what it had been like in that house, how cramped and suffocating the walls felt or what had happened in the Trap after dropping off my initial report. The storm. The tree. Michael and Stef, how they'd stared at me, coldness leering on their rugged, handsome faces. I'd dropped it and pretended it hadn't bothered me. It wasn't an omen. Michael was fine; he'd helped us get Hamden out of that mess in the woods. There was no threat. But if she wanted to go in that house and snoop around...

"Hazel, I don't know..."

"Not this very moment," she said. "Later. When we know they're gone. Right now, we've gotta get to class."

"Yeah, okay." I collected our bowls, rinsed them out in the sink, and went upstairs to finish getting dressed, ignoring the tinge of excitement and dread that came with the idea of setting foot in that house again.

*

WE HAD LITTLE idea of what to expect for the first day of classes at the academy. Our uniforms and PT gear had been handed out at orientation.

"You ready?" Hazel's uniform looked crisp. The shirt creases were stiff and slightly unmovable, the same way mine felt. The pants were thick, some material I'd never worn before but was already sweating through.

"Guess so." I ran my hands through my fresh cut, the undershave prickling my fingertips, with the top still long but not enough to get in my way. Hazel had practically shellacked her hair into a bun that sat at the nape of her neck.

We got to school twenty minutes later, and for the first time, campus buzzed with activity. Not an Oakley-level hum, but cars filled nearly every spot of the parking lot, and the walkways teemed with people carrying backpacks and campus maps and schedules in their hands.

Our first class met in the gymnasium. When we got there, a table of coffee and donuts had been set up. Some of the guys from our class already lingered around the table, while others had taken seats in the stands. I headed over to the refreshments. Hazel joined me.

The guy named Todd greeted us, shaking my hand and reintroducing himself. He and I basically had the same haircut. I brought it up; we laughed and started in with the small talk, which was boring and served such little purpose I had trouble concentrating on it.

At eight o'clock sharp, the doors banged open, slamming against the stoppers, and Michael's uncle, TO Gillespie, marched in screaming.

"Fall in formation! Fall in!" he yelled over and over. His cheeks were pink, and spittle sprayed from his mouth.

At first, nobody moved. But as he kept ranting, we scrambled into a line, mimicking what we'd seen done in military TV shows or movies—anything to get the guy to calm down. It didn't take us long, but apparently it took too long, so he commanded us to get down and complete ten push-ups.

Hazel finished last, and before she even stood back up, he singled her out, crouching in front of her. He berated her for being weak and slow and holding everyone back. He called her names, but stopped short of mentioning anything about her being a woman—probably because he had to. My jaw clenched. I bit the inside of my lower lip and stared ahead, homing in on the mats hanging on the opposite wall. Speaking up was bound to make things worse for Hazel, but it took every ounce of will for me not to do it. After she finished those first ten push-ups, he made her start over. Then he made the rest of us start over while she watched. She stayed quiet; we all stayed quiet.

I checked the clock: 8:10. *Jesus Christ.*

Suddenly, Gillespie calmed. Like a switch turned off, he stood in front of us with his arms clasped behind his back, panting a bit. A few specks of saliva adorned his mustache. "You will refer to me as Training Officer Gillespie or Sir."

No one responded.

"Do you get me?" Training Officer Gillespie screamed.

A deepening well in my gut formed, and it sloshed with all my indignation. Anything inside me that felt contrary or overconfident or human had to fit inside this well. Because—two years. I'd signed on for two years of this.

"Sir, yes, sir!" Somehow, we pulled off saying it in unison. Which was good because, no question, there would have been more push-ups or running had we not.

Movement near the double doors caught my attention. Several officers in full uniform—crisp olive-khaki shirts and pants, shiny black shoes, and hats pulled down low on their foreheads—had lined up. They held flags in front of them: American, Ohioan, and one I didn't recognize, maybe the county flag. They marched forward in perfect cadence, someone calling out the rhythm.

"Left, left, left, right, left." A low baritone voice filled the gymnasium and Training Officer Gillespie's demeanor seemed to cool further in response to the repetition and routine. When they got to the middle of the room, whoever called out the commands gave them a few more. Things I'd never heard before.

"Mark time!" And the flag-bearing officers marched in place.

"Halt." They stopped in unison.

"Right turn." They faced us.

Training Officer Gillespie yelled, "Hand salute!"

I'd never saluted anything in my life, but I quickly remembered my brothers in Boy Scouts, three little fingers on their right hands lightly touching the front of their caps with their arms snapped to attention. I copied that.

"Present colors!" The flag bearers adjusted their hold on the flags, and the banners waved free.

Then Training Officer Gillespie marched to the donut table and brought out a boombox from underneath. He hit Play and "The Star-Spangled Banner" echoed and bounced off the gymnasium walls. We all stood there and stared at the limp flags as some random recording artist warbled through the anthem. When the song ended, I kept my salute. Todd did not. He put his arm down, instinctively, which set off Training Officer Gillespie, instinctively.

Gillespie got right up in Todd's face. From my peripheral, I could see Gillespie's flushed cheeks and his beady blue eyes bulging as he demeaned the cadet. Was this for real? It couldn't be actual anger. Nobody got this pissed over such a small infraction. No, this was a display. A show of power. A test.

And it all seemed borderline psychotic.

After Gillespie finished humiliating Todd. The flag corps marched out, and we started learning marching drills. Some of the cadets took to it with ease. I struggled. It seemed like it should've been plain and simple; I'd been memorizing choreography for years, but my feet refused to match the beat. So maybe my body was just trying to tell me something—*get the fuck out of here*. A surge of panic coursed through me. Undoubtedly, I'd be targeted.

And then, Gillespie was there, screaming into my ear. I kept trying the steps, and he stayed next to me.

"What the ever-loving Christ is wrong with you?" he barked.

I fought the urge to shove him, knowing I could do it. He was sturdier, sure. With a thick chest and abdomen, he'd be difficult to topple, but I had a height advantage, along with the element of surprise. He wouldn't expect it. Only the image of him knocked on his ass helped me stay in control. I put it on repeat, my brain rewinding and replaying the imaginary scene, and blocked out every word he said. Even with his hot breath on my neck, all I could see was his ass on the ground.

Finally, after countless laps around the gym and my arms numb from push-ups, we were dismissed. Hours had flown by in the haze of Gillespie's shouting and physical regimen.

That well inside me, the one filled with all my natural instincts to talk back, to question and rail against authority, was already damn near filled to the brim. I was left with nothing of my former self, just a blankness to be imprinted upon.

And that was the whole damn point.

Day 837

From Within the House

For so long, I'd felt his presence loom over me, as ubiquitous as any god. But it was me, the ghost, watching and witnessing everything. I saw how his behaviors and demands would flip, like a switch, unpredictable and uneven. How he could be both charming and calculating. How he reeled people in and chose, so carefully, who could be manipulated.

As he lay awake, night after night, I scratched at his closet walls again. My fingernails made long, tearing sounds as I reached ceiling to floor. Animal noises weren't always effective. But I added a slow, measured hiss, surely terrifying in the dead of night, when only darkness blanketed him, and his friend tossed and turned nearby, suspecting nothing.

I left him notes. With an oily finger pressed against the mirror in the bathroom, I spelled out his crimes: liar, abuser, pyscho. The words, only appearing in the steam of each shower, were never strong enough to describe what he'd done to me for all those years. How he'd controlled my every moment, how he made me fear the consequences of disobeying him, how he broke me. It flooded me with a dull anger and pitifulness now, especially as I crept through this house of his. The walls became cramped, and I strained against them, wanting to feel them crumble as I pushed.

It wouldn't be much longer now.

But, oh, I loved this stage of things, lingering on the dozens of ways to scare him, to make him fear me for once. His slow unraveling brought me such a sense of malevolent joy. His shiny brass look, now dull and green. The shade under his eyes spoiled, turning a deeper gray by the day. When he snapped and screamed at the others, the hate that glowed in their eyes was nearly feral—like an alligator's burning red glare at night. They waited, still as stones in the water, keeping vigil for the moment they must have sensed was coming.

Enough people knew or suspected his truer self, beneath the gleam of conventional looks and wealth, that when I finished with him, not one of them would grieve a golden boy.

Chapter Fourteen

September 6, 2001

HONESTLY, I COULDN'T believe I was going back. But I sat on the couch, dressed in my uniform, waiting for Hazel to get ready so we could leave for class. Today should be different. Classes had started—the physically sitting at desks or tables in a schoolroom type—so my expectations for the day were positive, mostly. Yesterday's PT and screaming session had me wary though. I'd left feeling empty, kind of hollowed out like a cracked open and shucked peanut shell of myself. And that was...concerning. I'd allowed my brain to check out during training, taken chunks of myself and stuffing them deep inside to get through the day, full-on disassociated, and that didn't seem healthy.

Hazel sat in front of the computer, half dressed. She had her uniform pants on but only wore an undershirt.

"We're gonna be late," I said.

"Just a sec." She stood up and swung her shirt off the

back of her chair and around her shoulders.

"What is it?"

"Doug sent me an email. Thinks he found another victim of the Creeping Cop." She grimaced, hating that stupid name.

"Really?"

She nodded, buttoning her shirt and not taking her eyes off the screen.

"How many have you found?"

"Four so far. This would make five."

I crossed the room, interested. "And what's your process? How are you finding them?"

"Trial and error, really. Doug found this website that had archived all of the newspapers from Shirlee's town. Over the summer, he sent me a 911 call log, and then we went from there."

I leaned over and scrolled through the file Doug had sent. He'd been thorough, including a logged call, two other articles that seemed to correspond, any pertinent information he could find about the woman, city crime stats, and proximity to the Creeping Cop's hometown—which meant accessibility. One of the articles reported the nature of the crime: woman, cop, rape, and the possibility of an internal affairs team needing to come in and lead the investigation. The sheriff's interview, which had probably been meant to be reassuring—they were following all leads, doing everything they could, exhausting all resources—ended up reading like preprogrammed sound bites. The last line encouraged anyone with information pertinent to the case to come forward.

"What are you planning to do with all this?"

"Don't know yet." She bent toward the computer and clicked Save. "We've just started spiraling out from where Shirlee grew up."

"You haven't contacted local cops?"

"Not yet."

"Why?"

"I don't know. I guess, at first, it felt more like a shot in the dark than anything useful."

"You should definitely turn this stuff in. Oh! Maybe Detective Patterson could use it. I've still got her card somewhere—"

"It's old, Maeve. Statute of limitations is, like, five years in Indiana."

"I think that just has to do with coming forward if you're the victim. These have been reported, so they're legit cold cases. You can't just hoard this information because cops make you nervous—"

"I'm not!" She grabbed her keys and backpack. "I'm not doing that."

"Okay, fine. Is Doug holding you back then?"

"No. God." She rolled her eyes. Doug had officially become a sore subject between the two of us.

"You need to call her." I turned and ran upstairs to get Detective Patterson's card. I kept it in my jewelry box with the spinning ballerina that Yaya had given me when I was little. Back downstairs, I handed over the card and waited. I wasn't going to let her put this off any longer. Doug was good for her, but I pushed her to go beyond herself. To be uncomfortable. To take risks.

She reached for the portable phone, smelling of soap and coffee, and dialed.

We locked eyes as the phone rang, and then her gaze flicked away as she left a message.

She hung up. "There. Done."

"Okay, good. We've gotta go."

"There's no way we'll make it in time."

"I know." And my stomach cramped just thinking of how Gillespie might handle tardiness.

*

IT WAS BAD. Like vomiting in the grass, world swaying in front of your eyes, whole body burning with strain bad. The traffic gods had been lenient, and it almost seemed we'd make it in time. But we didn't, missing the start of class by seven minutes. Seven minutes. Four hundred and twenty seconds. A tiny amount of time. But late was late, and we had to pay for time wasted and the interruption. Gillespie hadn't backed off the entire time. He hauled us out of the classroom, and we did PT until we puked.

We were home now. Hazel sat on the couch with her leg propped up and a bag of frozen mixed veggies on her knee, her face still splotchy and pink from the exertion.

"We should have just stayed home," I lamented.

"For real," she said and moved the ice pack to her forehead. "We won't make that mistake again."

"Yeah, guess Gillespie really showed us. If you're going to be late, just be absent." Sarcasm leaked throughout my tone.

My mother's words, *you can always change your mind*, had rung like a gong every time he made me do another push-up. I couldn't quit though. They'd see it as weakness. That I couldn't handle Gillespie's yelling. That the physicality was too much for me. If I gave up, I'd fulfill all their fantasies about women not being strong enough for this line of work. So it wasn't really true, what Mama had said.

Except who were *they*? And why did I care so much about *them*?

I sat in front of the computer, chugging Gatorade and checking my email, thinking about writing Mama, when Doug messaged.

GuidedByNachos: You there...

GuidedByNachos: OK, maybe you're still at class.

GuidedByNachos: What did you think of what I sent you? Meet up today?

"Doug asked if you want to meet up."

"I'm not moving from this couch. Tell him to come over when he's done with school." She'd fallen on the track, and her knee had taken the brunt of it. The joint was a swelling mass of purple and blue. It was just like our first day of classes last year when she'd come back to the dorm with a similar-looking bruise. That had been the first time I'd ever attempted to talk to her. Most people would've described her as shy, but really, she was just in her own head, living her whole life up there. Sometimes it seemed she had to fight to stay present in this world.

"Tell him to bring pizza," she added.

*

DOUG ARRIVED A few hours later with an extra-large pizza and a two liter of lemon-lime pop.

"Savior!" Hazel said when she saw what he carried.

"Just a lowly delivery man at your service."

Ugh, banter. I turned away to roll my eyes and grab some cash for the guy. We spread the food out on the floor and ate while watching the *Behind the Music* special on Fleetwood Mac I'd seen a million times because it was that good, and it was always on. After we finished eating, I turned down the volume on an explanation of a massive coke habit and asked Doug about what he'd found.

"I printed everything out." He pulled a file folder from his backpack and handed it to me. "Here."

I'd read all this when we got home from the academy. Hazel had given me access to the saved files on her computer. Each file contained an initial 911 call that had been traced back from a newspaper article mentioning the detail about the police uniform. It seemed that aspect of the serial rapes had been leaked a few times.

"How'd you start finding these?"

"Hmm?" Doug stared intently at the TV screen.

"I mean, did you just randomly start looking for these?"

"Oh—I searched and found all the news articles about what happened to Hazel's mom. Then I figured there were more victims with similar articles."

Hazel's gaze narrowed. "Wait. What?"

"It was just a matter of looking."

"You researched my mom?" she asked.

"Mm-hmm." Doug twisted the cap off the two-liter, which hissed as he turned. He poured himself a glass, then took another slice of pizza out of the box.

He didn't seem to notice Hazel's flushed cheeks. She stared at the floor in front of her, at the file in my hands.

Flimsy little printouts were all she had left of her mother. And apparently, they were available to anyone with internet access.

"I gotta get some air." She stood and headed for the back door.

"Way to go, Doug," I said as I stood.

"What did I do?"

I just rolled my eyes and left. The TV volume rose behind me.

Something crashed outside. It sounded like a garbage can being knocked over by raccoons...or an extremely upset person. By the time I got to her, Hazel sat under the neighbor's big tree, her back leaning against the trunk. With her head tilted back, I couldn't tell if she was crying.

A car door slammed somewhere in the distance. Voices carried, and snippets of conversations made their way to us as people strolled along the sidewalks. Peals of laughter erupted from the open window of a different set of neighbors.

I stepped carefully toward her, over the grassy mound under the tree, and sat next to her. "Hey," I said quietly.

She didn't respond.

Comforting people didn't come naturally to me, or so I'd been told, but I knew Hazel's feelings, the ones she worked so hard to hide, were up at the surface. Something about Doug's ability to research her mother without her knowledge or consent had brought everything bubbling back up.

"You had to know he'd done that, right? Like he's gotta start somewhere." I couldn't believe I was defending him.

"Yeah," she said quietly. "I knew. It's just... Sometimes

I still can't believe that's all I have left of her."

"But that's not really true."

Her eyes met mine, dry yet anguished.

"Your mom—" I swallowed; we never talked like this, or about this. I had no idea how she might react. "—is more than what happened to her." I crossed my legs, muscles aching from Gillespie's punishment. "Like, sometimes I think that's what's so tragic about these things. Not only did your mom go through all that, but then she became defined by what that man did and caused. Her story...her whole life outshined by some..."

"Him."

"Yeah, but it doesn't have to be that way."

"How? Doug looks up my mom on the internet and *that's* what comes up. That's all that comes up."

"So...change that."

"You make it sound easy." She let out a half snort. "How would I do that?"

"Make a website dedicated to her. Or write her biography or something. I don't know."

Hazel made a little noise in her throat, maybe considering it.

"So what'd'ya knock over?" I asked, changing the subject.

A little smile crept across her features. She jutted her chin toward the neighbor's front porch. Trash always littered their stoop, so I couldn't even tell what she'd done.

"You wanna go back inside? Finish dinner?"

She shook her head. As I stared at the house in front of me, the colonial revival with its old windows like eyes, an idea formed.

"Come on." I stood.

"I just need a few more minutes," she said.

"We're not going back to our house."

Her eyebrows scrunched together, and a quizzical look painted her features. "Where are we going?"

"There." I pointed at the neighbors' house.

"What? Why?" But she'd already leaned away from the trunk—interested.

The house stood quiet and dark. Why did I want to go in there? I'd witnessed what these guys were doing to one another, had seen Hamden's reaction, the disassociation. It didn't seem that far off from how the police academy and TO Gillespie had made me feel. *Fuuuuuck* that.

"What you're doing with Doug is great. It might even lead to closure for some families. But this"—I indicated the house again—"is action." My lifeblood: I wanted to *do*. Jump in. Worry about consequences later. The thought of walking into that house and snooping around made me feel more like myself than I had in months. "The house knows what's going on inside its own walls. So let's prove it."

Excerpt taken from *The Oakley Book of Lacrosse*

Item #5: Silence is our bond.

What happens to the team, for the team, stays within the team. There are no exceptions. No rats. No squealers. Ever.

Chapter Fifteen

September 6 (continued)

"WHAT ARE YOU thinking?" Hazel asked. She stood near our apartment, the kitchen light backlighting her in yellow, surely about to reject this plan.

"We can't solve *that* tonight." I motioned toward our house, meaning to indicate everything that had happened to her mom, everything that Doug had been helping her with. Her past. Her present. Probably a large part of her future too. "So let's do something about *this*." I turned toward the colonial house. Its dark windows and loose shutters stared soulless under the first stars of dusk. "That house has secrets. Big ones." I stepped toward her and wound my arm across her shoulders. "Let's find them."

Was I trying to distract her from how Doug digging into her mom's past had upset her? Yes. Was I trying to show her that she should always choose me to work with?

Yep, that too.

"Maeve, wait. You can't just barge over there."

"Watch me." I smiled slyly, then turned and stomped through the grass, fully grasping the idiocy of this idea. I'd already gone into their house once, and it had been a close call. But why shouldn't I keep challenging them? I'd just spent the day at the police academy being screamed at and demeaned. If I could manage that, these guys couldn't touch me. These guys weren't little deities, even though most folks treated them as if they were.

"Maeve, wait! I'm coming with you." She stood beside me, and we matched our stride toward the house.

"What about Doug?" I asked. "You wanna bring him?"

"You know he won't come."

"What is with *that* tone?" I struggled to keep my expression neutral. "Do I detect scorn?"

"No. He is who he is. And I won't let you go in there alone."

"Oh, I'll be fine. They're not home."

"You don't know that, Maeve. We've seen this group of guys do really weird shit to one another; what do you think they'd do to some random girl breaking in?"

"Whatever."

"Yeah, whatever." Now she used sarcasm with me. "You need me."

"That's true." And I tried to keep my voice from sounding as if it dripped with lovesick syrup. We were friends, nothing more. That was the way Hazel wanted it. I was positive of that, at least.

The house was quiet, disturbingly so because usually it brimmed with people and noise and disgusting smells. We stepped onto their porch and the boards creaked under our weight. A couple of soft spots in the wood would give out before too long. And because of that, I walked gingerly, testing the porch's sturdiness, not wanting to fall through to whatever hell existed just under the surface.

Hazel knocked, but no one answered. She turned the knob and the door opened, unlocked, unbarred. So we went in.

"We should go back," she whispered.

But neither of us made a move in the opposite direction. Instead, we stepped forward, passing through the gray, dingy rooms, each tinged with a kind of reversed wonderland vibe, with their stained, shaggy carpets and couches that had long ago lived better lives. Nothing bright. Nothing vibrant. A mound of trash littered the coffee table: plastic cups, some tipped over and some still half full, mold growing on the top; fast-food wrappers and used ketchup packets; mini-lighters of every color; a pack of cigarettes—which I took; several cashed bowls; and a baggie of weed—which I almost took, but then remembered the academy's random drug test policy. The place reeked of stale beer and smoke. In some areas, the carpet squished wet under our feet.

Hazel followed the hallway that led to the kitchen and immediately turned back around.

"You don't want to go back there."

"Well, but now, I kinda do." I didn't though. I'd seen their kitchen once, and it had already been bad. I could easily imagine the filth piled there now. Plus, whatever secrets lived here, they weren't going to be found in the kitchen or the first floor.

"This place is disgusting," she whispered.

I nodded, then indicated the stairs and pointed toward the ceiling. "Up?"

As we climbed, images of those guys being marched up these very steps with hoods covering their faces flashed through my mind. The grunts of pain. Hamden screaming at the river. The cries—pain or pleasure, I couldn't always tell—that came all weekend long from this place as they threw their mega parties. What could we possibly be walking into? The living quarters downstairs offered two easy exits, up here though? We'd be trapped.

As we broached the top of the stairwell, the house remained gloomy but asleep. The landing was a long hallway with several doors off it, one of which was open and led to the bathroom. The door outfitted with a sliding lock on the outside was where I'd stood and watched the first beating.

I walked toward it, Hazel following close behind, and slowly slid the bolt aside, then turned the knob. The hinges creaked the whole time the door slid open, and there was nothing I could do about that except grit my teeth and wish it weren't happening. Once the door was fully open, we stayed on the threshold. Waiting for the big surprise, a reveal, some guy who'd been here all along, plotting and planning for us to open that door and shove us inside, locking us away. But nothing happened. The house remained silent, so we pressed on.

Inside, the room seemed a little cleaner than the rest of the house. The hardwood floor had been swept. A bench butted up against a bay window that overlooked the front yard and, beyond that, the city skyline. All the windows were nailed shut though.

"What is this place?" I swallowed, anxiety creeping up

my esophagus.

Hazel turned in the center of the room. "I don't know. There's always so many of them here. It seems like a waste to have a whole room open and empty like this."

From the window seat, I could clearly see inside my own bedroom, all lit up, having never hung up that sheet. Had anyone ever sat in this spot and watched me? Had they been locked in this empty room? Had they needed help while I went about my business next door, worrying about cop school and pining for my roommate?

I turned away and noticed what I assumed was a closet. As I opened the door and walked in, I realized it led to a hall that opened into another room. A secret room. Or what might have originally been a nursery.

"Hazel," I whispered. "Check this out." An old desk had been positioned on a kind of platform in the center of the room. Newspaper articles plastered the walls, some recent, some brown with age. The older ones were mostly about lacrosse and past teams. Newer ones mentioned a missing teenage girl. I ran my hand over the stories, feeling the glossy texture of dried glue and overlapping paper, the wrinkles like hardened veins creating random patterns.

"What is it?" Hazel stepped through the dark corridor into the hidden space. "This is—" She took her time choosing the right word. "—odd."

"Totally," I agreed. Even the windows were papered over, the words too sun-bleached to read, especially in the dim evening light. What was the point of this? This was supposed to be a sports team, nothing more. Yet these two rooms pulsed with a frenzied, hostile heart. Something was *wrong* here. Something old and dark. Something that grabbed hold and didn't let go. A beast.

Hazel opened a closet door and pulled a string hanging from a bare lightbulb. It clicked and brightened up the space. It was big, a walk-in, rare for this type of house. Along the closet walls hung...instruments: the rod I'd seen Michael use, a wooden paddle, a pitchfork, even a whip. Bundles of rope and pillowcases—all mismatched in solid grays and whites and blues, mixed with striped and plaid patterns—lay in piles atop the closet floor.

We stepped away from the closet, not saying anything. Hazel went over to the far corner of the weird little room and lifted the lid on a cooler. She held up an ice pack like the ones taped to the guys' junk out by the river, then dropped it back inside and tapped the lid. It closed with a soft *thwack*.

Nothing littered the desk's surface, no clutter, no knick-knacks. I scooted back the chair, sat down, and opened the top drawer. Stacks of notebooks stared back at me. Each front cover indicated a year with pages inside of lists, stats on every player. It was standard stuff like we'd seen online, if not a bit obsessive. I shuffled through them, the earliest dated 1998.

The second, and much bigger, desk drawer was locked. I sat there, biting the inside of my cheek, weighing options. The lock wasn't anything that couldn't be easily picked or broken, except someone would notice.

The team had people in and out of this house all the time. There was no reason they'd connect a broken lock in a hidden room to us. Unless we got caught. We'd been in the house for a while now, and the pressure of time running out, slipping away from us, crept through the shadows. With each *creak* and *crack* and *moan*, the house gave out a warning.

Fuck it. We were already deep in this. And anything that'd been locked away needed to come out eventually.

I scrounged around the narrow middle desk drawer, looking for something to use until I found two paperclips. I stretched them out and went to work on the lock, thankful my brother Evan had shown me how to do this on Dad's liquor cabinet years ago. Using one paper clip to hold the pins and the other to apply pressure, I turned until the lock released. *Click.* I opened the drawer and found a worn leather portfolio.

"Hazel," I whispered, "come look at this."

She'd gone back inside the closet and emerged, swiping cobwebs from her hair. "There's so much weird shit in there. Including what I think might be a hidden passage. What did you find?"

"I'm not sure." The leather flaps were thick and puffy under my fingers, someone else's oily prints all over them. I'd seen this; Michael had read from it the night I'd shown up at their party. He'd held it up to me as proof he hadn't been doing anything wrong. I opened the cover, and inside, we found the handwritten letter to the team dated 1972. Past the letter, we found pages with "items" listed. The writing style, strange and aggressive, contained little snippets of rules left to follow or to be widely interpreted, like a gospel.

"This is what? Passed down from team to team?" Hazel asked.

"Seems so."

"Since when?" Hazel stood next to me, reading over my shoulder. Her wild hair tickled my arm.

"First entry says the seventies."

The manual contained only seven entries, each about a paragraph long. Empty blue lines filled the rest of the note-pad's yellow pages. Except for an imprint on the very last page. I ripped out the paper, searched for a pencil, and started shading over the inscription. A name appeared: Hamden Stevens, the kid we'd pulled out of the woods. A straight line slashed through it. What did that mean? Had he been eliminated? Quit? Dropped from the team because he wouldn't go along with all of this? Had he put up too much of a fight? Was he dead?

A *slam* sounded from downstairs, a screen door banging shut. Someone was home, possibly multiple someones.

I looked at Hazel, sure my eyes were as big as hers. She tiptoed to the closet and pulled the light string. I'd never heard a louder click, except maybe the trigger engaging on Shirlee Hensen's gun, but the room became engulfed once more in the gray, dying light of the day. Not dark. Not light. I folded up the book and hesitated; *should I take it with us*?

Hazel pantomimed for me to follow her, mouthing, *Come on.*

No time to think, I stuffed the ripped-out sheet back in the portfolio and carried the whole thing against my chest.

We entered the dark closet, which was much bigger than I'd initially thought. Past the ropes and instruments tacked to the walls, the closet became a dark hallway that ended at another, much smaller door. Hazel grabbed the doorknob and pulled, but it didn't budge. Then came the low murmur of voices in the adjoining room.

"The door was wide open, dude."

"I don't know what to tell you, Stef. I locked up."

Stef. The unpredictable one.

They came closer, their footsteps thudding over the floorboards. Hazel struggled with the door. Either painted shut or swollen with time, it wasn't opening. I set down the portfolio to help. She tugged on the doorknob; I felt along the edge, looking for a place to wedge my fingers. Near the bottom, I could fit them underneath and pull, but we had to coordinate our efforts in the dark without making a sound. Hazel tapped my shoulder and indicated the number three.

Got it. One. Two. Three.

The door sprang open with a deafening crack. We scrambled down a set of stairs, no longer caring about how much noise we made. They were too close for us to care. If we could get out of the house without them seeing us, they could never be sure *we* were the ones who'd been here.

The dank stairwell smelled of mold. We breathed in all manner of spores. The house had gone rotten from its core to the skin. Nothing could save it. I just hoped it wouldn't infect us, wouldn't grab hold and lock us in.

My fingers grazed over the lath and plaster of the interior as we raced down the steps. Hazel stopped suddenly, and I ran into the back of her, her hair soft against my face, her back firm against my chest. The stairwell was as dark as a cavern, and I couldn't see much except a line of light showing near her feet. We stayed silent, listened. I felt like a mouse, hiding in the walls, heart beating rapidly, scared to death of being caught in a trap but also not wanting to live in the labyrinth.

Pots and pans banged just beyond where we stood. The crinkling sound of plastic bags made its way through the walls where we hid.

Someone yelled, "What for? I'm getting ready to make noodles." They sighed and muttered something under their breath, then everything went quiet.

Had they left? Should we make a break for it? Or wait until it was the dead of night to leave? We didn't know where the hidden passage let out, but I guessed the kitchen. What might we be walking into? Thoughts, intrusive ones, gripped me by the throat. *What if they locked us in*? *What if we stayed here in these walls forever*? No. No more waiting. I could barely breathe for fear of the walls, of the space constricting. Hazel turned the knob. The door came open with one quick shove, and the two of us fell into a cluttered, dusty pantry.

The back door, leading out of the kitchen and into the real world, was in view. Together, we crept toward the end of the pantry. I peeked inside the kitchen—all clear. We raced for the door, tore it open, and fumbled outside. The screen door banged against the frame behind us. We took off running—god knew where, not back to our place—just running. By the time we slowed, panting and sweating, we'd come to the edge of the ravine, blocks away from home.

When I bent over, hands on my knees, trying to catch my breath, I realized I didn't have the leather folder.

Day 838

From Within the House

They were here. Two girls. One of them, I recognized as the neighbor. The other, I may or may not have seen before. They risked a lot, coming here, creeping through the walls like me. If Michael had come upon them as they went rifling through his desk...oh, the things he might have done to them. They're in more danger now than they could ever possibly imagine.

Especially after I spied my brother. Stupid as he was, he'd put it together that they were the ones who were here snooping. He'd tell Michael; I was sure of it. Loyal like a big dumb dog, that one.

But it was fine.

I would hasten my plans.

Keeping more women safe from the monster within this house would be just another motivator.

Chapter Sixteen

September 6 (continued)

"WE HAVE TO go back," I panted.

"What? No. Why?" A sheen of sweat covered Hazel's forehead.

"I left that folder thing in the closet."

"Then it's gone." Hazel, hands behind her head, drew in slow, measured breaths. She looked out over the ravine, the tree limbs casting a tangle of shadows across her face, the sunset giving her skin a golden-pink radiance.

I rolled my lips, considering her words. If I left the portfolio behind, it would only ever be our word against theirs. "It's proof though. Evidence."

"Of what?"

"I don't know; that it's systemic."

"It's just words, written a long time ago even. It doesn't prove anything." She wiped her brow with the hem of her T-shirt. "What's your end game here?"

"To make things right," I said incredulously, not understanding her hesitation. "Like we did last fall."

"That was different."

I stepped back. "How so? There was an injustice. We fit the pieces together before the police could. Handed their case right to them."

"And I nearly died."

I had no counterargument to that. "Yes, but—"

"Yes, but?" Her eyebrows were high up on her forehead. "You're gonna 'yes, but' my stabbing?" She started down the sidewalk, leaving me behind.

"Hazel, wait!" I rushed to catch up with her, dodging someone riding a bike on the sidewalk. "You know that's not what I mean. I was there. I saw you"—my voice cracked—"get hurt." She spared me a glance, the look on her face unbelieving. "It was the worst night of my life. And I'm not trying to minimize that. What I meant was, what's going on in that evil, fucking house—that's the kind of thing we signed up to fight against. Right?"

"Sure. Yes. Okay, so you want to storm back in there, at huge risk since they know someone was sneaking around, to steal a folder and do what? Take it to the police?" Her arms flailed as she spoke, her voice near a frantic pitch. As we passed another house, someone on their porch mocked her movements while their group of friends laughed. She pretended not to notice. I flipped them off.

"Fuuuck you," I drawled at the group.

"Anytime, baby!" One of them yelled, cracking open a beer.

"What would the cops even say?" She paused for half a

beat as if she expected me to answer. "Nothing. They'd do nothing but pat you on the head and send you on your way. You already reported to the university. No one's even contacted you."

"You're not wrong. I know no one cares. But what about that guy? Hamden. I don't know what's happened to him or who he's talked to, but I bet if he knew about or had that portfolio, he'd be in a much better position to bring this shit to light. So we skip the police; get the notes to him."

She didn't say anything, just continued back toward our apartment in silence. I knew she was thinking, taking her time with what to do next, like always. And maybe we weren't compatible in that way. I rushed in; she held back, weighed out options, and planned.

By the time we got back to our apartment, the sky had turned indigo. Doug sat on the couch in our living room, watching TV. He clicked the remote, and the screen went black as we walked in.

"Hey," he said. "Everything okay?"

"No," we said in unison. But we didn't make eye contact or laugh at the congruity. An invisible wall had built itself between us, and where, normally, I stormed through these things, this time, I only had the energy to walk away.

"I gotta—" But I had no excuse really. "—go." I took the stairs two at a time until I reached my bedroom.

Inside, I stood with my back to the door. Dirty clothes littered the floor. I needed to throw a load in the wash if I wanted a clean uniform for tomorrow's class at the academy. I tossed a pair of pants, some socks, and the stiff, button-up shirt of my uniform into my laundry basket. As I turned to leave, that house, Michael's house, caught my eye. A window lit up—the one I'd stood on the other side of not more than twenty minutes ago, realizing there was a clear view into my room—like a wide-open eye, watching my every move. I continued cleaning up, pretending not to notice how it stared. How it tracked me.

They knew someone had been inside. They would have either found the portfolio in the back of that closet, or if not that, noticed it had been taken from the desk, the lock picked. They'd feel anxious about being discovered, which made them more dangerous.

When I looked up, it wasn't just the house staring at me. A dark silhouette stood there, framed by the window. The shape, the face, remained hidden. They were protected. I was exposed. I rushed to my doorframe and turned the light off. Darkness came down in a flash as if I'd closed my eyes.

I crept back toward my bed and watched, unsure what might happen next. The figure shined a flashlight over their face. They wanted me to know who they were. I struggled to make out their features from this distance, until it clicked. Stef—the one even Michael was wary of, who was more unpredictable than the rest—smiled, holding the flashlight under his chin like some stupid slumber party trick. He put his finger to his lips, then held the leather folder into the light.

Excerpt from *The Oakley Book of Lacrosse*

Item #6: Only the strong survive.

There will be no weakness. No softness. Neither vulnerability nor fragility will be tolerated. The weak never win. To be victorious is paramount. This is the time of your life. You will look back on your team years with fondness and pride because not only did you survive. You dominated.

Chapter Seventeen

September 7, 2001

THE BRIGHT RED numbers on my alarm clock changed from 3:10 to 3:11 a.m. I had to be up for the academy in just a few hours, but my mind kept spinning around that folder. Plus, the neighbors' genre-warping, country/hip-hop music pounded through yet another night. It rattled my bedroom window alongside snippets of yelled conversation, pulsing chatter and laughter.

It never ended, all the shit that went on over there—the drinking, the partying, the abuse—just kept going and going and going. Who was gonna stop them? I'd reported them to the university. Hazel had been right; no one had even gotten back to me. So what person in power would tell these guys, *No. Stop. There is a line, and you've crossed it. This is where all your privilege ends*?

There wasn't a soul.

Knock knock knock

I sat up in bed, gripping the covers. The September heat hadn't waned overnight. The air still felt sticky with humidity. My ears strained to hear over the blaring music next door. But nothing. I eased my breathing, willed my heartbeat to slow. It could have been anything: a tree branch banging in the wind, an animal scavenging through the trash can, even part of the party next door.

Knock knock knock

The knocking became banging, louder now. I pictured a fist pounding the wood frame, rattling the glass panel. My heart quickened, a pulsing glob in my throat. What was I supposed to do? It was the middle of the goddamned night.

"Hey!" A voice sounded, muffled and distant, traveling through the same walls that had me trapped inside.

I got out of bed and quietly crept out of my room, keeping the lights off. At the top of the stairs, I stood, perched next to Hazel's closed bedroom door. Was she home? I didn't know; I couldn't remember what she'd said about her plans.

Knock knock knock

The voice, clearly coming from the front door near the bottom of the stairs, called out again, "I know you're home!"

I descended the first few steps after hearing the tremor, a frantic oscillation in the person's tone. Something was wrong. They could need help, but as I bent at the waist, peeking toward the door, I made out the shape of the person and it matched the deep register of their voice. It was a guy— a man. And that sealed his fate: I would not answer that door. No matter what.

He rattled the knob, found it locked, and beat on the

door again. This time, the sound was less a knock and more a slap. His palm smacking flat against the wood, I imagined.

"Answer the door! Fuck!" he said, apparently talking to himself. His silhouette shifted away from the entrance. His head turned, looking back at the street, hand raised as if in greeting. He laughed, fake-like. He turned the knob again, still locked, then took off running.

Guilt, heavy and deep, weighed on me. How was I supposed to be a police officer if I couldn't even answer my door in the middle of the night? Everything my family had warned me about, everything they'd been worried about when it came to me being a woman on the force, rushed through me.

Screw that.

I went back to my bedroom and threw on some regular clothes. My bedframe squealed as I sat to tie up my sneakers. The guy was probably far gone by now, but I'd seen the direction he went. This was more about proving something to myself than anything else. I couldn't be scared of a man just because he was a man. Just like I couldn't be scared of the dark just because it was the dark.

The dark doesn't hate you though. It doesn't call names or grab as if it owns.

I pushed the thought away and looked up. Hazel stood in my doorway. "What are you doing?" Her eyes were puffy with sleep, and she stifled a yawn.

"You're here?" I asked.

She looked confused. "Uh, yeah."

"I thought you were at Doug's."

"Maeve, I don't spend the night with Doug. I've told you this a million—"

"Somebody was knocking on our door just now. I didn't answer, but I think they were in trouble. They ran off a few minutes ago. I'm following them."

"Not without me you're not." She finger-combed her hair into a ponytail and went to her room, where she hopped around, grabbing shoes and putting them on. She didn't bother changing out of her pajamas—an old T-shirt and boxer shorts.

"You sure?" I asked, thinking of how we'd argued earlier.

"Yes, I'm fucking sure."

Outside, the muggy air clung to the skin. The screen door opened, and Hazel joined me. She turned to lock the door, and using the small flashlight on her keychain, we completed a quick search of our front porch. Nothing indicated anyone had even been there, except one of our porch chairs was tilted at an odd angle.

"Which way did he go?"

"That way." I pointed, and we headed off. As we walked farther from our house, the sounds of the neighbors' party faded. My shoulders dropped back to their normal position, and I loosened my clenched jaw. I took a deep breath. The absence of sound, those loud, manufactured beats, backed me away from the razor's edge I'd subconsciously been balancing on.

Most of the homes along our block were dark, whole households asleep, tucked safely in their beds. Occasionally, we passed a lit window with the flickering blue from either a video game or TV show.

After a few blocks of encountering nothing, we came to an intersection and stopped.

"Well, what do you think?" Hazel asked.

"I guess we should probably head back. Whatever happened isn't something we can help with now."

"Right." She swung her flashlight wide as we turned back toward our apartment.

Out of the corner of my eye, I saw it. Even though I wasn't quite sure what "it" was.

"Hold on." I stopped her, grabbing her arm. "Shine your light over that way again."

She did, and a single shoe came into view.

We crossed the street to get a closer look, Hazel's flashlight creating a shifting circle of light on the pavement. Up close, the condition of the running shoe looked either new or very well taken care of. From the size, I'd guess it fit a man. It sat at the top of a set of rustic stairs, wooden beams positioned into the hillside that led into a gulch. A few expensive houses dotted the top edge of the ravine, but mostly it was a wooded area—a place to avoid at night.

We both knew we were going down there, didn't even bother checking with each other. We stayed side by side, the little keychain light bouncing and bobbing through the trees as we descended. The quiet that had brought relief earlier, now brought a new sense—a kind of sharpness. Every *creak* and *crack*, every animal chitter, sliced through the darkness and set me on alert. As time ticked forward, one thing became ever clearer: Something or someone had been chasing that guy who had been knocking on our door. His frantic pounding, the tinge of panic in his voice, the way he'd greeted someone, his lost shoe: I'd let that whole thing play out. I'd decided I shouldn't help; I'd failed.

At the bottom of the stairs, beside a shallow creek, a

paved path wove through the trees. Streetlamps dotted the trail, but they were few and far between. Darkness spread between them, an oil spill of sorts.

We scanned the area, looking for any indication of where the guy might have gone, but it seemed deserted.

"Which way?" I whispered.

"Without clues, I say we go right."

"Why?"

"Most people are right-handed. You said yourself the dude was in a panic, so maybe turning right would be more instinctual for him in the moment."

"Right, okay." I loved the way her brain worked. But now was not the time for adoration.

With no indication to go any other way, we followed Hazel's instinct. She swung the light from side to side as we walked. Seconds turned to minutes which turned to long stretches of blank, eventless time. Hazel stopped short. A little whoosh of air, a *yeesh*, escaped her.

Up ahead, a family of raccoons stopped whatever they were tearing apart and looked at us with cold, assessing eyes. I stepped ahead of Hazel and widened my arms, making myself appear bigger. I didn't know a thing about raccoons except my dad hated them, calling them "vicious little bastards."

The biggest one moved away from their find—a big, crumpled bag marked with a fast-food logo—and led the others off the path. Thankfully, the rest followed, and we both let out a breath.

Coyotes yipped and barked in the distance, another warning. We hadn't found any evidence down here, save the shoe. And it had been at the top of the steps, so it didn't necessarily mean our guy had made it to the ravine path.

"How much longer do you wanna look?" Hazel asked.

I shrugged. I couldn't beat back the feeling that if we just went a little farther, we'd find something. How could we stop looking when the next clue might be just ahead?

"What time is it?" I asked.

Hazel checked her phone, pressing a button that made the face light up a turquoise shade of green. "Nearly four."

"You think we should head back?" I asked.

We stood under one of the few lamps that lined the path, so I could see how half her mouth scrunched as she bit the inside of her cheek, mulling it over.

"It's hard to make that call. They could be right there." She indicated the velvet dark just ahead of us.

"That's what I was thinking too. If we turn around, we could miss something by inches."

"Let's set a time limit. If we don't find *anything* else in the next fifteen minutes, we head back?"

Reasonable. I agreed, and we pressed into the darkness.

"Hey, I'm sorry about earlier," she said.

"No, you were right. There's no way we could've gone back into that house and gotten the folder safely." Stef's maniacal grin replayed in my mind. "Pretty sure they know we were there."

"I mean, about all of this. You've been the one taking what's going on over there seriously, and I'm sorry I've been...distracted."

"Oh. It's okay."

"It's not. I've been—"

"I get it, Hazel. What you and Doug are doing is for your mom. That stuff comes first."

She sighed. "Yeah, for a long time it has. I don't really know how to set it aside and, like, figure out other *things*."

And with that emphasis on "things," I thought maybe we weren't talking about her mom anymore. I glanced at her but couldn't read her expression. The flashlight flickered. Hazel banged it against her palm until it came back on, but the beam had weakened. If our time out here weren't limited before, it was now.

"We should go back," I said, keeping my voice low. "The lamps along the path are really spread out."

"Yeah, I don't like the idea of having to walk around in the dark."

The flashlight flickered one more time, then died. It took a while for my eyes to adjust to the black. But eventually, Hazel emerged beside me, like a shadow of herself. Nothing but the pale moon illuminated her face, so it was cast in a silvery-gray light. Not a shadow or a ghost, Hazel was more enchanting than either of those things. Maybe a nymph, one of the Meliae of the ash trees.

She reached for my arm, her fingers like an electric spark along my skin, and I let her take it. My heart fluttered, and I wondered if she felt it too. I thought of that night, nearly a year ago, when we'd spent time smoking and talking by the river. There had been a moment, one where we nearly kissed, but it was disrupted. And everything since then had been similar, one interruption or disappointment after another.

Until now. Nothing stood between us now. No Doug. No Ryan. No Creeping Cops. We were alone out here, just the two of us holding on to each other in the quiet gloom of the wood. Our own kind of fairy tale.

Of course, it could all mean nothing to her. Prick a finger, shatter the glass slipper, let that last petal fall, she could never be mine.

But then her other hand grazed the waistline of my jeans and pulled me closer, my lips mere inches from hers. I reached for her hips, lined up against mine. Her fingers trailed up my forearms.

My eyes met hers, and I hesitated. Not because I was nervous but because I loved this feeling. The moment—just before everything changed—hung between us. Its intensity pulled tight through my whole body. We were on the edge. A precipice. The cliff.

And then footfalls, heavy and fast-paced, ran toward us. I put my finger to my lips, my heart beating from lust and fear all mixed up together, and guided us off the path into the trees.

The trunks were thin, and we separated to hide. I kept my eyes on the trail, the pounding footsteps steady like a telltale heart, guilt-ridden and consistent. They grew louder, and the person passed under the closest lamplight. I caught a shock of blond hair and a wide chest, a white T-shirt and jeans. Was it the same guy who had pounded on our door? Had he gotten away? Was he safe? Or was this the person who'd chased him away?

He'd just passed us when Hazel shifted her stance and rustled some leaves. The guy stopped midstep. Only moonlight and shade painted his features. He looked around, obviously curious about the noise. If we could stay still for just a little while longer, he'd be sure to think it was only an animal. Coyotes barked again, closer than they had been before, and the guy didn't hesitate. He set off at a fast clip.

I blew out a long, deep breath once he was good and far away. The two of us stepped out from the brush and onto the path. We silently trudged back toward the ravine entrance.

A thought occurred to me. "Did we make the same mistake we made last time?"

"What do you mean?"

"Should we have called the police? Instead of trying to go after that guy?"

"Oh." Hazel shrugged. "I don't know. I thought you were talking about the other thing."

"What other thing?"

"If you don't know, it doesn't really matter."

Day 839

From Within the House

I approached him while he slept. The plan: Straddle him, making him think I was just another girl, one of the many he brought up to his room and fucked into oblivion. His eyes would start to open, and he'd see me instead.

I'd relish the look on his face when he recognized me as a living and breathing being. No longer the missing girl, no longer the ghost. What would he do then? Push me off? Try to flip me around and take me from behind, all the while his brain working out what ways he could control me next. He'd think he'd won. That I'd come back to him after all this time. His little pet.

And that was when I'd swing the rubber mallet I'd found in the basement. Not at his face. Not at first. I needed him to recognize that I was the one ending the poison that bloomed between us. That I wasn't lost or stolen. No, I'd healed, and he would no longer be the theme of my story or anyone else's.

It would have been the perfect end.

Except for my brother.

When I stepped toward the bed, it wasn't Michael's eyes that opened but Stef's. What was he doing in the bed? He'd been sleeping on the floor since I'd ruined Michael's mattress. They'd switched places? Before I had answers to any of my questions, a set of warm fingers wrapped around both my wrists. A person pulled my arms behind me and brought their chest up against my back.

"Look who it is," Michael whispered, his hot breath wet against me ear, making goosebumps rise along my neck. "In the flesh."

"Stef?" I whispered my brother's name, pleading. He just lay there, staring up at me, maybe transfixed by the sight of me alive. Either way, he'd helped Michael spring this new trap. All my plans, all the work I'd done to heal myself, started to crumble. I started to disintegrate. Michael's fingers were like chains. "Stef..."

"He won't help you." Michael nipped at my earlobe, and I suppressed a whimper. "He's never been able to help you. You both are mine."

He twirled me around to face him, his eyes searching mine. "It's really you," he said, a tinge of awe accenting his tone. He gathered both my wrists in one of his hands, his grip constrictor-tight, and then he brought his fingers to the base of my jaw, stroking lightly. "I knew it the moment I saw you in the attic. I'll admit, it surprised me! Went to my uncle and everything. Then you started pulling tricks around the house. Did you really think I'd fall for it? That I'd be scared of a ghost?" He licked his lips. A maniacal smile painted his features, all shades of blue and black in the darkness of the room. "Nothing haunts me, Stonie. Nothing at all."

Chapter Eighteen

September 7, 2001

There was a dead body in our basement.

Excerpt from *The Oakley Book of Lacrosse*

Item #7: Eliminate weakness. Eliminate threats.

Period.

Chapter Nineteen

September 7, 2001

I SHUFFLED A few steps closer to try to identify the person. Their face lay in shadow, and it was badly bruised and had swelled to curious proportions. Parts of the head even seemed...a bit concaved.

I steadied my breathing, doing my damnedest to ignore the metallic tang of blood in the air. I swallowed panic and suppressed a gag, along with the bile threatening and burning the back of my throat. *Do not puke. Do. Not. Puke.* I stepped away from the corpse, scrubbed at my eyes, an immature attempt to wash away what was so clearly before me.

I'd *just* come down here to get my uniform from the dryer. I'd planned on making coffee while relishing the fluttering feeling that had come with another near-kiss with Hazel. She'd chosen me. Anything was doable, fixable even, because we would be together in the end.

But then...this.

Forced to deal with a dead body.

Again?

How did that not smother anything that might have sparked in the ravine?

I reached and pulled the string to the light—a bare bulb attached to a rafter. *Click*. The room went back to a myriad of grays and blacks. I was alone in the dark with the body, large and ghastly. A beast in the basement.

I turned and made my way to the bottom of the stairs, considering how the dead person might rise again. I even listened for a *whoosh* of breath or a low moan of pain. The person *could* come creeping and slithering across the dirty cement to grab at my ankles through the open risers as I plodded up the stairs. But no. Nothing but the occasional drip of water sounded. What once had been a person was no more.

Show some respect. My yaya's voice rang in my head. *Someone has died.*

I climbed the stairs, and only the basement's quiet mustiness lingered at the threshold of the kitchen. I had to tell Hazel. I had to figure out who was down there. I had to puzzle together how someone might've dragged a body or chased them through our apartment and why.

I stumbled through our place in a daze. Standing outside Hazel's open bedroom door, I knocked softly on the doorframe. She turned. One eye seemed brighter and larger than the other, a mascara wand still in her hand. She had coffee already—must have made it while I was down there, in what seemed like another world—and took a sip from the mug on her vanity.

"What's up? You don't look so good," she said.

I paced into her room and sat on her bed. I wiped my palms, gummy with sweat, on the comforter. *How do I say this*? *How do I tell her about another dead body*?

"There's...something in the basement."

"What? Like a leak? Call the landlord, I guess." She turned back to her vanity mirror and continued applying makeup, swiping thick black smudges over delicate lashes. "Not that it will make a difference. They still haven't come and fixed the back door." She screwed the cap back on the tube and tossed it into her bag, annoyance showing on her features.

"No, it's not that."

"What, then?"

"It's a person." I watched her face in the mirror. Her brows knitted together, and the corners of her mouth turned down. "And they are not alive."

"What?" she practically whispered. She'd been through this before. More than once. More than me.

"There's a dead body in the basement, Hazel." Time folded in on itself as I repeated nearly the same phrase from last year. Words that had started this whole path toward the police academy. What if I had never said them? I'd been curious about what had happened in the Trap last fall, and at the time, I wouldn't have considered missing out on all that drama. *Drama, oof*. What if I'd stayed in the dorm that night instead of urging Hazel toward some grim fascination of mine? If we'd never allowed all this death and mystery and trauma to be stirred up between us, where would we be now?

"What?" she asked again, confusion painting her

shimmering eyes. She rolled her tongue over her front teeth, then bit her bottom lip—calculating, I thought. "How can that..."

"We should call the police." I stated the obvious before she had time to suggest anything else. "And we'll need to call in our absence at the academy. It's gonna be a long day."

"Who is it?" she asked.

"I'm not sure. They're...pretty banged up."

"Do you think it's the person that knocked on our door last night?"

"I have no idea." Mostly because I hadn't gotten around to thinking that way yet. But it was possible, maybe even probable. "Could be."

"Let me see." She stood quickly, and the bench seat fell over backward, banging against the floorboards. "Let me see." She looked lost, like a trapped animal, a virtual deer caught in headlights. She stumbled over her own feet but righted herself. "Take me to see it."

"Okay." I got to the door, and we faced each other, just staring, eyes searching.

"We do this together," she said.

I thought she'd be shaky or weak, but all I picked up on was her steely resolve as she turned and headed down the stairs ahead of me.

We made our way to the living room, and I stopped to turn off the lamp. Nobody needed to think we were here, or awake, or that anything weird was happening, especially if any of last night's partyers lingered out back. Their laughter and chatter seeped through the brick walls, oozing through the crumbling mortar, even when they'd quieted. Always there. Haunting us with their version of a "good time."

"I don't think we should have the lights on," I whispered, even though I didn't need to. "If this has anything to do with the neighbors"—It absolutely did; I knew it already—"someone might be keeping an eye us."

"You think it's them?"

My gut said yes, but I'd been ignoring what my gut had to say for months now. "I don't know," I lied, shrugging. My intuition sang: *Stop ignoring me.* "After everything that's happened? Who else might dump a body in our apartment?"

"Right," she agreed. "It's either a total, random coincidence that someone's been killed, and the murderer just happens to stumble upon our empty apartment while we were chasing after someone else. Or—"

"Our place was a logical choice. Easy access. Look." I indicated the back door, scooting around Hazel to get a closer look. The wooden panel that had been used to replace the broken window hung loose, the two nails along the bottom edge no longer embedded in the door.

I crouched, examining the whole thing closer. A spattering of burgundy dots had collected on the floor. "They weren't very neat about the whole thing." Sure enough, a tiny bit of maroon stained the nail closest to the doorknob. "Must've scratched themselves on the way in."

"That's good." Hazel sifted through the designated junk drawer. "For us, I mean. When we call the police."

"True."

The doorknob hung a little loose, out of place a bit as if it had been handled roughly or even kicked.

"I can't find another flashlight, but we have these." Hazel held up a pair of candlesticks.

"You're kidding." I stood and took one of the long white

candles.

"Nope." She struck a kitchen match, and a tiny flare brightened the room. "They were in the emergency box Aunt Liddy put together." She lit her candle, shook the flame out of the match, and leaned her burning wick toward mine.

"What on earth would we do without Aunt Liddy?"

"I can't even fathom," she said, her gaze focused on the flame.

We reached the bottom steps, our candles casting a golden hue along the old walls. Shadows lengthened and deepened against the flickering flame. I moved forward, to where I'd found the body, and for a moment, I thought— *hoped*—they were gone. Vanished. A dead person disappeared, like in the movies. But this wasn't Hollywood, and they lay exactly where they'd been before, unmoved and unliving. Unchanged...well, except for the whole ecosystem of decomposition currently underway.

Hazel's breath hitched when she saw them. Blood wasn't the only smell in the room. A hint of turned meat, a slight rottenness hung in the air, a spoiling. I thought of the lacrosse house—decay everywhere, down to the studs. Hazel stepped to the other side of the body and knelt.

"I think there's something in their mouth," Hazel said. "Hand me a towel."

"I don't think we should..." But I gave her my candlestick and grabbed a clean towel from the stack atop the dryer. As I stepped toward her, my ankle rolled where the drain dipped. I tried to catch myself, to grasp at anything, but there was nothing to do except fall and get my hands in front of me to protect my face. I landed on the corpse's legs, which felt like two thick rolls of clay, spindled out like snakes.

I jumped back. "Fuck." I'd touched it; I hadn't meant to touch it.

"It's okay."

How was she managing to stay calm?

"We've been through this before," Hazel said. "Remember?"

Of course I did.

She took the towel and covered her hands, then pressed against the person's mouth, prying it open. Before I could respond to her comment or ask what the hell she thought she was doing, a bulky ring with a giant, shimmering ruby popped out.

Day 839 (continued)

From Within the House

Eight hundred and thirty-nine days. One hundred and forty weeks of scrounging for food and hiding behind walls. Over 20,000 hours spent observing and healing and slowly peeling myself away from him. Only to have him grab me by the wrists and win.

No.

No.

The Stonie in this timeline, who mended her own wounds with plots and ideas, she would not go quietly into his grasp. She'd become feral, scavenging for her survival. Foraging for herself. She had teeth to bite with.

And bite, I did, as Michael couldn't help himself from coming in close and making sure he took up all my space and all the air I breathed.

"The things I have planned for you," he whispered. His cheek, his ear, the pulsing vein at his neck, all parts exposed and weak. I turned my head only slightly before the salt of his skin lit up my tongue. My teeth grazed his prickly,

unshaven neck, moved up toward the flesh and gristly cartilage, then sank in.

"Ah! You dumb bitch!" He shoved me, but that was a mistake because I didn't let go. Blood flooded my mouth, and still, I held on. He pushed again with enough force to send me flying across the room. My backside rammed into the bookshelf, and I fell to the floor. Textbooks tumbled from the shelves.

On my hands and knees, I spit the bit of his earlobe that had torn away. It landed on our old yearbook, a wet and slimy chunk of meat, a piece of him.

This time, I took a piece of him.

And now, for all the rest.

Chapter Twenty

September 7 (continued)

WE TRUDGED BACK up the basement stairs, passed through the kitchen, and stopped in the dining room. The morning light, white with a tinge of gray-blue, streamed through the windows. A trance of spiraling thoughts swirled through my head. How could this have happened? Why did that ring look familiar? What were we supposed to do now?

Call the police. We hadn't last time, and Hazel was nearly killed when the murderer came after us. I headed right for the phone on the computer desk.

"Hold on," she said, stopping me.

"No." I shook my head. "No, Hazel. We have to go to the police this time. I can't watch you—"

"No, I know. We're definitely calling the cops. I'm not talking about that." She indicated our neighbors' house. "Look."

I set the cordless phone on the dining table and noticed the quiet. The house, usually lit up and loud and spewing people onto its front porch and lawn even at this hour, was dark again—like it had been when we broke in and found their little folio of sins. It seemed vacant, devoid of life. It was as if somehow in the last hour or so, they'd all packed up and moved away. But that couldn't be possible. They'd been partying; I'd heard them, seen them. It hadn't stopped. Until now.

"This might be the only opportunity..." Hazel said.

"First we make the phone call. Then we go get that portfolio."

"Okay." Hazel turned toward me, her eyes serious and dark. She blew out a steadying breath and nodded. "The house seems empty enough."

"It's not." I smirked. "They're in there. And if they had anything to do with the person in the basement, then they'll expect us to call the police. They've shut down the party because—"

"It's the cover-up."

"Maybe the beginnings of one. I'm only, like, 95 percent sure they know who's in our basement and how they got there." I picked up the phone.

"Maeve," Hazel started.

"Yeah." I pressed Start, and the distant, corresponding beep followed.

"The ring."

"Is it familiar to you too?" I pressed nine-one-one—*beep, beep, beep*—then brought the phone to my ear. "I can't remember where I've seen it."

The ringing had already started, and then a gruff voice

said, "Nine-one-one. What's your emergency?"

"Michael," Hazel whispered, her features wide with re-alization.

His name brought a memory: a flash of deep-red, the shine of gold turning on his finger. The ring was Michael's.

"Hello? Is anyone there? Nine-one-one. What's your emergency?"

What did it mean that Michael's ring was stuffed into the mouth of the person downstairs? Was it Michael, lying there while cells deteriorated and bacteria flushed through his system? Or was leaving it with the body a tactic, a terri-torial marking like some animal pissing on a wall?

Hazel took the phone from me and answered the dis-patcher's questions, her voice sounding far away. I stumbled backward into a chair and sat, staring at the old house. The shutters in an upper-story window blew closed and opened like a winking eye.

I shook my head. No, the house wasn't alive. But it played a part. It held on to secrets and let bad things bloom in the shadows, not a difficult thing to do when the whole world was trained to look the other way. I bit my lower lip, tearing at a piece of chapped skin.

"Not today." My backpack hung over the back of the chair, and I rifled through it until I found what I was looking for—my knife. "They're not getting away with it today," I mumbled under my breath.

I paced to the still-broken back door. Its knob hung loose, the boarded-up window unattached at the bottom edge, the wood around the chain lock splintered and shred-ded, and the drops of blood spattered along the edge and floor—all of it evidence. I shouldn't use this exit.

I stalked toward the front door, thinking of the body downstairs. Who were they? My mind immediately conjured up Hamden—the guy who'd had enough at the river, his name crossed out on in the leather padfolio. He'd seemed a likely person to have gone to the authorities about what the team, what Michael, was doing to its newest members. But the detail about Michael's ring? How did that fit? Why would Michael set himself up in such a way?

"Okay, they're coming." Hazel eyed my knife, then turned and grabbed hers from her purse. "Are we really doing this?" Our eyes met; I tried to convey how resolute I felt without words. She nodded. "Okay. We're going back in there."

"Whatever happened to the person downstairs, that folder is part of it." I'd convinced myself in the moments it took for Hazel to share information with the dispatcher: Our neighbors were responsible for that body. Their macho little system of proving themselves had been part of it. That was the piece we had to hand over to police before they questioned us over and over again about what might have happened to the dead person who'd just happened to end up in our home.

We stepped outside. From a perch high up on the power lines above us, a mourning dove cooed, sounding much like an owl. *Whooo-woo who who-who*. Instinctually, we trailed back toward their kitchen, heading for that pantry and the secret passage. The siding of the lacrosse house sagged and warped away from its bones, a greenish-gray fungus clinging to the outer layer.

"Unless someone confesses," Hazel whispered, her breath misting in the cool morning air, "it's circumstantial evidence."

"Could show motive," I said, moving ahead of her.

She continued as if I hadn't said anything. "But even that would be iffy to prove in court. Anyone could write anything in that book. To be honest, the real evidence is in our house."

I stopped just before my foot landed on the back porch steps, doubt seeping through all my forward momentum. Hazel ran into me, shoving me forward.

"Ope, jeez. Sorry," she whispered. So Midwestern. So cute.

Voices carried from the kitchen. The house wasn't asleep. Neither were the people inside.

"Shh, listen," I whispered and crouched, stepping back to the side of the porch, out of view from anyone inside.

"This is insane."

I recognized Stef's voice, his tone lit with panic.

"What do you suggest we do, Stef?" a woman asked. A *slap* sounded, something flat—a notebook, or a *leather portfolio*—tossed onto a table or counter.

"I don't know. I don't know."

"Let me remind you, we are making things right," the woman said. "You didn't mean for things to go as far as they did. But...they did. And, well, now, we gotta get our stories straight, right?"

Stef mumbled his agreement.

I couldn't see how many people were in the kitchen; so far, I'd heard two distinct voices—Stef and this woman.

"So when's the last time anyone saw him?" she asked.

"There's no way to know," Stef said. "People started showing up around ten and were in and out all night long."

His voice was low and difficult to hear. "I saw him a few times, and then...I saw you."

"Okay, good enough," the woman said, obviously in control. "Then that's it. The party gives us enough cover for no one to really know what happened. You tell your friends to say whatever—that they were too drunk to notice, they hooked up with someone, they left for White Castle; I don't give a fuck. But nobody saw him after one or two, got it?"

More mumbling. More agreement. Some movement.

Toward the back door.

They were coming outside.

I crept backward to avoid being seen, motioning to Hazel without making a sound. Once we got far enough away, we broke into a run, rounding the corner of our row house and not looking back till we stood on our own front porch.

"Who was that? Who was in the kitchen?" Hazel asked, taking a seat on the stoop.

"Stef, for sure. I don't know the other person."

"What do you think happened?"

"Who knows? Anything I come up with would just be a guess at this point."

"Yeah, okay," Hazel said. "But let's put all the pieces together—what we know goes on in that house, a guy running away, the portfolio."

"You're assuming all those pieces are from the same puzzle."

"You don't think they are?"

"No, I do. I mean, it's possible. I don't know." I shrugged. "It could also be possible that guy running away last night tried something with that woman, and she fought back. Maybe their little portfolio doesn't play into the murder at all. But the dead person's face was destroyed. You think a woman could do that?"

"Given the right tool—cast iron pan, baseball bat—sure, yeah, a woman could do that much damage. Shirlee did her worst work with just a box cutter last year. And it sounded to me like Stef helped."

"True." I paced in front of the steps. "But how and why did they end up downstairs in our apartment?"

"Well..." She sat on the stoop and picked at the weeds growing through the pavement. "Maybe the guy led them here. Like he broke in thinking he could hide out. But they cornered him."

"They. Just the two of them?"

"Stef and the woman, for sure. Maybe more? I don't know." Hazel pressed her fingers to her temples and rubbed a circular pattern. After a few moments, she sighed and opened her eyes, her hands falling back into her lap.

It had happened again, one of those electric moments between us. I searched her eyes, hoping to bring back a brief glimpse of the magic I'd felt in the ravine. But it was gone, snuffed out by our shared sense of duty. What sometimes lingered between us became a job once more.

"Do you have your cigarettes?" she asked. "I could really use...something."

"Yeah, just a sec." I stepped around her and opened the front door. My purse lay flung across the couch, and I grabbed it quickly, not wanting to spend any time in what we'd once thought would be our perfect first apartment.

I walked back outside, the screen door slamming behind me, sat next to Hazel on the steps, and handed her the pack of cigarettes. She pulled one out and lit it. I did the same once she handed it back to me.

"Can't get coffee, I guess," I said. "We probably need to limit our time inside."

"Right," Hazel looked to the sky and exhaled a plume of smoke. "What's next?"

"Nothing." It hurt to say. Since when did I step back and get out of the way? Well, maybe I'd learned a little something. "We let the police do their job. Tell them what we just overheard. Tell them everything." I took a drag off my cigarette; the burning sensation in my throat fit the morning. "And hope to hell they don't arrest us for murder."

*

THE REST OF the morning sped by while I spent most of it on the sidewalk in front of the row houses. Beyond the area cordoned off by the police, it seemed the rest of the neighborhood had gathered to watch the spectacle. At some point, someone handed me a coffee. It tasted awful, overly bitter and somehow dry. But it was something warm to hold in my hands, something to do with my mouth when I wasn't answering the same questions over and again.

When did you notice the door had been broken? After I found the body in the basement. I ran back upstairs to tell my roommate. And that was when we noticed the door. My roommate called you guys then.

Do you know the person in the basement? I didn't recognize them, no. I wondered about the ring. Had Hazel left it down there?

Have you noticed anything out of the ordinary in the neighborhood lately?

"Yes."

The officer looked up from her notepad. Clearly, she hadn't expected confirmation. Her cap rested low on her forehead and nearly covered her eyebrows, yet now, they disappeared under the bill. "Care to elaborate?" she asked.

"You saw our back door. The missing windowpane. How it's painted over."

She nodded, scrawling something onto her notepad.

"They did that. The guys in the house behind us broke the window, then painted a slur on it one night. They fixed it but... They're athletes at the university."

"Oakley. Right, okay." She wrote something in her notebook.

"They party *a lot*—"

"Well, that's campus for ya—"

"No, this is different."

"You wanna cut to the chase here?" She huffed, her chest rising with impatience.

Another officer squeezed by us. "'Bout done in there, Mary."

"'Kay. Thanks, Tom." She turned her attention back to me. "You were saying?"

"I've seen some things next door." I explained about Michael and the caning and the river. She asked some questions but mostly listened. I told her everything I knew, everything I thought: Their secret handbook, how I hadn't seen Hamden after the river incident, and how he'd threatened to kill them. How it had seemed like he meant it.

"And who's Michael?"

"They're leader. Captain. Of the team or whatever."

"And you think this is all related?" She spread her

fingers and made a circular motion with her hand, looking like a witch casting a spell.

"You don't?"

"I'm just gathering information, ma'am."

It was the first time in my life I'd ever been called a ma'am.

"Well, yeah. I think it's connected," I said. "That place is fucked up."

She didn't stop writing, but her eyes narrowed, considering and judging. "Did you report any of this to anyone before today?"

"Yes! I dropped off a complaint form at the athletic department a while ago. Listen, have you been over there yet?" I asked. "They have this room; the door locks from the outside. My roommate saw it too."

I started feeling defensive, a little pissed even. What if she didn't believe me? "Look, a guy ran up to our door last night—morning really. Knocking like crazy, like he was being chased. My roommate and I didn't let him in...because, well, it was the middle of the night. But we did go after him. When we got back, the house was like this. The party next door was over and quiet. I've seen them beat the shit out of one another with my own eyes. I've confronted Michael about it, multiple times. He'll tell you." At least, I hoped he would, but maybe that was wishful thinking. More likely, he'd fall back in with his boys. Not say a word. Protect his friends. If he was even alive. "And we overheard some of them talking this morning, working out alibis."

"You heard them? Who? And where?"

"Right outside their place."

Her eyebrow cocked. "And when was this?"

"Right after we called you. We walked over there." There went her eyebrows again, disappearing up under the brim of her cap. "We thought we would…" I let my speech trail off. How to explain?

"Okay, okay. Calm down. Who did you hear?"

"One guy, Stef. I heard someone, a woman, use his name."

"All right, we'll look into it." She folded up her notepad and fit it into her utility belt. Her demeanor was all business. "Do you two have a place to stay?"

"I…" Hadn't thought of that. Hazel stood near the curb talking to another officer taking her statement.

"This is officially a crime scene. You'll need to call someone or get a hotel room until we clear the house."

"How long will that take?"

"Depends."

"Helpful."

The officer's mouth flattened, but she didn't add any information.

"Can we grab some of our stuff?"

"With an escort, yes."

"Right, okay. Is there someone I can call later? To, like, check on the status of the house, when we can come back, that kind of thing?"

"The lead detective on this case will be in contact with you. They'll want you to come in and give a formal statement as well."

"And who is that? Do they have a card or something?" I asked. I hadn't planned for this part, the afterward. The last thing I wanted to do was walk away from our house empty-handed, with no information about when I could come back—if I even wanted to come back.

"There she is, Detective Patterson."

Bells rang, at least in my head. Officer Mary pointed to a black car that had just pulled over and parked. Detective Patterson stepped out in the same bomber jacket and oxford-style shirt she'd worn last fall. Her hair was longer, past her shoulders now. But there was no mistaking the woman who'd encouraged Hazel and me to try for the peace officer program trudging up the concrete steps to my apartment. She appeared laser-focused on the building, on the details. She examined the front door, finding something photo worthy as she called someone over to take a picture of a dent no one else had noticed. It could have been made by that guy banging on the door last night. Or it could have been made five years ago; I had no idea.

Then she turned her attention to the officer who'd interviewed me. It took a second for recognition to bloom across her features, but it came. She pointed at me, squinting as she tried to remember my name.

"Maeve," I offered. "Maeve Drakos."

"That's right. From the campus murder last fall." She inhaled deeply. "I'd hoped to see you again...just not like this."

"Yeah, well, guess I attract dead bodies."

Both Detective Patterson and the officer stared at me, unlaughing and serious. After an awkward silence, Detective Patterson said, "I better get inside. Anything I need to know?"

"Yeah, the house behind this one. She reported some strange stuff happening over there. Hazing and the like," Officer Mary said.

"Send someone over there; see if anyone has a witness statement to give."

"Will do."

"And later check call logs for complaints. When did they move in?"

"'Bout the same time as us, first of August," I answered.

"Go back that far," said Detective Patterson and she turned to leave.

"Yes, ma'am."

Officer Mary turned her attention back to me and continued, "So, about where you'll be staying..."

"My parents'." I gave her the number, and she told me someone would be in touch, then walked away.

I scanned the area for Hazel, who looked to be finishing up with the officer she gave her report to as well. Our eyes met, and I felt a bunch of things at once: astonishment, regret, curiosity.

I made my way to the street corner where she stood. The morning had risen with the temperature creeping through the mugginess of yet another late summer day. Hazel still wore her pajamas and sneakers. I hadn't showered, hadn't swiped on deodorant, or brushed my teeth. The two of us had been totally overtaken by this.

Randomly, the other apartments we'd looked at a few months ago came to mind. How we hadn't chosen one of those because of Hazel's aversion to carpeting. I'd take old, matted carpet over a corpse any day.

"Hey," I said, greeting her as the officer walked away. Our near-kiss in the ravine faded with last night's moon, still there, just not shiny and bright—lightly haunting me, even while reality crumbled around us.

Her features pinched, the sunlight making her squint. "You going home?" she asked.

I shaded my eyes and watched officers go in and out of our front door, swarming like ants. "I'll call my mom here in a bit." I raked my teeth over my lower lip, just thinking about how Mama would react. "She's gonna freak out so hard."

"Warranted, I guess. I haven't called Liddy yet."

Liddy lived about three hours away and would surely drive down in a rush to swoop in and help.

"You two are welcome to stay with us. We have room." My parents' house was one big ole empty nest.

"If I can, I'm gonna try to keep her from coming down here."

I snorted. "Like that's possible."

Hazel gave a weak smile. "I know. She'll ignore me. Come down with guns blazing, and I'll stay with her in whatever hotel she books. Until then, Doug already offered up his couch, so I'll probably stay there."

My whole body lurched at this news. "You called him? Already?"

"Yeah." A moment later, her phone buzzed, and she answered it, then ended the call quickly. "Okay. He's here. I'm gonna..." She made a weird hitchhiking motion that was meant to explain how she was leaving.

"Oh." My throat constricted; I could barely breathe let alone talk. I didn't know what I'd expected, hadn't really had time to think about it, but Hazel driving off into the horizon with Doug wasn't the scenario I'd imagined.

"Call me when you get settled, I guess." I grasped. "You think you'll go to school Monday? Want me to pick you up?"

"I don't know yet. I'll let you know."

The moment held an unreal quality. Her voice sounded inexplicably light and airy, kind of bouncy. Pops of yellow goldenrod swayed across the street. I sneezed, ragweed season. Police passed around us, marking our porch with caution tape. Nothing matched. Everything contrasted.

"Uh-um," I stuttered at all the incongruencies. "Can I use your phone? I should call my mom."

"Oh gosh, yeah." She handed me the little gadget, and I typed in my old house phone number, hoping she hadn't left for work yet, then clicked the little green button. The phone seemed so small, fragile even, in my hands and smaller still when I held it to my cheek.

It rang and rang until, finally, Mama's voice came through. "Hello?"

"Mama?" Just saying her name brought tears to my eyes, and I wasn't even sure why. I choked on the words I needed to say.

"Maeve, honey? What is it?"

The idea of driving myself, after everything that had happened, felt overwhelming. "Can you come get me?"

"Yep. Where are you? I don't recognize this number." She'd already started gathering her things; papers shuffled, keys jangled. The phone made a shushing noise, and I pictured her holding the receiver squeezed between her shoulder and ear.

"At my apartment."

"I'll be right there." She didn't need any more than that. And the relief of not explaining flooded through me. Tears came, and I quickly swiped them away, wishing I could pull it all back in, not just the tears but everything that had led to standing here on this curb feeling heartbroken while another murder investigation swirled around me. For the first time, I let the thought, *I don't want this*, complete itself.

I tapped End and handed Hazel her phone. Our eyes met once more, and everything I thought I'd once seen there slowly dissipated. It wasn't chemistry. This wasn't love. We were just two confused people who didn't know who they were, let alone what they wanted.

"I gotta go," Hazel said haltingly. She stepped toward me, though, moved as though she might touch my arm. But this time, I stepped back. Out of her reach.

"So do I."

Day 839 (continued)

From Within the House

When I said I could have ripped him to shreds, I meant every word. I wanted to see him torn to pieces, a pile of bits and shards, broken before me. So I rushed at him as he gripped his ear and marveled at his own blood dripping down his fingers.

"She bit me," he said, to whom I wasn't sure. My brother still lay helpless in the bed. I sprang, launching myself through the air, mallet held high above my own head. If it weren't for Stef, the whole thing would have ended right there, but the damn boy squeaked, and Michael turned just in time for me to bring the mallet down on his shoulder instead of his crown.

He grunted, his eyes full of disbelief and amazement.

I squared my shoulders, held my head high, and said, "You better run."

Michael laughed, but pain cut it short. What it didn't cut short was his condescension. He didn't fear me—a misogynist would never.

It wasn't until my brother stood and said, "You heard her," that he really began to understand his story would end—violently.

Chapter Twenty-One

September 7, 2001

I SAT AT the curb, waiting for Mama. Behind me, our apartment buzzed with activity. Emergency responders doing their thing while I lit up a cigarette and waited. Eventually some of the police officers sprawled out from our place, knocking on neighbors' doors for their statements as well. Across the street, people lingered on the sidewalk. They surveyed the scene and sipped their morning coffee. Their gazes danced around me. Not one of them seemed bold enough to offer up a "Good morning!" or ask me what had happened. It felt like I wasn't there, as if I'd already gone. Like *I* might be a ghost haunting the neighborhood, and not the dead person downstairs.

Finally, someone did sit next to me. Detective Patterson.

"Can I bum one of those?" she asked.

As if I could say no. I offered her the pack, and she took one out and swiped it under her nose, taking a deep sniff, savoring it.

"I quit ages ago," she said. "Right after my son was born." She dug the lighter out from its spot tucked into the pack and lit up, inhaling even more deeply than she'd sniffed.

I nodded and blew out an exhale. Smoke mixed with the exhaust of the cars creeping by, held up by all the emergency vehicles parked alongside and in the road.

"So how've you been?" she asked.

"Not great, obviously." I gestured at the activity behind us.

"Yeah." She took another toke. "You and your friend sure have an ability to get yourselves in the middle of some weird shit."

I didn't know how to respond, so I stayed silent and scanned the line of cars for my mom's van.

"I'll take your formal statement later." She tried to hand me a card, but I told her I still had the one she gave me last year. "Right, right. Hey, did you two end up taking my advice? Sign up for the academy?"

"We did." I stubbed my cigarette out on the cement, the ash creating little black smudges against the rock. "It fucking sucks." And a bubble burst inside my chest. The "me" I'd been holding back, the one who said what she meant and didn't mince words or play games, broke through—still there.

Detective Patterson huffed out a laugh. "True. It's no walk in the park. You gonna quit?"

"I don't know yet." I met her gaze and judged the

character I saw there. Beneath the no-nonsense, direct persona was someone who actually cared. "I gotta make sure I signed up for the right reasons."

She coughed into her fist. "Oh, now that sounds interesting. And what are the wrong reasons?" Her cigarette burned past the halfway point.

"A crush."

"Mm, you're right about that." She didn't laugh, and I liked her even more. "Want some advice?"

I shrugged, spotting Mama's van inch down the street.

"Police work has to be something you love. The only other thing you gotta love more is community."

My face reacted before I could control it, my brows scrunching, lips turning to express nothing but doubt. I'd only attended two classes, but expressing a love for *community* was not the vibe.

"You should see your face." Detective Patterson laughed. "Don't let that macho shit plague your learning. Good police know what's up."

"Well...thanks for that." I stood. Mama waved from the driver's seat. "From what I've seen so far, I don't know if I believe you. I gotta go." I indicated my mom. "I'm going home. Don't know how long."

"I'll be in touch."

"'Kay."

I carried only my purse. All my clothes, toiletries, anything or everything I might have wanted, I left behind, placed under lockdown in the apartment.

"Hey, Maeve," Detective Patterson called out. "Who're your TOs?"

"Main one's Gillespie."

"Oof." She pulled a face I understood to mean she knew of him, and not for anything good. "Hang in there, kid."

I walked away, not thinking about the academy or training officers or bodies in basements. Instead, I focused on my old bed in my parents' home and how good it would feel to pull up the covers and burrow. When I opened the passenger side door of the van, the fake pine smell of air freshener wafted over me, the little tree-shaped deodorizer swung from the rearview mirror, and Bette Midler's *The Rose* played through the speakers. Mama turned down the volume as I climbed in and buckled up.

"*What* is going on?" Worry and fear painted her tone and her expression. She gaped at the emergency responders in front of our apartment.

"Somebody died," I said.

"What? Who? Where?" She fired off three of the five *W*'s in rapid succession.

"Hazel and I found a body in our basement this morning." I couldn't see her face because I'd set my head against the headrest, and my eyes were closed.

"How the—Why didn't you—Are you okay?" she sputtered.

"Not really. Can we go?" Cars honked behind us.

"But nothing happened to you?" She ignored the traffic. "You're safe?"

"Yeah, Mama. I'm fine." I was nowhere near fine. Soon, she'd make me tell her everything that had happened in microscopic detail, but for now, I hoped she'd let me sleep. For hours. Days. Maybe weeks. Without a single, blaring note of shit music to disrupt me.

Day 839 (continued)

From Within the House

The hardest part was over. Or so I thought.

He was dead and gone. I could move on, except...my brother hung about. He stashed me in his bedroom and kept generally freaking out about what we'd done to his best friend. His best friend? How could he dare say such things to me, his twin? He'd let that conniving son of a bitch come between us. Never said a word about what he'd seen and everything he knew Michael to be. Never stood up for me. Until last night.

He paced the room, swiping his big dumb hands through his slick black hair. His blue eyes flashed in the daylight. He obsessively checked the window, watching the scene play out next door.

"Come away from there," I said, not wanting him to see the body bag. It wouldn't have surprised me if he ran out there and confessed at the clank and roll of the gurney wheels on the pavement.

"What am I supposed to do?" he asked.

"Grieve."

"Somebody's gonna find out, Stonie. And you! You're alive! We've got to get you home. Mom—"

"I'm not going home, Stef."

"What do you mean? Why wouldn't you go home?"

I sighed and broke away from his gaze. I sat on the bed, propping my back against the wall and willing myself to not check on the progress next door. The longer Stef focused on me, the less time he worried about the police swarming outside.

"Stef, I'm not that person anymore. I can't go backward. Does that make sense?"

Confusion pained his features.

"No, of course not." I took another deep breath. "It wouldn't make sense to you. You spent your whole life happily being who you were while I played the part Michael laid out for me—"

He made to interrupt me, and I almost let him, with my throat a bit raw from talking so much after so long, but I held up my hand to finish.

"I never had a chance to be myself. So while you may still think of me as Stonie, your twin sister, that's not who I was forced to become."

A car, or ambulance, slammed shut with a deep and final-sounding thunk. Good, maybe they're finishing up over there.

"So who are you, then?" he asked.

Such a perceptive question from my puppy-dog brother. "Well, we're starting to see, aren't we?"

"Guess so." Stef nodded, clearly not quite understanding. He popped his knuckles, one by one, the cracking like that of a nut at Christmas, and took up his pacing once more.

"Enough about me." It was obvious I would have to coach him through this. "Let's talk about you. What you're going to need to do now."

"Jesus, Stonie." His whole face collapsed—not good. His shoulders folded inward, concaving his great big chest. People would either think he was overcome with grief, or he was guilty as hell. And with his drinking... It would only be a matter of time before he told on himself.

And on me.

"As his best friend, you'll need to plan something. A get-together, a memorial."

"Like a funeral? Won't his family do that?"

"Yes, Stef. I mean for the team. So as not to raise suspicions."

"Oh, okay. I can do that."

He'd never done anything alone.

"And the police will want to talk with you." As I said it, a knock sounded from downstairs. Stef turned ghastly pale.

My confidence in his success was slim. I bit the inside of my lip, entertaining one thought. If my brother was a liability, what then?

Chapter Twenty-Two

September 8, 2001

I WOKE UP in my old bed in my old room, unsure about where I'd slept and how I'd gotten there. Memories slowly fell back into place: frantic knocks, the dark of the ravine, an almost kiss, the body.

Who was it? Setting up a meeting with Detective Patterson might lead to an answer to that question. I reached for the phone on my nightstand, dialed her number, and made an appointment for the afternoon.

My parents' muffled voices carried through the walls, snips and snaps of an anxiety-ridden conversation. No doubt, they would literally ask me one million questions the second I stepped out of my bedroom, so I prolonged the inevitable until I absolutely had to use the bathroom. I peeked into the dim hall. All the other bedroom doors were closed, and I quietly closed mine behind me, hoping to stay undisturbed. My toes sank into the hall carpet, and it felt luxurious, like a cloud or mossy undergrowth. After using the bathroom, I crept toward the computer room.

The thin door was practically weightless—prefab, nothing fancy—and it closed behind me with a swoosh and a soft click. Mama had stripped Nicky's posters of hair bands and bikini-clad models off the walls soon after he left for college when I was in junior high. It had surprised everyone; apparently, she was supposed to memorialize him or something. Instead, she'd pasted up a thick floral wallpaper, the pattern swooping and unfurling with blooming petals in varying shades of pink without a single conversation about it.

I sat at the desk, centered along the far wall, and booted up the computer. The chair wheels rolled along the plastic mat on the floor. When the dial-up connected, I logged on to instant messenger. Only a smattering of old high school friends I hadn't spoken to in a long time were online. I kept the "door" open though, hoping Hazel might make a sudden appearance.

I clicked on Internet Explorer and navigated to the Oakley campus newspaper—the *Echo*. They'd cut back on their print editions, only publishing several days a week, but kept their website up to date.

I didn't know what I'd expected. I was fairly certain the body belonged to a member of the lacrosse team, but to see Michael's shining face and broad, muscular frame on the front page stole my breath. The headline read "Lacrosse Star Found Dead in Nearby Campus Apartment." Yet, the article read more like an obituary than front page news. It consisted of bare facts, most of them contained in the headline, and the police were unwilling to share any pertinent information at this time. One item caught my attention though—a memorial. The team planned to gather in the Trap tomorrow evening to pay tribute to their captain. That should be interesting since some of them were culpable for either his murder or covering it up.

Replaying everything I knew—the beatings, the power structure—it was highly likely one of Michael's teammates had snapped and killed him. Hamden sat at the top of my list of possible suspects. But also, Michael's friend and shadow, Stef, because of his supposed unpredictability and that conversation Hazel and I'd overheard.

AIM's tinny, computerized sound of a door creaking open announced that one of my contacts had logged on— Hazel. I sent her a quick message about the memorial, adding that we should go.

Haze731 was typing...*Yeah, okay. What time*?

Paper says 4 o'clock tomorrow. When are you meeting with Detective P?

Haven't called her yet. You?

This afternoon.

I told Hazel I could pick her up for the memorial, but she said she'd ride with Doug, and then we both logged off— an all-business interaction. *Damn.* I headed downstairs to talk one of my parents into giving me a ride to my car.

As I descended the stairs, the smell of bacon permeated. Mama didn't make full breakfasts often after all the boys had moved out. She and Dad served themselves, pecking and grazing through each day until dinner. So all this had been made for me: bacon, egg casserole, biscuits. She'd gone all out. Dad sat in the TV room, watching ESPN from the sound of it.

"Good morning!" Mama sang.

Her cheer raked over my nerves. Michael was the second dead body that had taken over my life in a little less than a year; nothing "good" about that. I sat at the island. She came around, greasy spatula in hand, and wrapped her arms around me.

"Mama, stop." I squirmed out of her embrace.

She kissed my cheek anyway and asked, "Coffee?"

"Yes, please." She grabbed a mug and the carafe, then poured me some. It tasted like perfection. Mama never skimped on coffee. She refused to buy brand name cereal or laundry detergent, but not coffee.

She took the empty plate in front of me and filled it. "Eat," she said, setting it before me with a clank.

I didn't argue. The food tasted amazing. I'd eaten nothing but cereal or toaster pastries for breakfast since I'd moved out.

Mama leaned against the opposite counter, just in front of the sink, her own coffee mug in hand. She took slow, assessing sips, surveying damage.

"Now talk," she said once I'd finished most of what was on my plate. "What is going on with you?"

"I don't know"—I pulled my shoulders into a shrug— "why dead people keep affecting my life."

She made a noise deep in her throat, a clearing of the throat that had the power to dismiss my last statement. "Maeve..." She stepped forward but then looked away and started wiping down the glass cooktop with a damp towel, only smearing the spattered bacon fat. "That boy—"

"Man."

"That man's body was found in your basement. How

can that be?"

"You think I had something to do with it?" I asked, dropping my fork, my heartbeat clunking.

"God, no." She crossed herself. "I would never think something like that about you. But tell me how this happened."

"I don't really know, Mama." I spoke up about the guy knocking at our door and being chased away. "I mean, that was probably him. Probably Michael. God, what if I'd answered the door?" Emotion bubbled up from some unknowable place, and my vision blurred, watery with tears. "He'd still be alive."

"Oh, baby." She came around the island and sat next to me. Her hand gripped mine. "If someone was going after that boy, they would've caught up to him eventually. You can't take the blame for that."

There was so much I chose not to tell her: the things I'd seen Michael do; the way the members of the team had always felt dangerous, a threat living in our backyard from day one; my own assault on the trail last year—so minor and distant it now seemed. Barely a blip. A miniscule thing to bring up when my world kept getting littered with the dead.

After a silence I felt she'd accept, I wiped my eyes and focused on the present. "Can you take me to my car this morning? I have a meeting with Detective Patterson later."

"I can do better than that; I'll come to the station with you."

"No. It's no big deal."

She gave me some serious maternal side-eye.

"Seriously. It'll be fine, Mama. I'm fine."

Chapter Twenty-Three

September 8 (continued)

I WAS NOT fine, but I was able to talk her into letting me do this myself anyway.

Mama pulled away. Her van—bought when she was toting us all around for school and extracurricular shit—seemed outdated and oversized, big and bulky, only ever carrying one or two people now. It bumbled away, down the side street where I'd parked. I focused on her license plate, inhaled the exhaust, and tried to ignore the guys' house and its simmering, hateful gaze.

All I had to do was unlock my car and leave. Drive into the city, grab lunch, meet with Detective P, then go home—safe. I didn't have to confront anyone or anything.

But all I could think of was how those assholes, with all their privilege and swagger, had derailed all my plans. My future, the one I'd envisioned with Hazel and me solving crimes and kicking ass, dissipated by the second. And it was their fault. Because how could we come back and live here? Jesus, how could we even face Training Officer Gillespie after what had happened to his nephew?

Yet...storming back up to that house? That was something I could *do*. An action. It would serve nothing—unless I got my hands on that leather portfolio.

I shouldn't risk it.

Hazel and I were probably on the list of suspects, even though the police seemed to have bought our side of things. They saw the broken back door. The blood spatter on our kitchen floor. They had to know we had nothing to do with what had happened to Michael. But if I were to go snooping around and get caught...

I unlocked my car and got in, then forced myself to fit the key in the ignition. But I didn't turn the key. Leaving felt wrong too.

Outside the car, crows cawed, screeching their indecipherable warnings. *Go*! *Stay*!

I should go. How many red flags needed to fly before a person realized that the path they were on was the wrong one? I turned the key, and my car wheezed, sounding like a smoker near the end. *Great*.

I tried again. Another coughing stutter. Again. And nothing.

Well, decision made. I removed the keys from the ignition and tossed them in my purse while fear prickled the back of my throat. I found my pack of cigarettes and lit one, the initial inhale overriding my anxiety. I could do this. I was supposed to, obviously, or my car would have started, and I'd be on my way downtown. Cigarette pinched between my fingers, I crossed myself, like my yaya taught me, and stepped out of the car.

The house appeared dead behind its black, glossy windowpanes. No noise emanated from within. The rot taking over the front porch seemed to have hastened, with boards pulling away from the frame in a crumbling kind of frown. A sense of vacancy overpowered the place. And that made sense. A murder had happened among the team, so families had closed ranks, spiriting the rest to safety.

A flutter of yellow caution tape across the back door of our apartment nabbed my attention. The unfixed plywood panel with black dripping paint covered the word *cunt* underneath. They'd ruined everything.

Anger pressed through the rest of my hesitation, and I moved forward, stepping along the cracked pavement that led to the mouth of the lacrosse house. I snubbed my cigarette out on the porch railing, the soggy wood practically sizzling. I checked the windows. Everything was gray and silent inside. Nothing moved except dust motes floating and falling above the coffee table.

I tried the doorknob—locked. Instead of walking to the back door, assuming it locked as well, I pushed on the frame of the window they used to prop speakers in, and it slid open easily. I crawled over the threshold.

I stood in one of the downstairs side rooms, then moved toward the front door, unlocking it in case I needed to make a quick exit. I didn't want to linger too long and headed right upstairs, back to those weird, little rooms.

The lock had been removed from the outside of the door. Only four small holes remained, along with a slight discoloration in the shape of the sliding lock.

Inside the room, the nails that had kept the windows shut had also been removed. In fact, one of the windows had been left propped open, and a little bird trilled from the sill, then flew away. I paced through the corridor that led to the office-like anteroom, and only the desk had been left behind, all its drawers emptied. The walls were stripped of the old newspaper clippings, showing only new drywall in need of paint. Ramrod, and all the other "tools," had been swiped from the closet.

At that point, I held no hope in finding the portfolio.

But I kept on, unsure what exactly I looked for but searching nonetheless, touring the other rooms this time. The bedrooms hadn't been completely cleaned out. Dressers and bedclothes remained, along with closets still cluttered with sports equipment and a few collared polo shirts. A low, wooden bookshelf, containing textbooks, filled one corner. I scanned the spines. One stood out as unique. Among the thick coursebooks, a high school yearbook hid. I picked it up. Flipping through the pages, I searched for any of the three names I knew: Michael, Stef, Hamden.

Messages filled the back cover. *See you next year, Bro*! *Go Oaknuts*! *Don't ever change, Michael*! So it was his. There among all the cliché comments something different stood out. A bit of tiny, pinched handwriting fit in among the rest. "If fear can't hurt you any more than a dream"—I couldn't help but whisper the words as I read them, written in that cramped, overly precise style—"then the Beast is something you can defeat."

What an odd thing to put in a yearbook. And something about it read a bit threatening. Unfortunately, the comment wasn't signed or dated, so I had no idea who or when someone had written such a thing to Michael.

I sat on the corner of the bed and flipped to the senior section, heading right to the *G*'s. Michael Gillespie's senior picture looked like all the others. A black tuxedo jacket padded his already prominent shoulders, bowtie at his neck, hair parted and combed just so. The soft-focus filter added a haziness to his features.

Another face jumped from the page. A few rows down, Stef, last name Guenther, gazed back at me. So they'd gone to high school together. Stef's black, flopping fringe was styled across his forehead, and his eyes were a shocking blue—intense, but not his usual roaming, predatory look. Here, he seemed content, at ease, jovial even.

An image of a girl with similar features—white skin, black hair, full lips, same dimple in the same cheek, and piercing blue eyes—took up the frame next to his. Stonie Guenther.

"His sister. She's missing. Been missing for awhile now. We don't have much hope..."

Michael had mentioned her. I skipped toward the extra-curricular section, past sports and theater, on through to the baby pictures, and came across a kind of memorial page for the girl. The page consisted of a collage of all her different senior picture poses. In one, she leaned against a crude fence post. And then there was a close-up of her face, rose in hand, a mirror reflecting light into her eyes. In another, she stood barefoot in a white studio, wearing a pair of jeans and white T-shirt, a violin tucked under her chin. The phrase "Gone but not Forgotten" was printed across the bottom of the page. What had happened to her?

I closed the yearbook and checked the high school name

on the front: Riverview High, Home of the SkullDogs. I knew the place. Riverview was a huge suburb. We spent most of the forty-five minutes it took to drive to my hometown circling around it. A rivalry between their high school and mine had been born long before my time, but only in the sense that our suburb hated their suburb because they always won and never really viewed us as competition.

Checking the date, they—Stonie, Stef, and Michael—would've only been a year ahead of me. A girl about my age, and from the town next to mine, had gone missing and possibly died. And I'd never heard of it? Maybe she'd run away. Something like that might not have made it through the rumor mill in a neighboring town. Except why the memorial page? Runaways were absolutely forgotten, alongside a kind of shame swept under the rug. There must have been suspicious circumstances. Either way, my curiosity was piqued. Two people, Michael and Stonie, from the same class, likely the same friend group, had big mysteries surrounding them. A Venn diagram of unfortunate doom with Stef Guenther between them.

The crows started making noise again. Louder this time, so I considered it a warning. I moved to put the yearbook back on the shelf but then decided against it.

Day 840

From Within the House

My hands, I hardly recognized them. I hadn't so much as glanced, let alone examined myself, in a mirror in a long time, and now, I couldn't take my eyes off who I saw reflected. The previous version of myself would have shuddered. The shadows under my eyes looked like smudges of black ink. My wet hair, stringy and limp, hung past my shoulders, dripping rivulets down my back and chest. But the strength—a power I'd had all along, I just had to figure out how to claim it and unleash it—beamed forth from my gaze, a threat in and of itself.

The house let out a creak, an alarm. Someone was here. Damn. I'd thought they were all gone for good. Or at least long enough for me to clean up, gather what little belongings I had, and move on. I didn't have much by way of plans, but leaving the city was atop the list. Run away, for real this time, and start a whole new existence. Sounded easy compared to the rest of my life.

Creak.

I scurried back to the nearest entrance to the house's innards and waited. My heart beat so fast, tittering against my lungs. I was hiding again, as weak as ever. Then came the anger, hot and flushing my system. I would never be weak again. I quelled my initial instinct, the panic. Fear could not hurt me, only men had done that. And look what had happened to them?

A figure passed the peephole, too close for identification. They, too, crept through the rooms, their movements slow and calculated as if they didn't want to disturb the house while it slept—wise.

From my vantage, I watched a pair of legs pace the length of my brother's bedroom. The person was tall, their core and posture straight, like one who'd been trained to not bow down. I envied them.

They crouched in front of the bookshelves and took one from its place—the yearbook. They sat back and flipped through its pages. It was the girl next door, the one I'd seen with Michael a few times, the one who'd challenged him, called him out, and didn't let his mask of "nice guy" completely fool her. She'd handled him in all the ways opposite me. Yet look at her—a whole person, unchanged by her interactions with him. Even having his dead body in her basement hadn't phased her. If I were a vampire, I would have sprung forth and sucked all the righteous will from her body. Since I was a murderer, and she was snooping, I stayed put and calculated the risks.

Chapter Twenty-Four

September 9, 2001

MIRACULOUSLY, MY CAR had sputtered to a start, and I made it to my meeting with Detective P. yesterday. It had gone about the same as the last time I'd met with her and given a statement. Then, her overly warm office had smelled like whatever tea she'd brewed. This time, it was something with a citrusy orange. The space felt tight and uncomfortable with barely any room to cross my legs or do anything but sit with my hands in my lap, ankles crossed. I'd told her everything I knew about the guys next door, except for what I'd seen in the yearbook—the missing sister. I'd kept that to myself because the connection felt too weak, barely a hunch.

"Are we out of pop?" I called from the kitchen, letting the refrigerator door slam shut. Mama used to always keep a cube of it in the fridge.

"I don't buy that crap anymore." Mama sat on the

couch, her arms crossed as she watched a recording of the soap opera *Days of Our Lives*. "Your dad and I don't drink it."

"Oh."

"I can put it on the list for you. There's iced tea."

I didn't want tea. She used the powdered kind with no sugar, and it tasted way too bitter. I let out a sigh and sat next to the couch in the plush, leather recliner. The chair sighed, too, *swoosh*.

Mama turned down the TV volume. "Are you okay? How did it go with your detective?"

I'd already told her how it went. But Mama kept asking questions, wanting me to explain over and again.

"Do we need to get you a lawyer?" she asked for the tenth time.

"I don't think so, but if it'll make you feel better, sure."

Detective Patterson had made it clear I wasn't under arrest. They were still in the information-gathering stages, but for now, it seemed Hazel and I didn't need to worry.

"I should call my sister. Her boy, Patrick, is always in trouble. He probably knows a good lawyer…"

She was mostly talking to herself, so I didn't make the smart-ass comment about how no matter the lawyer, Patrick would surely end up in jail given enough time. 'Cause maybe that was true of me too. How many times could I dodge the dead body bullet?

A commercial played on the screen. An old man walked a dog, the name of some prescription drug flashing behind them, and all the possible symptoms in small, unreadable text.

"Hey," I interrupted before she hit the fast-forward

button. "Do you ever remember something happening to a senior girl over in Riverview?"

"Like what?"

"Some girl went missing. Dead maybe."

"Why do you have to blurt it out like that?" Her eyes grew wide, her brow creased.

"How else am I supposed to say it, Mama?"

"How about 'She might have passed away.' Or 'She's not with us anymore.' Say it like that."

I tried not to roll my eyes. Why be so precious? All it did was distort the meaning. "Fine. A girl from Riverview, who would've graduated the same year as Evan, is no longer among us, Mama. Do you remember hearing anything about that?"

Mama huffed at my phrasing. "Such a smart-ass," she mumbled. A snappy jingle about dish soap hummed through the TV speakers. "Now that you mention it...I do remember something. Evan's age, you said?"

"Mm-hmm, class of '99."

"Yes, a girl did go missing. I think it was right around spring break. She didn't come home from a party and was never found. So tragic."

How did I not know this?

"You look confused," Mama said.

"Just wondering how I hadn't heard of this before. I mean Riverview's not far from here."

Mama waved her hand. "You were all wrapped up in your own world. Like most kids that age."

"But still..."

Mama shrugged. "Why are you asking about this now?"

"No reason."

"I doubt that very much." Sarcasm leaked through her tone. Her show came back on, and she turned up the volume.

"Where are you going?" she asked when I got up.

"To the library. I have to go to Oakley afterward."

"Will you be home for dinner?" she asked. The dreamy string of chords and notes announced that her show had come back from break.

"Probably not."

She and dad liked to eat early, and the memorial didn't even start until four.

"All right, be careful," she said.

"I will." I let the empty promise stand between us, and quietly closed the front door behind me.

*

I DIDN'T HAVE a ton of time. Michael's memorial started in two and a half hours. But the library was located just down the block, and I needed access to a stash of old newspapers. I had a time frame plus a name, so it shouldn't take too long to pull up anything written about Stonie Guenther.

I passed the much-loved diner, practically regarded as an institution, where my parents had their first date—hot dogs and milkshakes. The library's modern architecture, with lots of white beams and reflective glass, seemed a bit out of place situated amid the more traditional style of housing. We lived in an older suburb of the city, not like the planned communities that cropped up all the time, but where every house was nearly the same, either a Cape Cod or something split-level.

As I walked through the library foyer, air conditioning hit me like a gale, and goosebumps broke out all over my arms. I headed right for the main desk, not willing to waste time aimlessly looking for what I needed. The librarian greeted me, and I requested access to the *Ledger* from the months of March–May 1999. She handed me a request form to fill out, then led me to the microfilm and microfiche machines and indicated for me to sit.

"I'll be right back with your request," she said and disappeared among the stacks.

I waited, slowly realizing this might have not been the best time for this. Combing through months of daily newspapers could take a long time, and I *needed* to see the faces of Michael's teammates at that memorial. I had to be there, judging their every move, every facial expression, and nervous tic.

The librarian reappeared carrying several small boxes. She showed me how to load, zoom, scan, and print, then left me to my search.

I didn't have to look too hard before I found a front-page headline. Pretty Suburban White Girl Gone Missing sold some papers. I clicked and printed, skipping most of the reading for now. This mission was for gathering information, but some details were difficult to ignore. A photo of the scene, a river beach like the one Michael had led his team to, stuck out. It was strewn with party trash, like their yard was most mornings, but one segment had been cordoned off by police tape. Later in the article, another image showed a closer view of the sectioned-off space. In it, I could make out some torn clothing, wet and stained, possibly signs of a struggle, and what might have been a half-crushed sandcastle. I'd do a deeper dive later. Three whole articles. That was all I could find. More than some, but not nearly enough. The last article was an anniversary piece, an interview with the family. I scanned it as it printed and learned Stef and Stonie were twins.

I fed dimes into the printer and copies of the articles fell into the tray. The paper was wet with black ink and warm from the machine. Once the articles were dry, I folded them up and stuffed them in my purse, then returned the boxes back to the main desk. Checking the clock above the librarians' heads told me I was right on time.

*

I PULLED INTO a campus parking lot and waited for the attendant to give me a pass. I parked and rode the shuttle toward the university center—the Trap. As I watched campus roll by, my mind meandered back to last fall, when this place had been home. It wasn't the first time I'd felt a kind of nostalgia toward Oakley.

The shuttle bus slowed, brakes hissing and whooshing to make the next stop. The driver opened the doors, and I got off, the Trap, the university's heart, not too far now. I passed through the brand-new business majors' section of campus, where all the buildings had been artfully designed to look old and classic, situated around a cement pad of a courtyard. A large fountain in the center of the courtyard sprayed treated water, the bleach-like smell tinging the air around it. Beyond that, the flat roof of the main library peeked atop the trees surrounding the Trap. Its Beaux Arts-style grandeur, limestone columns, and symmetry crowned the leisurely greenspace. The historic oak, nothing more than a stump after lightning struck it in the last storm, marked the middle. But the university had already planted a new sapling nearby. Apparently, each year someone from the Ag department saved a handful of acorns in case something—like lightning—happened. I'd read about it in the *Echo*.

A small crowd had gathered around the stump. The team wore their maroon jerseys, and some of them held a frame with, what I assumed was, Michael's uniform pressed against the glass. Their heads stayed bowed; their stares focused on the stiff and patchy grass of late summer.

Hazel and Doug sat near the group but not too close. The pair of them exuded quite the vibe, a comfortable way of being together. Hazel noticed me and waved me over. I steered away from the mourners and sat next to Doug, who scribbled notes on a legal pad.

"What have I missed?"

"Not much," Doug said. "They just started." He wrote down jersey numbers. "We can use the team webpage to put names to these numbers later."

Hazel angled her body in a way that didn't directly face the team. She wore headphones and sunglasses, even though the sky was a hazy, mixed blend of gray.

"You recognize anyone over there?" I asked.

"Just that guy Stef," she mumbled. She bit at the cuticle around her thumb. "No Hamden."

"Hmm, think it means anything?" I asked.

"Maybe." She shrugged. "Maybe not."

I turned to look at the crowd. Stef hadn't taken lead. Some other guy led the service. He asked them all to bow their heads for a prayer. A small group of women stood behind the team. "Think one of them could be the voice we overheard that morning?" I asked.

"No way to know without talking to them. And even then, how could we be sure?"

I nodded and watched them pretend to mourn what had happened to their supposed friend. As if Michael had just happened to die.

The speaker handed a bunch of candles to Stef, always the right-hand man, and he passed them out dutifully. His once-apparent unpredictability was not on display; he'd gotten himself under control.

"Stef had a sister. A twin." I picked at a hangnail on my thumb, tearing the skin. A bead of blood welled up, and I pressed on the sore spot. "She went missing after, or during, a party along the banks of the Skullkey in '99."

Hazel cocked her head toward me. "How'd you find that out?"

"Found an old yearbook with a dedication to her. They were all in the same class—Michael, Stef, and Stonie."

"So they're connected."

"Seems like it. Check this out." I pulled Michael's yearbook from my bag and flipped to their class pictures.

"Where did you get this?" she asked.

"I snuck back into their house."

"What?" Doug chimed in. "You messed with evidence?"

"Uh, no. Their house isn't the active crime scene, buddy."

"But it is!" His voice registered a little too loudly, his cheeks flushed. And he stopped writing. "And you know it." He brought his voice back down to a whisper. "There could be all kinds of useful information there, and the police need to be the ones who sift through it first. You shouldn't be interfering. And you definitely shouldn't be taking things out of that place."

"Too late. The house is deserted. The families have gone and moved everything out, cleaned up most of the team's secrets." I grabbed his notebook and waved it in his face. "And isn't this interfering as well?" Why was he being so sensitive about this?

"That's different."

"How?"

"I'm not withholding anything from the police. I'm just putting names to numbers. Stuff that can be found online, not sneaking into crime scenes."

"*Our* house is the crime scene," I countered. "And I haven't laid a finger in it since I found Michael's body."

He huffed, seemingly flustered by me, but that wasn't anything new.

"Doug, it's fine," Hazel reassured him. I rolled my eyes. "The police should have already done a preliminary search of Michael's things and collected anything they thought might be pertinent to the investigation. For lots of reasons, an old yearbook would be considered useless."

"That doesn't matter," Doug said. "If you think it's connected to what happened to this guy, Michael, then you should turn it over to the detectives working the case. It's the right thing to do."

"And who, exactly, has said I haven't shared all this with Detective Patterson?"

Hazel's gaze connected with mine, but the lenses of her glasses were dark, so I couldn't get a read of whose side she was on. I broke eye contact, peering back at the team. Stef had lowered himself on one knee. A boombox sat in front of him, and he pressed a button. Sugar Ray's "When It's Over" serenaded us all.

I had to bite the inside of my cheek to keep from laughing. This whole ordeal was *not* funny. Someone had died. I should not be acting like this; Mama would kill me. But when I checked back at Hazel, her lips were rolled inward, stifling laughter as well.

"Stop it," I said, but the words came out with a cough of laughter. Hazel smiled, and the tiniest of cackles emerged from behind her lips.

Then Doug started packing up his stuff.

"Wait, what're you doing? Are we leaving?" Hazel asked.

"I'm not doing this again with you guys."

His comment drained the dark comedy out of the moment.

"Come on," Hazel said. "Don't be so dramatic."

"No. You two don't take any of this shit seriously. You withhold stuff from the police, and I was with you last time because I knew you were innocent. But if this is some kind of—pattern, I'm out." He shoved his notebook into his bag.

"Dude! What is your problem today?" I asked.

"Not helping," Hazel said.

"Take what you found to the cops," he hissed.

"Hey." Hazel pulled off her headphones and sunglasses. "You were fine monitoring these guys just minutes ago. She's right; that's interfering too."

"It's different, and you know it." He stalked off.

She sighed, then started packing up her stuff.

"You're going too?" I asked.

"Guess so," she said, dejection coursing through her tone.

"Why? You can just stay with me at my parents' place."

"I better make sure he's okay. He's helping me with all that Creeping Cop stuff—the cold cases, ya know?" She tossed her headphones into her backpack. "He's really good at tracking information online. You wouldn't believe what we've found."

"But what about this?" I indicated the yearbook and the newspaper articles in the grass.

"I can do both."

I rolled my eyes.

She stood, took an exasperated breath, and paused, making a "stop" gesture with her palms pressed out.

"Fine," I murmured. I didn't want her to go, to choose working with him over me, but I ended up just looking the other way, exasperated myself.

The memorial service continued to play out. Present team members silently stared at the flames of their dripping candles while their stupid song choices lilted through a tinny set of speakers.

Chapter Twenty-Five

September 9 (continued)

I SLIPPED MICHAEL'S yearbook into my bag. My attention flitted back to the memorial scene, but the group wasn't doing much except appearing to grieve. All of them. No one seemed happy or relieved or even guilty. Not even Stef, and I'd heard him talking about what had happened to Michael with my own ears. I wasn't naïve enough to believe he would be out here high-fiving the others and cheering Michael's demise, but I didn't expect this much earnestness in the attempt to mark the passing either.

A song ended, and Stef stepped in front of the others to deliver some words. A legit eulogy of his friend, the speech detailed some of Michael's milestones as the lacrosse team captain and ended with the memory of their first meeting. When he spoke Stonie's name, my ears perked up. He eloquently painted a picture of the three of them meeting at the beach, one of the manmade banks along the Skullkey, when they were only four years old.

"Stonie spotted Michael playing alone—he didn't have any siblings. She walked right over to him and asked if he wanted to build sandcastles with us. That day started a friendship that would..." His voice trailed off.

Be cut suspiciously short, I thought.

"Change the course of all our lives," he finished. "RIP, brother." Stef's face crumpled and turned a bright pink before he added, "I miss them both."

A breeze picked up, and big, dark clouds rolled over the horizon. Everything I thought I knew about Stef, Michael's warnings about his unpredictability, his highly aggressive stance toward Hamden in the woods, none of it fit together very easily. How did that person reconcile with this person, crying over sandcastles and friendship? Could everyone exhibit all these shades of darkness and light? Were we all just sliding along a continuum of good and evil with only the impulse of any given moment to guide us?

The expectation was that people fit into two little boxes—good or bad with no overlap. Or there were patterns and explanations for every single behavior. But what if there weren't? What if we were all too random and chaotic, too influenceable, to predict?

The crowd broke up. I gathered the news articles I'd tried to show Doug and Hazel when something sent my hackles up. I looked, and Stef Guenther's gaze met mine. His dark and foreboding essence, the one I was more familiar with, fell upon his features once more.

I didn't flinch or run. Instead, I clenched my jaw. He didn't know what I'd heard him say yesterday morning or that I'd gone back to the lacrosse house and had Stonie's picture fit neatly into my bag. He didn't know I thought him capable of murdering his best friend. He couldn't see the sickle of fear slicing down my throat.

He stalked toward me, and I did not look away. My brain flickered through the details I'd witnessed at the river, the blood dripping down Hamden's leg, how the man coming toward me had carved his initials into another man's flesh for no reason other than to exert power. How someone vomiting in his kitchen had distracted him enough to not assault me. This confrontation, and it was sure to be that, could go very wrong. But then, that was true of so many moments, even seemingly innocuous ones. I zipped up my bag and stood because I'd be damned if I let him tower over me.

"Stef!" One of his friends called for him from the stump.

"Just a sec," he said.

"You need a ride?"

"Nah." He turned to address his teammate, still coming toward me but now stepping backward. "Don't worry about it."

The wind picked up. They were all leaving. I would be alone in the Trap with this complete question mark of a person. My heartbeat ticked up. My armpits poured sweat. I wanted to run—desperately. But I stood firm.

His cologne hit me first, smelling sweet, spicy, and woodsy all at once. And then this short, athletic man, looking like he'd been built of bricks, stood before me. The similarities between his sister were even more prominent this close. They both possessed a mischief in their eyes, but his carried a threat.

"You're the neighbor," he said.

"I am." I forced my voice to be strong and true, no wavering in this moment. I couldn't let him think he could affect me in all the ways he was affecting me.

"What the fuck do you think you're doing here?" he asked.

"It's the Trap. What do you—"

"My friend's body is found in your basement, and you have the fucking nerve to show up at his funeral."

"Wait, what?" I checked around, but the Trap had completely cleared of people. Streetlamps dotting the walking paths flickered on, one by one. The wind, relentless now, sent a few pieces of trash skipping along the grass.

"You heard me?" His fists clenched, unclenched. His jaw clenched, unclenched.

"The Trap is a public space."

"How come you're not arrested?"

"We both know the answer to that." The words came out like a slap, an involuntary reaction to his antagonism. I knew more about him than he knew about me, and that was power.

Surprise danced around his eyes. He couldn't pretend to be clueless about Michael's death with me.

"I heard you." This time *I* stepped forward, into the three feet of polite, required personal space between us. "After we found him, I heard you whining about what to do next in your own kitchen. You know *exactly* what happened to your captain, and you know it doesn't have anything to do with me." I paused, deciding whether to press him further or walk away.

Lightning flashed. One, one thousand. Two, one thousand. Thunder cracked through the moment.

The hunch that had started the moment I'd flipped to Stonie's memorial page, an idea like Frankenstein's monster, half stapled and sewn together, sputtered to life. I decided to go for it. I'd never get another opportunity to ask. "What happened to Stonie, Stef? Is she who you were talking to yesterday?"

"Don't say her name! Don't you put her name in your mouth!" He, too, crossed into the zone of space separating us, leading with his chest and stabbing his forefinger into my neck. Red splotches crept up his stubbled jaw. "She's an innocent."

"Okay." I swallowed fear, grappling with what to do next. Where could this interaction lead? The facts: He wanted to pretend Hazel and I had something to do with Michael's death; he had a hair trigger when it came to his sister; and I couldn't walk away without putting myself at more risk. Turning my back on him could cost me everything. All I had were words. "Look, I'm not trying to upset you—"

"The fuck you aren't!" Spittle gathered at the corners of his mouth and sprayed my face.

"Just—" I blinked. "What happened to her?"

He took a step backward, swore again, and turned around, frantically running his hand through his short hair. His breathing became more like gulping, and his eyes bulged. Panic. And that meant I still had the upper hand.

"Hey, hey," I said, then swung my bag around and grabbed the spare bottle of water I usually kept in there. The cap crackled as I twisted. "Sit down." He did. "Here." I handed him the water.

Tear streaks wet his cheeks. He sipped, then chugged once his breathing steadied.

"Sorry," he apologized after a few minutes passed. "And thanks." He held up the empty water bottle and crushed it in his fist.

"Eh, you can't really control those."

"What?" he asked, his question not much more than a rasp.

"Panic attacks." I stayed standing next to him, not trusting him enough to get too much closer. "That happen often?"

Even in the growing dark, I could feel his gaze, his anger, targeting me.

"Talking about it might help," I offered lamely.

"Oh, yeah?" His voice held a gruff quality, as if his words had to fight to move beyond the vocal cords. "What do you know about it?"

"One of my brothers started getting them a while back." Evan still had them. "Therapy's helped, I think. I don't know." It was just something to say, something to offer up that didn't mention Stonie Guenther or Michael Gillespie when all I wanted to do was steer the conversation back their way.

The silence grew between us, amplifying the surrounding night sounds. Leaves protested against the coming storm, and a distant clock tower chimed.

"I don't know what happened to her," Stef said meekly. "One night, she just disappeared."

"Then what?"

"Then nothing. Michael's family helped out; they've got connections. But the consensus was that she must've run off, got pregnant or some shit. Maybe even killed."

"Is that what you think happened?"

He didn't answer, the tic in his jaw came back as he stared into the middle distance, where the team had just gathered for Michael.

"What's your name?" he asked.

He didn't even know my name, although it shouldn't have surprised me. Michael had been the only team member to ever ask.

"Maeve Drakos," I said, and his eyes met mine. "Irish mom—"

"Greek dad," he finished.

"Yeah, that's right." I let suspicion linger through my tone. *How'd he know that?*

"Stonie knew a Drakos. He introduced himself the same way."

Wait, what?

"You from around here?" he asked.

"Not the city. A suburb." The conversation had made a marked turn. It pressed against me now instead of him. Suddenly, we were talking about *my* family and *my* home, instead of Stonie and whatever the fuck he had done to Michael. He was either way more intelligent than I'd suspected or this was a true coincidence. Either way, I wasn't entirely sure I wanted to stick around and find out.

Darkness fell between the coming storm and night, and I still had to hike to the shuttle station and then on through the parking lot. He'd calmed a bit, so there might be a reasonable expectation he wouldn't try to follow me.

"Look I gotta—"

"You got brothers? Cousins?" he interrupted, stalling any progress I might've made again.

"Several of them." Where was this headed? "I need to

get home," I managed to say and turned to leave.

"Evan!" he yelled. "Evan Drakos!"

I stopped walking, an icy prickle of realization preventing me from moving on.

"That was his name! You know an Evan?" he asked.

I forced myself to take a step and then another. Stef couldn't be talking about *my* brother. Why would this asshole know anything about Evan? Good, sweet Evan would never have hung out with these douche bags. *And murderers. Don't forget murderers.*

"He was there—"

I whirled around. "Stop it!" He was just trying to get in my head, attempting to twist things around because I knew he had something to do with his so-called friend's death. "Now it's your turn to keep a name out your mouth. Got it?" I backed away, taking slow measured steps.

"Yeah, I understand," he said. "But I've got something for you."

Our gaze remained locked, neither of us made a move.

"There's something you should know about Michael," he said. "He wasn't the golden boy everyone thought he was, you know? I think your brother knew that much. Stonie did too."

I gritted my teeth, knowing whatever he had to say, I needed to hear it, even if it involved Evan. But I didn't trust myself to talk, so I waited.

"The portfolio. I know you saw it that night."

I nodded.

"I have it."

"Okay." Surely, he wasn't just going to hand it over. I wasn't even sure it meant anything anymore, just a guide for the team culture, started way back in the '70s.

"Michael wrote it."

"Huh?" Confusion crippled any coherent response I might have had. "What?"

"He *liked* to do what he did—stuff like that, those things you saw. And more."

"But—"

"He told everyone it was part of the team's history, that it had been passed down generationally. But that was a lie. He just wanted to see what he could get away with."

"And you—"

"I was the only one who knew what he was doing. I covered for him." His head drooped between his shoulders. "Way too many times," he mumbled.

I could barely form a response. Michael had seemed like an okay guy. Not awesome, but not a complete monster. All those times I'd seen the damage the team was doing—the caning, poor Hamden's leg... "No, it was you. Michael said you were unpredictable, not to be trusted. Hamden said you carved your initials in his leg."

I couldn't be so wrong about someone's character, could I?

"Me? No." Stef pulled a cell phone from his pocket. He dialed. He put it on speaker and held up his forefinger while it rang. *Wait*, he mouthed.

"Hello?" a voice answered.

"Hamden, it's Stef."

"What do you want?"

"Look, I know you probably don't want to talk to me—"

"That's an understatement."

"But I need you to answer a question."

"What do you want, Stef?"

"That day by the river—"

"I'm hanging up now."

"Wait!" I said.

"Who is that? Who's there, Stef?"

"One of the girls from next door."

Hamden blew out a long breath. "Jesus," he whispered. "Fine. I'll answer, but only because she's there."

"Who carved their initials into your leg, man?"

"Michael," Hamden said, and then the line went dead.

My brain reeled back to the moment, trying to remember what Hamden had originally said. Had he even used Stef's name? Or had I just made an assumption?

"See. Wasn't me." Stef tucked the phone into his pocket. "It was all him. But if you don't believe me, ask your brother."

"Michael didn't kill himself though, Stef." I started backing away again. "I saw his face. I heard you in the kitchen afterward, trying to get your story straight.

"Did you tell the cops that?"

"No," I lied, because safety. "I just told them we'd heard someone knocking on our door late that night, and we'd followed them to the ravine. Then when we came back, we found...him."

"Good." Stef nodded. "Good." He rolled his tongue over his front teeth. "Then we might be okay here."

"You don't have to worry—" At some point, I had to turn around and walk away. I couldn't walk backward out of the Trap. "—about me or Hazel."

He hadn't stepped forward, so maybe this confrontation had come to its natural conclusion. Maybe he would let me leave. I'd have to just trust—in god, in the universe, in fate—that he'd leave me the hell alone.

So, I did it. I took my eyes off him and left him standing there. I hunched forward as I walked, wanting to make myself smaller, hoping for invisibility. Everything inside me fought to confront what Stef had said about Michael and my brother. *He was there...* Where? I should have let him finish that sentence.

Several minutes passed, and nothing happened. My breathing slowed. The main library looked like some historical mansion on the eve of a ball, all lit up and bright. On any normal day, I'd call it endearing or romantic, but tonight, it felt sinister, leering and imposing. A monster hidden in plain sight—just like Michael. I checked behind me, and Stef hadn't followed; he was gone. I picked up my pace, jogging toward the college of business.

What did Evan have to do with all this? He was my nice brother. The one who'd always included me. He'd graduated in the same class as Michael, Stef, and Stonie but from different schools. So how could he have been connected to them? How would their paths have even crossed?

An evening class let out, and I was jostled into the stream of students, all chattering, chewing gum, and laughing like they hadn't a care in the world. Because they didn't. Their lives weren't filled with nice brothers and dead neighbors and missing twin sisters.

I raced to the shuttle station, eager to get back home and track down Evan. Ignoring the conversations of other waiting passengers around me, I picked at a string along the hem of my T-shirt—unraveling someone else's hard work.

Rain pattered on the station roof, a steady stream

beating down. There'd been no starting drizzle, no easing into the storm, only downpour. The bus, wipers swiping fast, pulled to a stop in front of the station. I stepped on, rain pelting me in the few seconds it took to load up.

In my seat, I bounced my knee up and down, sitting still being a kind of torture in that moment. Evan filled my thoughts, alongside Stonie and Michael. What had happened to them all, and how were they connected? My thoughts were so concentrated I nearly let the driver pass my stop. I smacked the stop tab, *ding*! Brakes screamed and hissed, and then the doors popped open. I thanked the driver and stepped into the squall.

The pouring cold rain took my breath away as it snaked down the back of my shirt. I stalked through the parking lot toward my car while the world around me dissolved into nothing more than a blurry mess. I wiped my eyes and blew a stream of water away from my nose. The asphalt gleamed slick and shiny, glossy black with puddles of indeterminate depth reflecting headlights and streetlamps, the warning red of brake lights. I tiptoed, uselessly. My shoes and pant legs, hair and T-shirt, were soaked. I swiped the stream of water rushing down my face and out of my eyes.

And then I saw them.

At first, just two random figures appeared. But as I moved closer, certain details became familiar: the emerald-green of his Honda; the clothes they'd been wearing; her backpack, and the long, wavy tangles of her wet hair.

Doug and Hazel.

Embracing each other.

Passionately.

Chapter Twenty-Six

September 11, 2001

"FRIEND ZONE" WASN'T actually a thing people got to be mad about. No one ever owed anyone a romantic relationship.

Yes, sometimes love emerged from a friendship. But if not reciprocated, then it was literally no one's fault. Therefore, no hard feelings. I wanted Hazel to be happy. Period. If she wanted to be with Doug, I supported it. I might've spent the last few weeks being mildly jealous of the time they spent together, but that had been an asshole move. And now I was over it.

At least, that was what I told myself on my way to meet my brother where he worked. Romance was fleeting and could be redirected easily. Sitting at a stoplight, I noticed an attractive person casually window shopping. They carried a coffee and a bag from the used bookstore. I imagined what it might be like to hop out of my car, introduce myself to a stranger, and fall in love in a day.

See, totally over it.

Someone honked behind me. The light had changed, and I hadn't moved forward. I stomped the gas and took the first parking space on the street that didn't require parallel parking. I locked up and walked the rest of the way to Evan's coffee shop.

Bells jangled above the door as I entered and immediately spotted my brother. He paced behind the counter, wearing a brown baseball cap with the store logo on the front and a matching apron. He hadn't shaved recently, and under his eyes, the thin skin appeared discolored, blueish-gray like a half-healed bruise. We hadn't spoken since he showed up at my apartment with food from Yaya, so I had no idea about his current life status. He smiled when he saw me, then held up a finger—*just a minute*—while he punched some lady's order into the cash register.

I found an empty table and waited, watching him twirl around behind the counter, coaxing machines to rattle and grind and then hiss—a kind of dance. He laughed at something one of his coworkers said. The environment had a very laid-back and cool feel to it.

"Hey, sis," he said as he walked toward me. He put two large coffees, light brown with cream, on the table. "What's up?"

"*What's up*? How 'bout you call me back every once in a while to find out."

He scratched his neck. "Sorry."

"That's the best you got?"

"Hold on." He held up his index finger, then took back

off toward the counter. He returned and placed an almond croissant—my absolute favorite—in front of me. "Peace offering?"

"Fine, fine," I said and took a bite. "Did Mom tell you what happened at my place?"

"Some real crazy shit." His hands busied at untying his apron. Then he pulled it off in one smooth motion and piled it in the empty chair next to him. He adjusted his cap, took it off and ruffled his hair, then put it back on, curling the brim. This was classic Evan, stillness an impossibility. "You okay?" he asked.

"Yeah. No. I don't know." I wrapped my hands around the paper cup, and the coffee's heat warmed my palms.

"What do the police think happened?" he asked.

"They don't really go around telling people that, Ev."

"Well, what do you think happened? You're the one training to be one of them, right?"

I winced involuntarily.

"Right?" he repeated, his eyebrows arching upward.

"Uh, sure."

"Don't sound so convincing there, sis."

"Mm." I made a guttural sound. "Drop it, yeah?"

"Whatever you say." He shrugged, a half-smile tweaking his features.

"I need to talk to you about something else."

"What is it?"

"How did you know my neighbor, Michael Gillespie?"

"What?"

"The guy who ended up dead in my basement, you knew him. In fact, seeing him freaked you the fuck out that day you stopped by."

He shook his head, brows scrunched together.

"You said you thought you recognized one of them."

"Oh, that. No, I didn't. I was mistaken." But his lip quivered, his tell for when he lied. Poor guy never could hide it. Mama always called him on it.

"I don't think you were, Ev." I pulled the yearbook from my bag and showed him the page with Michael and Stef. His gaze softened when it hovered over Stonie. "Did you know all of them?"

"She used to work here. We went out a couple of times. But..."

"She's missing."

"Yeah," Evan said. "For a long time now."

I tapped my finger on Michael's picture. "He ended up dead. Beaten to death, by the looks of it. And this is his friend, Stonie's brother. He remembered you."

"Like I said, Stonie and I went out a few times."

"What do you think happened to her, Evan?"

"Nobody knows." His jaw tensed, and his cheeks flushed. "Consensus was she's either dead or run off. Long gone, either way." His breathing appeared to cause him effort. He stared at the table.

"Did the police ever question you?"

He seemed to come out of whatever memory played on the tabletop. "The police talked to everyone here, and I told them we'd gone out, but that was it. Guy was a real prick though. I might still have a card somewhere." Evan pulled out his wallet and sifted through a collection of business cards. "Here it is. I don't ever clean this thing out." He tossed the card toward me.

"Thanks." A little frisson ran through me as I read the

name on the card. Dick Gillespie. As in Training Officer Gillespie? He'd worked Stonie's disappearance? I tucked the card in my back pocket. "What aren't you telling me?" I knew my brother.

Silence.

"Did she run away, Evan? Was she pregnant? Stef mentioned it as a theory." I sipped my coffee.

Evan shook his head. "I don't know. I guess it's possible."

"But you don't think probable? Seems logical enough—"

"No," he interrupted. "I don't think she was pregnant."

"Okay, so what's that leave on the table? Kidnapped? Killed by some rando maniac? Could she still be alive? Out there somewhere? I haven't ruled out Stef being involved either. Most women are killed by someone they know. And, like, his sister ends up missing, then his best friend winds up dead two and a half years later. Is there a connection? It's worth—"

"I don't know, Maeve." He tossed his hat on the table. "I'm not like you. I try not to think about that stuff."

Right. Normal people scooted away from conversations like this. Only Hazel had liked to dive deep into the macabre with me. I scratched my temple, feeling perturbed and more than a little hurt by her absence, by her choice, by her... *Move on.* "Fine. Tell me what you know about Michael, at least."

Evan checked his watch. "I've only got a few minutes."

"You know I'll just follow you around asking questions while you work. In front of everyone." I checked the counter. "Even that really cute girl with the braids."

He looked over his shoulder and sighed. "You're so

annoying."

"Thanks."

"So, Michael was...." Evan leaned forward, both knees bouncing up and down. The table vibrated between us. His gaze flitted around the room, then came back to the creamy-tan coffee. He took a drink and continued, "It's hard to describe. Manipulative? Kinda creepy? Like... I don't know if you met him, but maybe you know the type. His whole personality was his good looks, and I got the feeling he came from money. Wasn't used to being told no." He stopped and took another sip of coffee.

"I got the same impression."

"But he had a darker side."

"What do you mean?"

"He was always sending Stonie these weird voicemails."

"Like what? She let you listen?"

"Yeah, sometimes. I mean, like, in one, he'd tell her how he wanted her to do her hair. In another, he'd tell her what to wear underneath her work clothes. Or what to eat so she wouldn't get fat. One time, he just called her names—slut, bitch. Sometimes, he'd make it seem like he was watching her at work. Like, if she'd be talking to a male customer too long, he'd leave a message asking what she thought she was doing, accuse her of all kinds of shit."

"Yikes."

"Once, he wanted her to, like—" He made a weird face as if struggling with how or what came next. "—*masturbate* in the walk-in. I think she got really embarrassed I overhead that in the back room."

"Ew."

"He had some kind of hold on her. They'd known each

other since they were little, and she said it was just like an extension of how they used to play. Only...it wasn't play anymore. Or maybe ever. This was real life."

"And you had a thing for her?"

"She was cute." He shrugged again. "But I kept my distance. I told her what was going on with her and Michael was fucked up and she needed to talk to someone, get help. It was like ten thousand red flags, right?"

I nodded.

"The night before she ended up going missing, I went with her to that party. All those Skulldog kids party at this one beach, and the vibe was just...well, nothing I'd ever experienced before."

"Frenetic? Misogynistic? Evil?" Those were the vibes I'd picked up on in the lacrosse house too.

"Sure, whatever you just said."

"What happened that night?"

"Booze. Loud music. People making out and fucking all over the shore. The usual."

"So what made it feel different to you?"

"That's the night I met Michael in person. And he was *not* happy to meet me." Evan huffed a little. "He acted all macho, kinda gets up in my face, makes fun of me. Posturing shit, right? Then he keeps pulling Stonie away from me. And, okay, whatever, but I don't know anyone there. I meet her brother. And he's, like, playing wingman or something for Michael, which is even weirder. But he's obviously trying to keep me occupied. And after a beer, I just took off. Couldn't even find Stonie to say goodbye. Took everyone a while to realize she was gone. Rumor was all they found were a pile of shredded clothes and a little blood on the shore. By then... Who knows what could've happened?" He blew out another breath. "Maybe I should've looked harder. Done more. I've been in counseling for that last bit. It's not my job to save anyone. But, like, the guilt is kinda heavy. I knew there was something really wrong happening, and I didn't do anything."

"It's not your fault." Everyone always said that, and the words felt lame coming out of my mouth.

Evan frowned. He took another sip, then checked his watch again. "I gotta get back—"

"Wait. One more thing—"

"This has been a lot, sis. Not really what I was expecting this morning. Ya know, going back through all that." He stood and flipped the strap of his apron around his neck and tied the strings behind his back.

I'd already turned to the comment section of the year-book and pointed at the tiny script. "Do you know what this means?"

"Hell, no."

"I think it might be a reference to *Lord of the Flies*."

"Never read that dumb book."

"You didn't?"

"Nah. Remember Melanie Constantine? She's the only reason I passed sophomore English." Evan fitted his work cap back on his head. "Stonie loved it though."

"*Lord of the Flies*?" I asked. "I hated it. Makes me cringe just thinking about it."

"Yeah, carried around a copy and everything."

"Huh."

"Everybody's got their thing." He shrugged. "Catch ya later, sis." Evan headed for the counter, then turned back.

"That guy was so sketch, Maevey. I honestly think he could have done anything to anyone. And I mean that for real."

He hesitated, seemingly unsure he should say anything more but added, "Maybe whoever got him did everyone a real big favor."

"I hear you." I'd felt something similar about Ryan Newsome's death last fall. It wasn't the neatest, nicest sentiment to cop to, but it was honest.

"How long are you at home for?" Evan asked.

"I guess the police will let me know when we can get back into the apartment."

"You worried? I mean, that you'll be pinned for what happened to Michael?"

"I probably should be." But for whatever reason, I wasn't. Detective Patterson didn't seem like the kind of cop that held on to a narrative just because it easily fit together. I trusted she was taking the time to look for harder evidence, real clues. And if she didn't, well, hopefully, I could find something else that looked as simple as Hazel and me beating some asshole to death in our own house. Something like a brother avenging his sister.

"Let me know if you need anything." Evan went back behind the counter.

"Hey, what did you think of the brother? Stef?" I asked.

Evan pulled his timecard out from his wallet. "Seemed okay. Some sidekick syndrome going on. I don't know if he knew what was really goin' on between Michael and his sister though. Why?"

"He's the one who kinda clued me in on who, or what, Michael might've really been." I paused and added, "Apparently, Michael carved his initials in another kid's leg as part of a team hazing—"

"What?"

"—ritual," I finished.

"You think Stef knew?" Evan scratched his neck.

"I think he did more than *know* about it."

"Then stay careful, Maeve."

"I will," I promised, even though I knew he meant *leave it alone*, and I wouldn't.

"Drakos!" A voice called from the back room.

"Shit, I gotta go. Coffee's on me, okay?"

"Later," I said and packed up Michael's yearbook. I slurped from my cup and headed to the condiment stand to grab a lid.

The bells above the door jingled again as I left. I walked back to my car, thinking about everything my brother had said. How differently he and Stef had described Michael from the guy I thought I'd known. Sure, I'd pegged him for an asshole on day one, but not a domineering, violent abuser, possibly a sadist.

And how the hell did TO Gillespie fit into all this? I took his card from my pocket, ran my finger over his name. There're plenty of Gillespies in the world, and maybe a fair number of them turned out to be cops. But still... I thought back to when Michael showed up at one of our first classes at the academy. "*It's not my jurisdiction anymore, Mikey.*" My stomach flipped. This felt big, bigger than a team beating gone overboard.

What if Stef had put a few of these pieces together, connected the dots between his manipulative, controlling friend, his missing sister, and a police force unable or unwilling to close the case? I remembered that female voice coming from the lacrosse house the morning we'd found Michael and thought of yet another possibility, one I hadn't been afraid to confront Stef with in the Trap, one he hadn't denied. What if Stef listened to that woman's advice because he already knew her? Because, hell, maybe they'd shared everything, including a womb.

What if Stonie Guenther really was still alive?

At my parking spot, I unlocked the car and got in. Before starting the engine, I grabbed my CD case. I flipped through the pages. Nothing stuck out or sounded good till I got to *Living in Clip*. I'd done a decent job of keeping thoughts of Hazel at bay, but the music brought memories of one of our first real conversations in the basement of Robin Hall. And then the concert where I'd told her I wanted us to go to the police academy together, way back when I felt like I could see the future.

Well, things change. Plans don't always work out. That's life.

Still, she was the first person I wanted to share my speculations with and the only person who'd care or even think I might be right.

I set the CD case aside, choosing the radio instead. When I turned on the car, I flipped to a local station. The news blasted through the speakers. I turned the volume down. Barely listening, I checked my mirrors, put the car in drive, and merged into traffic. Snippets of reporting caught my attention, pulling me out of my current and insignificant stress.

Something was really wrong.

In New York.

Planes, buildings, people—lots of them—were just gone.

Day 1

In the Absence of the House

I was out for the first time since Stef and I chased Michael into the ravine. The house behind me was a discarded cocoon. The urge to crawl back inside was strong. What did I do now? I stretched my arms, my head tipping back with the pull. There was not a cloud or threat of bad weather on the horizon. The purple-blue sky was so lovely and vibrant, I felt as if I could jump up and swim through it.

The neighbors' apartment beckoned me with its strips of caution tape that had pulled loose and fluttered in the slight breeze. I had a bit of money I'd managed to steal from the team, here and there. No ID. My clothes were pilfered from the guys' one-night stands. I needed stuff, and those girls had probably left a lot behind in the chaos around finding Michael's body.

The police had chained off the back door, but it was midmorning, and the neighborhood quiet. I'd watched the habits of everyone nearby since they'd moved in, so I wasn't too worried about being caught. A worn and damp blanket covered the couch on the guys' porch. Without a more subtle way to get in, I grabbed the blanket and wrapped a section of it around my forearm and fist.

The team had pulled out the girls' window screens and washed them a while ago, but they'd only haphazardly put them back in. So, with a quick pull, one came away in my grasp. I let it fall to the ground, and with a surprisingly small amount of force, I smashed my fist through their dining room window. Running the blanket around the edges, glass tinkled and shattered again as it hit their hardwood floors. I crawled through, over the threshold.

Dust motes floated through rays of sunlight throughout the lower level of the apartment. I moved quickly, making my way upstairs to find two adjacent bedrooms, with a linen closet between them. I started in the front bedroom. The bed had been left unmade, but other than that, everything had a place, and items were stored away. I searched the closet for a purse or wallet but found none. In the vanity drawers, I only found an array of makeup pallets and brushes. I grabbed a spare tote bag and a couple pairs of underwear and T-shirts that seemed like they'd fit before moving on to the next bedroom.

My curiosity slowed me; this was the room of the girl next door, the girl Michael had never tried to control. It was like stepping into a relief sculpture. I lingered over the posters on the wall, including what looked like a handmade copy of a Chagall hanging next to one for the movie Trainspotting. What a strange mix. She had no designated shelves for her books, leaving a small stack of them lined up along her dresser. Her bed was unmade; dirty clothes littered the floor. She wasn't here, but the bits and pieces of her personality were, and I stepped through them, selecting whatever I wanted. What was it about her that had kept him at bay? What did she have that I didn't?

A woodblock cutting of a name—presumably hers—sat atop the nightstand. "Maeve." I tried it out. Irish sounding. It reminded me of my friend, Evan and how he used to introduce himself. "Evan Drakos. Irish mom, Greek dad." I might have loved him as soon as he uttered those words, with his tanned skin and freckles across the nose. But it wasn't meant to be. Thanks to Michael. Thanks to who I had to become.

I needed a name too. What was another Irish name?

Chapter Twenty-Seven

September 11 (continued)

"*WHAT*?" I WHISPERED, even though I was alone. I turned up the radio, trying to pay attention to traffic. A light turned red, and I cranked the volume even louder. Tragedy. Chaos. No one knew what might happen next. Out of habit, I lit a cigarette and listened, trying to make sense of the words coming through my speakers. *Attack*? *Here*? "What?"

The stoplight changed to green, but nobody moved. I rolled down my window to let the smoke out and ended up making eye contact with the woman in the car next to me. Her stunned eyes were wide, tears already flowing. Neither of us smiled or acknowledged that we stared at each other. Finally, somebody honked. It seemed inexplicably rude, to make a sound, to force us all out of this moment of profound shock. But we shook our heads, moved forward.

I needed to get home. Call Mama at work. Check on

Yaya. *Oh, god. Yaya.* She'd be alone. I drove to her house first, my attention rapt on the radio, barely noticing the other cars around me. When I pulled into Yaya's driveway, I wasn't even sure how I'd gotten there.

Three pink plastic flamingos lined the sidewalk leading to her front door. I hardly ever paid them any attention, except today, they looked shabby and faded. The delightful kitsch of them had been lost with the news. How could anything be funny or cute again?

I could hear the reporters as soon as I stepped onto her little front porch area. Her door was opened, but the screen door didn't budge when I tried the handle. I tapped on it, calling out to her. "Yaya?"

From where I stood, the large set of sliding glass doors on the other side of her living room framed the silhouette of her profile. She sat on the couch, her hair swept into a bun at the nape of her neck, with the volume of the TV turned up unbearably high.

"Yaya! Come answer the door." *Knock knock knock.*

She turned, but her face stayed in shadow. I couldn't tell what she felt or thought. Was she confused? Scared? Weren't we all?

"It's Maeve, Yaya. Unlock the door."

She stood and slowly made her way toward me. "Maeve Helen. Can you believe this?"

"No...I can't."

Yaya unlatched the screen door and let me in. "It's like Pearl Harbor. Worse. All those civilians; *Ιησούς* save us."

"How are you doing?" I crossed into the living room, following the plastic floor runner to the couch.

"How am I?" A note of hysteria tinged her voice. "I just

watched two airplanes fly into skyscrapers on TV. How do you think I am?" She started to sit next to me but stopped to ask, "You want anything? I have cookies."

"No, I'm fine." I'd eaten with Evan, but my hands shook with either emotion or the extra caffeine. She indicated a plastic container filled with her homemade butter cookies on the coffee table, and I took several, ingesting them without even thinking, only watching the screen.

Obviously, I hadn't seen it yet. While driving I'd only imagined how it had looked based on the radio reports. Seeing it on the television was so much worse. The crash. The fire. People jumping. Pause, rewind, repeat. Again. And again. What were the anchors even saying? Who or what was next?

And then the south tower collapsed. Yaya let out a small yelp and grabbed my hand. My eyes filled with tears, and I covered my mouth with my other hand. All those people.

"Oh my god," I said.

Yaya's phone rang. She didn't seem to hear it.

"Yaya, your phone."

She made a waving motion. I got up and crossed into the kitchen to answer it, happy to look away, desperate to turn around and look back.

"Hello?"

"Hello, Eleni?

"It's me, Mama."

"Maeve?"

"Yeah, I came to Yaya's as soon as I heard the news."

Mama let out a loud breath. "Okay, okay, good. That's good. Your dad was worried about her, so he'll be glad she's not alone."

"Where are you?"

"At work, for now."

"Have you seen it?"

"No, there's no TV here so..."

"It's bad, Mama. Real bad." My heart beat hard in my throat. The line went quiet, neither one of us speaking. I could hear Mama swallow.

"Just stay where you are, okay. Stay with Yaya. I'm gonna check on your brothers and then...I don't know."

"Okay."

"I love you, Maeve."

"Love you too." Both of us paused before hanging up, but there was nothing more to say.

Nothing more to do except watch the horror as if it were a vigil.

*

HOURS WENT BY with me sitting beside Yaya on the couch, neither one of us speaking or touching, just staring at the screen. Eventually, it occurred to us that we should eat, and she disappeared into the kitchen for a few minutes. She reappeared with two lunchmeat sandwiches, and we ate, still watching, listening. A sort of desperation hung in the air as we waited for someone to explain it to us, but no reasoning came, none that made sense anyway. The newspeople just repeated the same details over and again. The same few hours rewound and replayed on the screen, and I expected something more, something even worse to happen. The death toll must be some staggering, god-awful number. In the many thousands, at least. Maybe it could happen here, closer, to people I knew and loved.

Soon it grew noticeably dim in the living room. A whole day had gone by like this. I invited Yaya to our house for dinner. She nodded, grabbed her sweater, and we left.

Outside, warm still tinted the evening air, inviting. Yaya's lawn was a deep, emerald green, the sky like a sapphire still. My eyes watered. I felt an inexplicable urge to just plant my hands in the grass. Surely, the soft spikes against my palms would root me to my yaya's place, her world, where buildings didn't explode and planes stayed in the sky.

How stupid. Just get to the car.

I opened the passenger side door for Yaya and let her hold on to me as she crouched and folded herself up to get in the car. When she let go of my arm, I walked around to the driver side and noticed everything: the scrape of my teeth against my lip, the weight of the bag on my shoulder, the smell of oil, the quiet of her neighborhood. I got in beside her and started the car. The radio blasted at a too-high volume, startling both of us. I turned it down, then turned it off.

As I pulled out of her driveway, Yaya rolled down her window and put her arm out. Her hand rode the invisible wave of the wind.

"As an elder, I should probably have some wise words to impart about all this," she said. "But I don't."

"You don't have to say a thing, Yaya."

"The world is a messed-up place, Maeve. Sometimes I think we won't ever get it right. But we keep trying. I guess that's about all any of us are good for—the trying." She rolled her window back up and pulled her cardigan tight around the middle. "Feels good to not be staring at the television."

"It does, yeah," I agreed. But also, it didn't feel quite the same as it had this morning. As if at any moment the road could crack open and swallow us whole. Now, we lived in a world where planes flew into buildings, and they collapsed, and thousands of people died before the West Coast had even had coffee. And that, that last part, I realized, had always been happening. I just pretended it hadn't. And now I couldn't.

In my parents' neighborhood, a couple of houses flew American flags from their porches. And it felt right. Brave. Defiant.

Even though it wasn't.

Mama's voice rang out from the kitchen, her phone voice. When we came in, her conversation continued, but she ran over and hugged us both, the receiver still pressed between her shoulder and ear. Her perfume and silky work blouse were decadently comforting.

"Okay, Anita. I gotta go. Eleni and Maeve just got here." She pressed a button on the cordless and turned to us. Tears flashed, threatening to flow over the tiny array of wrinkles surrounding her eyes.

"Mama, I—"

"Can you believe this?" she asked.

The answer was still no. But nobody answered her. Mama offered tea. I declined. My chest was tight as if my next breath might be impossible. And I needed to get the hell out of here. I mumbled something about the bathroom and left. Hurrying up the stairs, my feet pounded as fast as my heart and my head.

In my room, I sank to the floor. Tilting my head against the back of the door, I closed my eyes. The room's familiarity enveloped me, easing anxiety's hold on my lungs. I breathed in. Out. I swung my bag off my shoulder and winged it across the room. When I opened my eyes, Michael's yearbook peeked out from the bag. My folder with all the pertinent information and the news articles I'd collected lay beneath it.

How fucking pointless.

I couldn't put a case together around tidbits of information. I didn't have access to anything—or anyone—that might really help. Doug was right. I should hand over the yearbook, report what Stef had told me about the portfolio and everything, and let the actual police do their jobs. Yeah, that was right. That was what I should do. I crawled up into my bed and curled under the covers.

Day 2

In the Absence of the House

I pilfered Maeve's things. Couldn't help myself; I devoured every little trinket, every snippet of her writing, the books she chose to display. Her. Until I fell asleep atop her covers, her syrupy pheromones wafting up from the pillow.

When the sun came up, I walked to the gas station and called my brother at the payphone. He agreed to come pick me up. But he warned that our parents were keeping him on a short leash after what had happened to Michael. They expected him home, which I took to mean he planned on trying to talk me into going along with him.

I wouldn't.

I had other plans.

At the counter, I paid for a drink and some pretzels. The doorbell rang behind me as I headed outside to wait by the curb. The bag of snacks crinkled as I pulled it open and popped a few in my mouth. People stood at the gas pumps, their faces red with emotion or totally blank—like someone in shock. Some of them looked at one another and said, "How are ya?" The response came back as a sad shake of the head. It was...weird.

My brother finally pulled in, and I hardly let him park before jumping into the passenger seat.

"Jeez, Stonie. Let me stop the car," he said.

"Just drive."

"Okay."

He didn't ask where I wanted him to take me, so I assumed he planned on bringing me back to our parents' house in Riverview. The guy I needed to see lived over that way, so I didn't say anything about it. For now.

"What've you been up to?" I asked while we sat at a stoplight.

"You don't know, do you?"

"Know what?"

He turned on the radio, and the air between us filled with reports about an attack in New York.

A "wow" was all I managed.

"Wow?" He glanced at me, incredulous. "Thousands of people died, and all you can say is wow?"

"What should I say?" I asked, not even trying to be sarcastic.

A beat passed between us before he said, "I don't know." He sighed, his chest rising and falling melodramatically as if he cared for all those people. Please. My brother only cared about one thing.

"What's going on with the team?" I asked, to which he bristled.

"What do you think? The team's ruined. Games and practices are cancelled because of this." He gestured at the radio. "And some people don't even want to play out the season without Michael."

"I bet some do."

"Huh?"

"Nothing. And? Are you one of those people?"

He shrugged, pulled at his earlobe, and hit the gas when the light changed. "I've never played a game without him," he said quietly. "I don't know what it would be like."

Michael'd had power over my brother as well. I'd always focused on my own plight, how Michael had killed off parts of me. But Michael had done something similar with my brother, by always being there, always making Stef his number two. My brother never had a chance to develop into his own person. Michael had left the both of us devoid of an identity other than the one that existed through his looking-glass world.

"You'll be okay, bro," I said rather lamely. "You just have to keep to yourself and—"

"Like you did? Hiding for years in the walls of some shitty house? No thanks." He practically spat the words at me.

"I did what I had to... I don't know how to make you understand that."

"I won't."

"Fine." I crossed my arms and stared out the window. Sunshine and warmth filled the day, even though autumn should be right around the corner. Weather that didn't match all the big and little tragedies surrounding us. Such was life, such was nature. "Take me to Felix's place. I need a new ID."

He didn't even argue. Just followed directions. How very like him.

Chapter Twenty-Eight

September 12, 2001

I BLINKED, AND a pinkish-orange hue surrounded me as if I'd slept inside a shell. I pushed the blankets away from my face. My stomach growled. I'd skipped supper and fallen asleep in my jeans and T-shirt. The clock on my bedside table said it was quarter till seven. The details from yesterday arranged themselves in my head. Planes. Buildings. A whole city and country mourning.

I got up and stumbled over Michael's yearbook. The mystery of his life and death, what had been so intriguing to me, gleamed gray now. I was kidding myself, playing at being a real detective. Hell, I hadn't even been back to the academy, hadn't even considered going back since I'd stepped over his dead body.

I should hand all the information I'd collected over to the professionals. There were adult problems in the world, and I was nowhere near adult enough to solve a single one of them.

I stepped into the hall, and the house smelled like coffee. So I plodded downstairs. Mama stood in the kitchen, her back to me. She faced the little TV Papa bought her one year for Christmas. News flashed across the screen. She turned to face me, her skin already red and blotchy from crying. She cried still. When she reached for me, I obliged, even though I didn't want a hug. The camera panned over the missing people posters, walls of them, and I looked away, broke off the lavish embrace when so many mothers wouldn't be hugging their adult children ever again.

Standing in front of the cabinet with all the mugs, I picked my favorite and added milk. Surprise stained each mundane task when such tragedy unfolded elsewhere. And I reminded myself again, *This is always happening; you just have the privilege of overlooking it.*

"The president spoke last night," Mama said, turning the volume down.

"Oh, yeah?"

"I went in to check on you, but you were already out."

"Long day." Apparently, I only had two-word phrases to hand out this morning.

She nodded. Her long, springy auburn curls flowed down her back, dripping little pools on her bathrobe. The news replayed some of the president's speech. Words like *terror* and *evil* bounced around our kitchen as if they were born into the world just yesterday, as if only now must we accept them and act accordingly.

Evan skipped down the steps. I didn't even know he was here or had spent the night. Where was Yaya? Had she stayed too?

"Hey, sis," he said. He was shirtless, wearing only pale-blue athletic shorts.

"Hey. What are you doing here?" I asked.

"Came by to share the news last night."

"What news?"

"I'm joining the military. Pretty soon, you'll be looking at a damn marine."

"What?" I set down my coffee; the mug cracked hard on the counter. Little brown droplets collected and spilled from the now-present defect.

A sob escaped Mama. Her shoulders hunched under the terrycloth fabric of her robe.

"Why would you do that?" I asked, yanking some tissues from the box near the phone and handing them to Mama. She wiped her face and blew her nose. Pathetic whimpers emerged from some place deep in her chest.

"We're going to war, Maevey."

"You don't know that."

"You watch."

"Jesus Christ, Evan. Look at our mother."

"What? I wanna do my part. Like you, Maevey. I wanna help people."

I moved past him, stunned into silence. I headed back upstairs, reeling over his choice, his stupidity, his poor judgement, his decisiveness. Yet, if Evan could make a life-altering resolution in a day...

So could I.

The academy.

I hated it.

Hated being yelled at. Hated following rules just for

discipline's sake. Hated TO Gillespie and his dumb fucking face. *So. Change it.*

Organize and confront: it was what I did best, what I'd been stifling for months now. Well, not anymore. And a bonus would be that my quitting might make Mama cry less. Removing one of her children from harm's way meant she'd only have to focus on Evan's choices.

First, I called Detective Patterson and left a message that I had some new information regarding Michael Gillespie. Then, I headed to the computer room and booted the big ole thing up. The machine whirred and ground its gears, sounding as if it might die before it came back to life. The screen flickered black with white text, all gibberish to me. A logo appeared, and I waited for the chiming jingle. Finally, I logged on to AIM, but both Hazel and Doug were not on. Doug had some quote, likely a lyric, posted as his away message. Hazel had nothing. I wondered where she was now. Her aunt probably wanted to take her back to Lima. She might already be there. I should call her.

But not before taking care of this.

This, I did on my own.

I opened my email where a message from my advisor at ACC sat in my inbox. She asked when I'd be returning, that given the nature of my absence, my spot could be held open for up to a week. I clicked Reply and typed: *Thank you for the opportunity, but due to recent events—* I stared at the words, the cursor blinking, waiting for what came next. In a burst, my fingers flew over the keys. *I won't be returning to this program.*

Just the idea, seeing it on the screen, filled me with a giddy kind of weightlessness as if letting go of this path made room for my whole self to reenter my body. I had choices. And more opportunities would come. I didn't have to lock myself into one thing yet, especially when the one thing was based on a crush that had not established itself. I hit Send. And breathed.

This was easy—quitting.

I shut down the computer and headed back to my room. I picked up the phone and dialed Hazel's cell number. She answered after the second ring.

"Hey!" she practically shouted. "Where've you been?"

Confused, I answered, "At home, why?"

"I tried getting ahold of you yesterday, but no one picked up the phone at your place."

"I spent the day with my yaya, you know, because of everything."

"Right." She waited a beat. "Fucking crazy."

"Completely. Listen I—"

"Wanna meet for breakfast?"

"Uh—sure?" Not how I'd expected this phone call to go, but okay.

"Isn't there a diner near you?"

"Um, yeah. But where are—"

"Bring that yearbook. I want to go over it with you."

"Okay. But hey, Hazel. I need to ask you—"

"I don't need a ride. I'll meet you there in, like, what, thirty minutes?"

I checked the clock; it would be eight o'clock by then. "Okay."

Guess I'd be telling her I'd quit in person.

*

I LEFT MAMA and Evan arguing over him joining the military and walked to the diner. I needed the fresh air. It felt strange—not watching the news, meeting a friend for pancakes. Along our street, more neighbors had hung American flags; where had they all come from? I wouldn't even know where to buy one.

The diner came into view, its neon Open sign glowing a bright red. I opened the door and smelled bacon. The hostess greeted me and led me to a booth across from the counter seats. An old paisley-patterned carpet covered the floor. The booth seats were a shade between brown and maroon, and the curtains matched. A lamp hung over each table, giving off nothing but old-fashioned dive vibes.

I scanned the menu, but I'd been here so many times I already knew what I wanted. The hostess came back, and I gave her my drink order and told her I was waiting for someone else.

Hazel had sounded excited on the phone, and I kind of dreaded telling her my bit of news. I suspected she'd be disappointed, but maybe not. Maybe she didn't care whether we were in this together.

I hadn't sat facing the door, so I was mildly surprised when Hazel scooted into the seat across from me. It felt as if I hadn't seen her in years. But it had only been a couple days. My mind flashed back to the make-out session I'd witnessed in the parking lot and figured Hazel and Doug must be well on their way to a happily ever after by now. That was probably why she'd sounded so chipper over the phone.

"Hey," she said, picking up the menu. "What's good?"

Nothing, I thought. But she was asking about the food. "Anything. It's hard to fuck up breakfast." Her gaze met mine, and contentment glistened within her brown eyes. *Well, good for them.*

"Okay, Oscar," she said.

"What?"

"The Grouch."

"Oh."

She smiled slightly, gave a huff that almost sounded like a laugh. "So what have you been up to?" Her tone was light, too airy for the day or for how the world had changed.

"The last twenty-four hours?" I asked, annoyed. "I've been glued to the TV mostly. Like everyone else." Except maybe her? She didn't seem bothered by what had happened, the only change in her being a kind of brightness.

The college-aged waitress, wearing tight, low-rise jeans under a grease-stained apron and a pair of old chucks, interrupted us for our order. I went first, asking for their blueberry pancake stack, and Hazel ordered the pecan ones.

"Yesterday was nuts," Hazel said, her eyebrow crooked up as I watched the waitress walk away.

"That's an understatement." I sipped my chocolate milk. Thick and rich, it coated my tongue with sweetness, just like that waitress might. The thought was as crass as any my brothers might make, but I took at as a good sign. *See, I can move on.*

"What's wrong? You're all...closed off." Hazel waved her hand vaguely in my direction.

I rolled my lips, delaying my answer, wanting to get it just right. I needed to tell her I'd quit the academy. That Doug had been right; my meddling wasn't going to help solve anything. I didn't have the resources or the access needed to find Michael's killer(s). Every time I poked around, I just found another layer to a fucked-up situation—no answers. But none of that would form itself into actual words.

"Just...a lot's going on. Evan joined the military." I misdirected the conversation. What was it about her that made me not confront things head-on?

"What?" She practically did a spit take. "Evan? He doesn't seem like the type, maybe one of your older brothers—"

"How would you know?"

Surprise, as if I'd slapped her, alighted her features. She bristled.

"You haven't met them." I pressed further, my old self reasserting itself.

"You're right," she acquiesced. "I meant, from what you've told me, it doesn't seem like the military would be Evan's first choice."

"Yeah, well, everyone seems to be making *big* decisions lately." The comment was passive-aggressive, a feature of Midwestern Nice that let folks communicate what they knew and felt without ever having to say it outright. If applied correctly, she'd just walk away from this exchange feeling slightly eviscerated but wouldn't be sure why or how.

The sounds of clinking plates and silverware took over where our conversation left off. I refused to coax Hazel through her thoughts and feelings as if she were a puzzle I could solve. It had been reductive to think of her that way in the first place.

The waitress reappeared with a large tray and placed our plates on the table. "Anything else?" she asked, setting the syrup jar between us.

"I'm good," I grumbled.

Hazel gave a closed-mouthed smile, and the waitress turned away.

I cut into my pancakes, and the first bite chilled me out a bit. "Hey, so, about Michael—"

"Yes!" She jumped on the change of topic, on the work we did best. "What have you found out so far?"

"Just that he was a real controlling piece of shit. Stef has the portfolio, and he told me that Michael was the one making up the little entries we read."

"Wait, what? The ones from the '70s? Why?"

I shrugged. "To prove he could? I don't know. Also, my brother was friends with Stef's twin sister; they worked together. And he said Michael was always sending Stonie weird messages."

"So you think there's a connection?"

"It's possible. We heard Stef the morning I found Michael; he knows more. Maybe what happened to Michael was some kind of revenge for what happened to Stonie. I don't know... Proving it is the problem." I stabbed a portion of pancake. "I don't have the resources to pull anything together, so I'm just going to hand it all over to Detective Patterson."

Hazel's shoulders slumped, seemingly with disappointment. She lowered her fork to her plate with confusion showing plainly on her face.

"Doug was right." I met her gaze, both wanting and not wanting to see her face when I mentioned his name. "About my meddling in the case."

"Oh." She flinched and suddenly became highly interested in the wad of straw wrapper next to her plate. "I don't really see it that way." Then, because she was her, she changed the subject. "I can't believe you talked to Stef alone. He's kind of a loose cannon." Hazel picked her fork back up and held it suspended over her pancakes. "You should've waited...for me." She sliced into her breakfast, and a stray pecan shot off her plate.

I let out a huff. "Don't act like I had much of a choice."

Hazel looked up from her food, blinked at me.

I ran my tongue over my front teeth. "You left. With Doug."

"He was my ride," she offered.

"He didn't have to be," I countered. A quiet challenge hovered in the air above our booth. She wasn't going to tell me about what had happened between her and Doug in the parking lot. Fair enough, it was none of my business. But that was when I decided I wasn't going to tell her I'd seen them together.

"Also, I quit the academy." It felt good to take her by surprise, to deliver news that might hurt her.

She dropped her fork, and it clattered against her plate. "You what?"

"Quit. I hated every minute of it."

Her brow wrinkled in the way that used to make me swoon, but now—*I promise*—it had no power over me.

"I-I didn't—you hated it?" She tilted her head, angling it in a way that meant she had a sincere question.

I nodded, forcing myself to maintain eye contact. A stinging ache registered near my heart, and maybe it didn't feel so good, upsetting her. But it would be over soon. Soon, I would leave and be totally alone, not thinking about what made Hazel happy, not finding ways to force myself to be someone she might want. Away from her, I could remember me, who I was without and before she stumbled into my dorm room last year looking all...*precious.*

"We only went, like, three times. You don't think it would have gotten better?"

"Training Officer Gillespie is an asshole. *And* his nephew was found *dead* in our apartment. So, no, I don't think it would have gotten better."

She nodded, poked her fork around her plate and took another bite. "So you're just done?"

"Yeah, Hazel. I'm done."

"Wow. All right." She met my gaze, her brain working overtime. I'd thrown her off her game, if she'd ever had any. "Are we...okay?" she asked.

Are we okay? A reasonable question after all we'd been through and the ways we'd relied on each other. I didn't know the answer, but did I have the guts to say that? Yes, yes, I did. Because today, I embraced *me*, not her.

"I don't know, Hazel."

"What?" Tears welled up in her eyes. "Why are you doing this?"

Fuck. I didn't *actually* want to make her cry.

"I don't know." Was that a lie? Yes. My heart hurt, plain and simple, and the truth of how I felt for her just made it worse. So I offered up layers of excuses or none at all.

"The whole world changed yesterday, Hazel. Nothing feels stable or secure right now. And if I'm being honest, what's between us has always been kinda shaky. Where we go, people end up dead. And then we run around like chickens trying to piece together information? That's...nuts! Plus, this year, I've been doing it all on my own. You've been off with Doug"—she winced again—"working on your mom's thing"—she gripped the edge of the table, her neck flushed—"and that's fine. But..."

I lost where I'd been going with this little monologue, and I probably should have come up with a more delicate way to mention her mother. So I hit closer to the mark. "I've lost something of myself in all this, and I've got to get it back."

Hazel's fingers trembled as she pressed her palms together, then rubbed the quivering movement out of her digits. She pushed her emotions back down, regaining composure. Wiping her eyes, she let out an unbelieving little laugh. "Okay. That's fine. I'm sorry I didn't notice you were feeling"—she waved her palm in a circle—"all that."

Because you never notice me. You watch and you observe and you make guesses about other people, but you never see me. Right or wrong, I kept this sentiment to myself. It revealed too much, made me too vulnerable.

"I'm not saying our friendship is ending," I said. "I just need some time to figure stuff out."

She pushed her plate toward the middle of the table. Somehow through all this, we'd managed to finish a meal. My glass of chocolate milk was empty. Her ice water was nothing but ice. The waitress came back and asked if we wanted refills. Hazel said yes; I said no.

"Another water coming right up!" The waitress's cloying tone carried throughout the diner as she walked back toward the counter.

"I understand," Hazel said, looking back at me. "If anyone understands needing to remove yourself from everything to figure stuff out, it's me. I mean, I spent nine months doing that last year."

"You were healing," I said, feeling lame. I'd failed. At everything.

She nodded. "In more ways than one. What will you do now?"

"I have no idea."

"What about the apartment? Will you come back?"

I hadn't considered that yet. "The police will keep us outta there for a while. We should probably call the landlady and see what she wants to do. I don't want to pay rent for a place neither of us can live in."

"True." She bit her lower lip. Several beats of silence passed between us. "So who do you think did it?" she asked. "Who killed Michael Gillespie?"

"You want the list?" A creeping smile pulled at my lips.

"Of course I do."

"Do you have a list too?"

"Mm-hmm." She nodded as the waitress reappeared and set her refill on the table. "Thanks," she said to her.

"It could have been Hamden. Especially if he'd found out Michael was the one writing the entries for *The Book of Lacrosse*. Though I can't help but think that whatever had gone on between Stef's sister and Michael might've played into her disappearance. TO Gillespie even worked her case. So Stef's definitely in on it somehow."

Her eyebrows raised high. "He avenged her."

"It's a theory. What's yours?"

"Pretty much the same. I'd put Hamden and Stef on the top of my list, for different reasons though. I hadn't made the sister connection." She sipped her water. "Who do you think the woman Stef spoke to that morning was?"

"Not sure." I ripped my napkin into little strips. "One-night stand gone sour. Maybe Michael had started treating another girl the way he did Stef's sister... Maybe Stef couldn't see that play out again. Maybe it's Stef's sister come back for revenge."

"You think?"

"Who knows? Whoever she is, she brings in a whole other angle."

"One you don't want to figure out?"

My shoulders sagged, and I gave her my most sarcastic look, but I stayed quiet.

"I found Hamden's address," Hazel said. "I know you said you're out, but he doesn't live too far from here?" Her statement sounded like a question. "I thought maybe we could go pay him a visit."

Her eyes glinted with hope and excitement over the pro-spect of us driving out to some stranger's house and interro-gating him as if we knew what we were doing. As if I hadn't just told her I'd quit.

"Haven't you heard anything I've said?" I asked. "No."

"No?"

"No."

"Okay, well—"

"Look, I gotta go. My mom's freaking out about Evan."

"Sure, yeah. I understand." Hazel pulled the strap of her bag across her shoulder. She flipped open the flap and brought out her billfold. "I've got this."

She headed to the counter to pay, and I walked outside for a smoke. I lit up and waited for her. She came out, the door bells jingling behind her.

"Want one?" I held up my cigarette.

"No, I stopped again."

"D'you need a ride back to Doug's?" I asked. "We can walk to my house and grab my car."

She swiped her hair behind her ears. "Um...no." Her expression conveyed she was holding back something, likely the information I'd already witnessed in university parking.

"Okay, well. I'll see you later," I said. And I hoped it was true.

It felt awkward, us moving in completely different directions. I'd told her, and myself, I just needed time to reset. But I couldn't deny the vibe—finality. The moment came cloaked in the feeling of goodbye. Like, goodbye-goodbye. Like, "I'm not sure I'll ever see you again" goodbye.

She widened her arms, a question in her eye.

"*You* want to hug? You hate hugging."

"The moment calls for it, I think."

I flicked away my cigarette, the butt bounced on the pavement, the ember separating upon impact. I stepped toward her, and her chest pressed against mine, and then a lump formed in my throat—my heart. Her arms wrapped around my waist, and I flattened my palms against her back. Her skin smelled of soap and maple syrup. And I felt right on the edge again, the precipice of wanting her. I quickly blinked away tears. *Do not cry.* This was not the time. *Stop it. Stop it. Stop it.* I pulled away first, breaking the embrace.

Hazel wiped her eyes. Had she felt it too? If so, I needed her to say it. I couldn't be the one guessing all the time.

But she said nothing. Her eyes focused on the sidewalk, on the ember that had turned to ash.

"Okay, well, bye." My voice caught on the last word. And it sounded so vulnerable I hated it.

"See ya later," she said and looked up.

I stepped down from the curb and paced through and around the maze of parked cars, not looking back. I couldn't put my finger on why this felt so much bigger than I'd meant for it to, but I couldn't deny it. The aura of the moment felt huge, an oppressive end.

Chapter Twenty-Nine

September 12 (continued)

YOU PUSHED HER away. A truth.

I bit at a hangnail on my thumb and walked toward home. This was an end I wasn't ready for and didn't want. As I paced over the asphalt, a sense of wrongness swept through me. Quitting the academy had felt good. I'd known it the second I hit Send. This felt like shit. I made it to the edge of the parking lot before I turned back around.

But Hazel was nowhere to be found. A group of customers crowded around the diner entrance. Did she have a car now? Had she taken the bus from Doug's place? I scanned the parking lot, looking for a shock of her wavy hair spiraling up in the breeze, or her tattered black hoodie, a flash of the little purse/backpack she carried. Nothing. She'd already left.

The idea of working with her again, gathering clues,

putting the mystery together, tugged at my conscience. I'd call her once I got home. To tell her what, I wasn't sure. I had no desire to return to cop school. So where did that leave me but on a wide path nowhere. If I wanted to solve mysteries but couldn't hack the police academy, then I was kind of screwed.

But life wasn't all or nothing like that. Or at least, it didn't have to be. What had Mama said at the beginning of the year? *"You can always change your mind... You don't need to ask permission to live the life you want."* That seemed both too easy and totally impossible at the same time.

I crossed over a stretch of grass and onto the sidewalk. As I neared the parking lot entrance, a maroon Civic cut me off. "Hey!" I yelled, stumbling a few steps backward. "Watch it!"

The driver side window started rolling down. *Shit.* Another confrontation. Well, fine. I was the pedestrian here, so I already had the advantage. I stepped forward, steeling myself for whatever this asshole had to say for themselves.

So I wasn't expecting the nest of familiar chestnut hair or the smile I'd dissected the meaning behind a thousand times.

"Sorry," Hazel said. "I didn't mean to almost hit you. I thought you saw me waving."

"Uh, no. No, I was kind of in my head."

"Last chance? You wanna come with me to Hamden's? Or are you out-out? I won't ask again."

I took a beat, really wanting to make sure I was doing this for the right reasons and not because the sun caught her natural highlights giving her a kind of beaming halo around her face.

Fuck it.

"Let's go," I said and made my way to the passenger side door.

*

"WHOSE CAR IS this?" I asked because I didn't expect she'd had time to buy her own car on a day like yesterday.

"Aunt Liddy's. She drove down yesterday after the—"

Pause. There had to be a pause there because describing yesterday just didn't come easily to anyone yet.

"—attacks. We're staying in a hotel downtown."

"Oh." *Oh.* So she wasn't with Doug... I wondered about what had happened there. Maybe it was nothing. After yesterday, everyone wanted to be close to their families. Or maybe she hadn't been as willing a participant in their make out session as I'd thought. Or maybe I was doing *it* again and just needed to mind my own business and knock that shit off.

Hazel glanced over at me, barely hiding a smile. "Don't look so smug."

"Smug? Who's smug? I'm just sitting here, wondering if I can smoke."

"You're smirking." She clicked a turn signal on and changed lanes. "And no, you can't smoke."

"I am not *smirking*." I reached for the visor and opened it up. In the mirror, my reflection showed only a tired girl, with dark splotches under her eyes. I hadn't bothered with makeup because I almost never did and had only finger-combed my hair after getting out of the shower that morning. But I smirked the way Hazel said I did, and the dimple I'd inherited from my dad flared. The color of my eyes gleamed the shiny, wet brown of river silt, like always, and their almond shape was slightly upturned, just like my yaya's in pictures of her when she was young. This was me. It had been me all along. Even when I changed or lost my way. I flipped the visor back up. "Anyway, there's nothing to even be smug about."

"Well, you should know Doug and I—"

I braced myself, gripping the "oh-shit" bar as if she drove wildly down the street. I prepped a statement. *I'm happy for you both. Congrats. No really, you two make a great couple.*

"—we're..."

I tightened my abs because this was sure to feel like a blow to the stomach.

"...taking some time apart."

Whoosh. All the air vacuumed out of my lungs as if I were in outer space. As if I were trapped in an event horizon and could only accept an eventual fate of being stretched and ripped apart by gravity.

But *wait, what*?

I looked at her. Her gaze stayed on the road as she braked and slowed the car until we came to a complete stop at a red light. She glanced at me.

"You were right." Her mouth formed a tight, straight line. "Doug was interested in more than a working relationship," she said formally.

"I'm sorry."

"Yeah." She tucked her hair behind her ears and sighed. "I thought he was my friend."

"He was...is," I offered. "Look at how he helped you. Just give him some time. It'll be okay."

She shrugged unconvincingly and hit the gas as the line of cars started moving again.

I thought of what I'd witnessed in the parking lot, my whole heart breaking over a kiss she hadn't even been that into while I'd been convinced by what I'd seen. "Misunderstandings happen."

"You think I led him on?" she asked.

"Hazel, I haven't been anywhere near your relationship with Doug. I have no idea what happened between the two of you."

"How'd you know then? That he'd developed feelings or whatever."

"Just a hunch."

"I didn't see it," she said, then added, "How am I ever gonna be a detective when I can't even tell when someone has a crush on me?"

"You were gathering information that pertained to your mom. I think you can cut yourself a break."

"And now I don't even have that."

"Oh, come on. You probably learned enough to continue. And he sent you all the files, right?"

She nodded.

"Then keep at it. It's good work."

"I don't know what I'll end up doing with it."

"That doesn't really matter now. Just keep finding possible victims."

She stayed quiet for a beat, seemingly contemplating what I'd said and then asked, "Can I have a cigarette?"

"I thought this car was 'No Smoking,'" I said, already

reaching for the pack stashed in my bag.

"Screw it," she said.

I handed her one but decided against smoking one myself. She could break her aunt's rules, but I wouldn't. Liddy was a powerhouse and a half, and I did not want to get on her bad side.

Hazel lit up and cranked her window all the way down. Her hair blew around the car, tendrils like kite strings catching the wind.

I cleared my throat. "So where does Hamden live?"

"Not far from here, actually."

"Not Riverview?" They couldn't *all* come from the same place.

"No, Black Pool."

"Oh, okay."

Black Pool was north of the city, another wealthy suburb. Hazel merged onto the highway, and we headed that direction.

"Does Liddy know what you're up to today?" I asked.

Hazel flicked the remaining butt of her cigarette out the window and rolled it back up. The smell lingered though; she would totally get caught.

"Hell no," she said with a breathy laugh. "She knows I'm meeting up with you, and then I'm supposed to head to Detective Patterson's office."

"You haven't done that yet?"

Her mouth scrunched into a weird squiggle, and she shook her head. "We were supposed to meet yesterday, but..."

"Yeah." I didn't need her to finish that sentence. The way she'd said "yesterday" gave it all the necessary weight.

"So what's the goal here? 'Cause you realize we could literally be heading up to confront a killer, and no one knows where we are."

"I just want to ask him some questions. See what he knows, and who he thinks killed Michael."

"You think he's just going to offer up that information?"

"Doesn't hurt to ask?" She said it like a question.

"He has motive."

"Hey, Stef seems way more guilty, especially after that conversation we overheard, and you confronted him *alone*."

I didn't have a comeback that didn't take us right back to the conversation we'd had in the diner forty-five minutes ago, so I stayed quiet. Eventually, she clicked on the radio, and we drove the rest of the way to Black Pool, listening to the indie station programming amid the rush of traffic.

Day 2 (continued)

In the Absence of the House

STEF PULLED INTO Felix's driveway, and everything seemed smaller than it had in high school, even though this house was just as huge as the lacrosse house. Felix was the older kid who lived just outside of Riverview. For a cut, he'd gotten us beer and wine coolers. He never hung out, just handed shit off, and we'd leave with the goods. He had connections. If anyone could get me a new ID, it was Felix.

"What now, Stone?"

"Now I take back a life."

"That's not much of an ans—"

The *click-clack-punch* of the car door opening and closing shut out my brother. Gravel crunched under my worn sneakers. I needed a job and money and new clothes, but first, a new name.

The tall ash trees around Felix's parents' house swayed in the late summer breeze. Leaves rustled and shushed. Weed burned somewhere. The garage door stood open, and Felix sat on a beige couch smoking a bowl. An oval-shaped Oakley U rug covered a large portion of the garage's cement pad. Behind the couch sat a weightlifting bench, and shelves with dumbbells in all sizes lined the wall. Felix didn't look like he'd used any of the gym equipment in years; his limbs were long and lithe, thin, not muscular. His hair was a gingery-brown, and it fell to his shoulders, framing a thick goatee that he kept trim and neat. He blew out a toke of smoke and said, "Hey" as if he expected me.

"I need a new ID."

"Got cash?"

Felix never asked too many questions, except about money.

"Yeah," I said. "How much do you need?" If he recognized me, I couldn't tell. My guess was that he never paid much attention to whom he dealt.

"One fifty."

"I've got a hundred." I had more, but I wasn't about to spend everything in one place.

"Ok. That'll do." Felix's mouth formed a tight frown as if he realized he'd have to get up off the couch now. "Come inside. I gotta get your picture." He stood and stretched. His T-shirt rode up, showing the lower part of his abdomen. He yawned, then asked, "You gotta name you want, or can I just use what I got?"

"I've got something picked out."

"I'd love to hear it." Stef's footsteps crunched the gravel, just like mine had.

I rolled my eyes. He wanted me to stay who I used to be, and I didn't know how to explain to him that she was already gone. "Siobhan. Siobhan Drakos."

"Good name," Felix said and made his way inside the house.

"Irish mom, Greek dad," I said, but he wasn't paying me much attention, which was just fine. I'd just moved to follow Felix inside the house when Stef grabbed my arm.

"What are you thinking?"

"Nothing. Just moving on."

"You can't use the neighbor's name, Stone. That's just...effed up. We left a *body* in her basement. There should be zero connections between us now. If you're gonna do this, pick something else."

"Wait, her last name is Drakos? I picked that because of Evan. My friend."

"Stone, they're siblings. Be smart about this." His eyes searched mine, twin eyes from different continents. "You're *really* moving on, aren't you?" The realization washed over his features. He looked as if he might faint.

"Maybe you're finally getting it." I took both his arms in my grip, attempting to steady him. The muscles of his biceps grew taut and shaky under my palms.

"But I already lost you once..."

"Exactly, you lost me. She's gone. Maybe never even was. I'm putting together a new life for myself because...it's past due. Nothing—no one—will stop me this time." I kissed his sweet, dumb cheek and left him wilting on Felix's stained and singed couch. "This person is who came out of the walls."

Chapter Thirty

September 12 (continued)

WE DROVE BY Hamden's place before pulling into the driveway. The house sat a ways back from the road, nestled among the shade of too many ash trees. The structure was meant to be modern-looking, a kind of ranch-style home with floor-to-ceiling windows, a low-sloping roof, and stacked boxy shapes, more like an office. Dark-gray siding covered the spaces that weren't taken up by windows.

"There's a car in the driveaway. And the garage door is open," I told Hazel as we passed.

"Should we wait and do this later?" she asked.

"Maybe."

The neighborhood encompassed a private lane, so there was no place to park without looking like we didn't belong. We could either keep driving, give whoever visited more time and come back later, or do this now.

"Let's just go in," I said. "Interrupting never hurt anyone."

"I don't know if that's true." Hazel took in a breath and held it a few beats, considering my opinion. "But you're right. We're here, so why back down?"

At the next driveway, she turned the car around, and we drove back toward Hamden's place.

"What's the angle here?" I asked.

"Just gathering information. See what he knows, what he suspects." She parked next to the car already in the driveway. Someone had left the keys in the ignition and the driver side door propped open, so the *ding-ding-ding* was all I heard when I stepped out of Liddy's car. I couldn't see into the garage as it faced away from the road, looking out toward the wood.

What had been a bright and sunny day appeared gloomy under the canopy of all the trees on the property. We bypassed the open garage and headed toward the front door. Hazel pressed the doorbell, and an eight-chord melody played throughout the house. Muffled banter could be heard from within until, finally, the door opened, and Hamden stood before us.

"My mom's not—" He stopped once he recognized us. "Uh, hi?"

"Hi. We want to talk to you about the other night," I said. "You know, how Michael ended up in our basement." Why beat around the bush?

"Um...I've already spoken to the police." His brows scrunched with confusion. "I've got a lawyer and stuff."

"Sure, sure. This is different," I said. "We're obviously not the police."

"I don't think I want to..." The door started to close.

"You kinda owe us," Hazel reminded him. "We brought you outta the woods that day."

He raked his bottom row of teeth over his upper lip, obviously not enjoying the memory. "Fine, come in." He opened the door wider.

Hazel and I stepped into the foyer and waited for him to close the door. He then led us into a living room with high ceilings, a modern fireplace insert, and plush couches. An enormous TV stood taller than me against one wall.

Hamden sat and motioned to the other couch.

"Well?" He popped his knuckles and then his neck, fidgeting.

"So we just wanted to ask what happened the night Michael ended up in our basement," Hazel said, right to the point as she took a seat, and I sat next to her.

Hamden's mouth formed a dash, and he shrugged. "I don't know. I was already out of there by then. I never went back after—" He looked away, toward the sliding glass doors that led out onto a deck. He ran his tongue over his upper teeth. "—that day at the river. Came home and told my mom what had been going on. She got me a lawyer, and we were headed down that road when I heard about"—his nostrils flared—"his death." Hamden clenched his fists and rolled his wrists until they popped, too, *crack, crack, crack*. "Can't say I'm sorry 'bout it."

"He put you guys through hell," I said.

"Something like it, yeah." A tic pulsed along Hamden's jaw. "But it wasn't just him, was it? All those older guys let it happen. Nobody stopped it. Nobody stepped in." Hamden rested his elbows on his knees, seemingly ready to spring up and run. He folded his hands together as if in prayer. "'Cept you two. That's what kinda woke me up. Seeing your faces that day on the trail, I knew it wasn't just me who saw how fucked up it really was. It's when I decided to get myself out of there and also to fight back. I couldn't leave that shit for anyone else to go through."

"That's brave," I said.

He shrugged. "I don't know about that."

"Who do you think killed Michael?"

"Hard to say." Hamden unclasped his hands and massaged each knuckle. "I think he probably had a lot of enemies."

"What about Stef?" Hazel asked.

He grimaced with surprise. "Stef? Nah. He was Michael's biggest fan. Followed the guy around like he was on a leash."

Exactly, I thought. That was a kind of motive in and of itself. Couple it with the possible realization that his sister was alive, and he had a shot at avenging her? My brothers would have done it for me, without question.

"Do you know anything about Stef's sister?" I asked.

"Only that she disappeared a while back. I never met her. Most people think she's dead, been gone so long."

"Do you?" I asked.

"I don't have an opinion," he said and scratched his nose.

I couldn't tell if he told the truth because before I could ponder it, voices carried through a hall off the living room. Another man emerged. Agewise, I'd guess him to be slightly older than Hamden, scruffier though, with shoulder-length hair and a goatee. Probably Hamden's sibling. A woman trailed behind him, thanking him and staring down at something small she carried in her hands.

"Oh hey, I didn't know we had more company," the older guy said, eyeballing Hazel and me.

"They just got here," Hamden said.

Something about the girl caught my attention. She seemed small, delicate, and birdlike. As she tucked something in her back pocket, we made eye contact. She kept moving forward, staring at me all the while, her blue eyes like glacier ice—cold, distant...*unpredictable*. Stef's eyes. *Stonie's eyes.*

She blinked and looked away, following the older guy beyond the living room and into the kitchen.

"The cash?" he asked.

"Here you go," she said. "Thanks again."

At the sound of her voice, it all came together. The woman's voice in the kitchen the day we'd found Michael—it was hers. Stef's seemingly missing sister, who everybody assumed was either long gone or dead by now, had just waltzed past us. Very much alive. With very much motive.

"Maeve? Maeve!"

I looked around, unsure of where I was. Hazel's gaze brought me back to the moment, concern lingering there. *Hamden.* We were here to speak with him about what he thought might have happened the night of Michael's murder. But I had all the answers I'd ever need.

I swiped my hands through my hair, then straightened the hem of my T-shirt. "Sorry," I rasped. I didn't want to ruin this, especially for Hazel. But the longer I sat there, the more I felt sure the real murderer had just walked by.

"That girl? You know her?" I asked.

"No," he said. "Just one of my brother's randos."

"Why is she here?"

He shrugged, big and lazily like a Labrador retriever might after a long walk. "People are always coming here to get stuff from my brother. Beer, weed—"

"Nothing harder than that though." Hamden's brother leaned in the doorframe where the living room and kitchen met. "I promise you that. Why? You in the market?"

"Maybe," I said in unison with Hazel's firm, "No."

Her expression was one of pure confusion. But I had to keep pressing.

"What'd she get off you? Maybe I want that too."

"The girl that just left?"

I nodded.

"Just an ID." He scratched the scruff along his jaw.

"What's her real name?"

"I don't ask those kinds of questions, lady." He looked to Hamden. "Who is this?"

"Girls from school," Hamden said.

"We were his neighbors," Hazel added, probably seeking to regain the lead on this conversation. "The ones who found the team captain."

The brother scrunched his eyebrows. Hamden answered the look.

"The guy who died."

"Right," the brother said and yawned. "This is boring. I'm gonna go smoke if anyone wants to join." He turned and headed back toward the garage.

Hamden rubbed his thighs. "Welp..."

"We should go," I said, grabbing Hazel's elbow. "Now."

But she lingered. "Hold on—" She pulled her arm out of

my grasp.

"No, really, Hazel. It's time to leave." I turned to Hamden. "Thanks for your time." I dragged Hazel from the couch.

"Wait, I'm not—"

But Hamden was all too ready to show us the door. He followed us back to the foyer and closed the door behind us with a resounding *thwack.*

"Maeve! I wasn't finished!"

"Oh yes you are!" I marched back toward the car. "Do you have your cell phone?"

Hazel stomped her foot. "Yes, but what is going on? What's wrong with you?"

"Nothing." I turned back to her. She dug through her backpack and handed me the phone. "Just drive. I've gotta call Detective Patterson."

"Why?" she asked as we approached her aunt's car.

I opened the passenger side door. "Because that was Stonie Guenther who just walked through their living room."

Day 2 (continued)

In the Absence of the House

Shit. She recognized me, probably from the yearbook. I thought I had time—to change my hair, get fake glasses or something. But she was there, in Felix's living room, of all places. I should have put it together; Felix's little brother had been on the team. Coming here had been a mistake. And how many of those would I get before it all came crashing down and I spent the rest of my life in jail?

No. I'd already lost my first life; I wasn't going to lose this second chance—this metamorphosized self, the one I'd nurtured and cared for, was going to have a shot, goddamnit.

"Take me back to the lacrosse house."

"What? No. You need to stay away from there."

"I need to grab something from the girls next door."

"We should go home, Stonie."

"Forget it, Stef. I have a plan. For me. Myself."

So she knew about Stonie. But...well, I still had another chore to take care of before I spread my wings and flew the hell out of town. Something I thought of only when I saw her face. A face that reminded me of him—Evan.

"Drive faster."

Chapter Thirty-One

September 12 (continued)

HAZEL CLICKED HER seatbelt and looked over her shoulder to maneuver us out of Hamden's driveway. She popped the car back into drive. The ash trees melded together as we sped away.

"That was Stonie Guenther, Hazel. I can't fucking believe it."

"The missing sister…"

"Uh-huh."

"Just happens to show up needing a new ID. Oh. Oh wow."

"Yep. We have to talk to Detective Patterson."

"Get her on my cell. Now." I dialed and put the phone on speaker while we waited for her to pick up.

"Detective Patterson? This is Maeve Drakos. Hazel and I have kind of stumbled across some information about the mur—"

"Just stumbled across?"

"Yes, ma'am. We were just at Hamden—shit, I don't know his last name—one of the lacrosse players. We were just at his house—"

"Excuse me? What were you doing there?"

"Uh, nothing."

"Doubtful."

"Just talking. But that's not the point. While we were there—"

"Okay, okay. Listen, I'm in the middle of something at the moment. Hazel and I have a meeting later today. Can this wait until then?"

"Uh, no?"

Detective Patterson sighed. "So this is an emergency?"

"I think so."

Hazel spoke up. "Detective Patterson, this is Hazel. Can you meet us at our apartment? There's some paperwork there I need to grab, and this is something you'll want to know."

"Fine, fine. I'll be there to let you in ASAP," said Detective Patterson. "Give me half an hour to wrap up here?"

"Sure," I said and hit End.

Day 2 (continued)

In the Absence of the House

Up in the girl-next-door's room, I rifled through any notebook or folder I could find. She had to have something here with what I needed written on it. On her dresser, I emptied an old jewelry box—nothing. She had a small stash of well-loved novels next to her bed, and I flipped through them. And bingo. Tucked into an old copy of a Sweet Valley High title, I found what I'd come here for. An acceptance letter, by the looks of it, but all I needed was an address. I folded the letter back into the book, then tucked the envelope into my back pocket.

All I had to do now was plant the mallet somewhere. Stef had been driving around with it under the passenger side seat. I thought to hide it in the walls of the lacrosse house, but I couldn't quite make it over the threshold. The pull of the house, the safety I'd once felt in its walls, were like tentacles now. If they got ahold of me once more, I'd never break free.

So I just had to find a place for it here...

I moved to the front bedroom that looked over the street. The intermittent traffic sounds from the street rushed through the space, as if it were a wind tunnel or an ocean were nearby. The rolling sound was so convincing I moved to the bed and propped open one of the windows. If I closed my eyes, I could see the ocean, a sparkling turquoise splashing over white sand. A car door slammed, bringing me out of my reverie. I looked to the sidewalk, and that's when I saw them. Fuck. I'd just run out of time.

Chapter Thirty-Two

September 12 (continued)

THE PARKING SPACE in front of our place was open for once, and Hazel pulled over. She let out a shuddering breath and turned the car off.

"Got any more cigarettes?" she asked.

"All out." I scrunched the soft pack in my fist and tossed it back into my bag.

"I'm gonna head to the gas station and get some. I don't think I can just sit around and wait for her. You want anything?"

"Blue Freeze." I handed her a few dollars.

"All right. Be right back."

I stayed in the car, but the air inside grew too warm and stifling. I opened the door and walked up to the front porch, keys in hand. The pleasant afternoon air held the hint of autumn in the breeze. I sat on the stoop and waited for

Detective Patterson and Hazel.

I couldn't stop thinking about Stonie Guenther though, what my brother said she'd gone through. The things I'd witnessed Michael do to his team were weird and controlling and abusive; I shuddered to think what he'd be capable of doing to someone over many years. And he'd seemed like such a good guy. But that hadn't exactly been true. There'd been plenty of red flags; I'd just been socialized to ignore them. We all had.

"Maaa-eeve!"

I looked up, expecting to see Hazel coming down the street, but the sidewalk was empty. In fact, the neighborhood was unnervingly quiet. I supposed that happened after terrorist attacks; students had gone home if they could.

"Maeve Drakos!"

The hell? I turned, searching for where the disembodied voice came from but didn't see a culprit. I thought of my last night here, sitting on the stairs outside my bedroom and watching the man who had to be Michael pounding on my door. Clearly, Stonie or Stef, or both of them together, had been after him at that point.

"Maeve!" the voice called again.

This time, I stood, searching, but not finding anyone nearby. Was I just hearing things? Had all the stress torn my grip off reality? I ran back to Hazel's car, but the door was locked. I must've hit the button when I got out. My keys still in hand, I took the porch steps two at a time and reached for the screen door. I shouldn't go inside, but it felt the better option than being out here, all exposed. Detective Patterson would have to understand. And at that thought, I calmed down. People, actual police, were on the way. Yet, my fingers still trembled as I unlocked the front door.

The living room had an exhibitive quality, even though it had only been a few days since we'd sat here eating pizza and watching TV. I closed the door behind me and pressed my back against it. With shelter, my heart rate slowed. I felt safer inside than out. But...

Hazel. She'd be back any minute, and whoever had called my name could easily target her instead. Unless, I was really and truly losing it.

"Fuck." I opened my bag and fumbled my way through it, looking for my knife or the pepper spray.

"What a mouth on you."

I dropped my bag at the shock of that voice here, inside. A set of old running shoes descended the stairs that led to our bedrooms. Then came a pair of light-gray jeans with holes around the knees, a navy-blue hoodie tied around the waist, and an old baby tee of mine showed off a thin strip of abdomen. Their hair was long, straight, and a little stringy near the ends.

"Stonie," I said.

"At one time, yes, you'd be correct. But that's not my name."

"A fake ID won't get you a whole new life."

"Felix told! He shouldn't have done that." She took one step at a time, drawing the moment out. "How'd you recognize me?"

"I saw you in—" I realized there'd only been two places I'd actually seen this girl. In the newspaper and in the yearbook stashed among Michael and Stef's textbooks.

A smile crept across her lips. Her teeth had turned a pale, buttery yellow since her senior picture. "The yearbook."

I nodded, unable to make my mouth say words. If she knew I'd seen her in the yearbook, then she'd been there—somewhere. But that was impossible. The house had been totally vacant when I'd snuck back in there.

"Shocked?" she asked, nearly at the base of the stairs, close enough I could start to catch the smell of her shampoo. It smelled just like Michael's. "I lived there, you see. In the walls, the spaces you and your roommate escaped through the one time you went snooping. That place is like a maze within; no one ever suspected me. Well, until they did." She smirked, and her eyes, cold and blue, widened. "And that's when things started getting a little weird."

"A *little* weird?" My voice came back, sounding scratchy and dried out as if autumn leaves rustled down my throat. I swallowed. The only thing keeping me upright was the knowledge that, at some point, Detective Patterson would be here. That and my curiosity. What on earth did this girl want with me? She should be long gone, out of town, yet here she lingered. "You should leave," I said.

Stonie blew out a big breath, seeming cartoonishly frustrated. "I'm trying, you know. But then I keep seeing you. In the House, then at Felix's, and I don't know...feels like there might be some unfinished business here."

"I'm not stopping you from getting out of town. If you want to get away with murder, then you need to go."

She licked her lips, her shoulders deflating a bit. Her aura, chaotic and unruly, changed. "Do you know what he put me through?"

"Some of it. I saw what he did to the other guys, and my brother mentioned some...red flags."

"Evan," she whispered.

I nodded.

"How is he?"

"Okay?" I shrugged. "He thinks he wants to be a marine."

"Evan? Ha!" Her laugh cascaded around the living room.

I had no idea where this little confrontation was going, but as with Shirlee last fall, I felt if I could keep her talking long enough, it might stay...sane.

Suddenly, she grew serious, a hardness taking over her eyes like a pair of frostbitten marbles. "Why didn't he help me?"

"He would have, had you asked. He only understood some of what was happening between you and Michael, and then you were gone. I think he blames himself for what happened. 'Course he doesn't know you're actually alive. And you didn't need his help in the end, did you?"

"He's why I came here, you know? I wanted his address, wanted to tell him I'm going to be okay. He's a good person."

"He is." I struggled with what to say next. I thought of Stef, wondered where he was right now, realized that would probably be good information to have. "How 'bout your brother? How's he handling...all this?"

She snorted and made her way to the couch. It was then I saw the mallet she carried. I pictured Michael's destroyed nose, his concaved skull. I was looking at a murder weapon; every single burning cell of my body said so. And it also meant she hadn't come seeking peace. She meant to hurt me or Hazel or both of us.

"Stef? He's useless." She sat and set the mallet across her knees, staring at the braided rug.

"That's not entirely true."

Her gaze flicked back to mine, eyes narrowed.

"He helped. In the end," I said.

"It doesn't exactly make up for all the years he sat back and watched Michael destroy me."

"Eh, that's debatable."

She laughed. "I like you. Liked you since the moment I saw you call Michael out. You saw him for what he was all along, didn't you?"

"No, actually." I stepped away from the door and sat in the lounger Hazel'd brought down from Lima. "He had a really good mask."

She picked at a hangnail, appearing more fidgety the longer we spoke. It was difficult to get a true read on her or make a prediction about what she might do, but I stayed calm, even with the mallet still resting in her lap.

"You understand. No one would have stopped him," she said.

"I get it. He'd positioned himself as a leader. Everyone looked up to him. He was..."

"Golden."

"On the outside, at least."

"Hollow inside." She didn't look at me. Instead, she stared at the tan-brown brick of the nonfunctional fireplace. She stood and crossed the room, examining the photos we'd had developed and tacked to the mantel. "A hollow beast."

Beast. *Beast.* I'd seen that idea referenced before. I set my bag down, and it fell against my leg, the edge of the yearbook biting into my calf. The weird quote about fear being a dream and a beast that could be defeated—it had been her.

"So you decided to stop fearing him," I said.

She flicked the bottom of one of our pictures, one of me and Evan last Christmas. "That's when I really started to feel free. It's addicting, you know? Being in control of your own life."

"I probably would've killed him too."

She looked back at me, disbelieving.

"Honestly," I continued. "You watched him move on, keep his whole life, terrorize more people. If it were me? Yeah, I could see myself doing what you did. Ending it—him." I didn't know if what I said was true. I'd probably been angry enough to kill a person by accident, but plan a murder? To go through with each stage knowing the finale came when someone's life had been purposefully ended, all their potential snuffed out, the people who loved them left behind? Without blind rage or defense propelling me through it, who could say? But it didn't matter. I needed her to feel understood, wanted her to set down that mallet.

"Then, will you let me get away with it? Will you not tell the police about me? Possibly let someone else take the fall?"

I could've lied, but too quickly, Stonie saw the truth written all over my face.

"Right. That's what I thought." She let out a sigh, gripped the mallet handle, and stepped toward me. Her arms arched upward.

I flinched, cowered in the chair. But only for a second before I instinctually dove, springing forward, aiming for her middle. My shoulder slammed into her stomach, and pain bloomed across my back as she hit me. I wrestled her to the floor in front of the fireplace. She squirmed beneath me, but I was bigger, stronger. She swung the mallet again and again. It whistled through the air, missing me by inches until I grabbed her wrist in both hands and pinned it above her head. She spit in my face, but I was unmoved, banging her hand against the brick hearth until she dropped the hammer. She clawed my cheek, and pain registered again, but I wouldn't be distracted. This was life or death; she meant to kill me. She'd kill Hazel too. And I wouldn't let that happen. This had to be finished before Hazel walked in. A crash sounded near the back of the house, and we both stopped, looking up to where the noise had come from.

"Stonie! Stonie, are you in there?"

"Stef! Yes! Hel—"

I put my hand over her mouth, and she bit down hard, clamping her teeth into my pinky and ring fingers.

"Fuck!" I hissed. A burning sensation lit up my hand, and I smacked her to get her to release me. She did, but in that split second, she turned beneath me and reached once more for her weapon.

I got my arms up over my head just as the mallet smashed against my forearm. Lightning flared behind my eyelids; I saw the burning tree in the Trap. But this time, it was my own limb, broken, battered, burning with agony. I expected another hit, another fulguration. Another brilliant display of violence shattering me into a million pieces, like a broken mirror. Just like Stonie. Or like Shirlee. Only, they'd had the resolve to rise again. And if they could do it, so must I.

"Stonie! Stop!" The guttural scream came from the dining room. Stef stood there, his face red with emotion, his fists clenched. His presence, his barking orders, were enough to pause Stonie's attack and give me time to scramble backward, out of her reach. "What are you doing?

Stef asked. "You said you just needed to get some stuff out of the lacrosse house."

My arm lit up with pain at every movement, something broken, but I grit my teeth and moved farther away.

"You can't do this again," Stef pleaded.

I got my back against the door and cradled my arm against my chest. There was no blood, no bone sticking out, which brought a certain relief. It still hurt like hell, though, muddling my thoughts and actions. My bag lay nearby, my little cannister of pepper spray poking out the top. I just had to get to it.

"I don't *want* to, Stef. I have to."

"Why?"

"The opportunity presented itself, and she knows Stonie exists."

"So do I," he said. "And so do you. You keep telling me I don't understand what's happened to you and what you need, but I don't think you understand either. You can't just become someone new—"

"I can! I will," she screamed.

"You can't. It—what he did to you—it's already affected you and made you who you are. You have to deal with it."

"I don't want to live my whole life defined by him and how he treated me," she pleaded, her eyes rimmed red and teary, her chin wrinkled with emotion.

I inched closer to my bag, hoping the sad little scene continued with me going unnoticed.

"You don't have to, but you gotta, like, do therapy or something." He held his arms out toward her.

Stonie considered his words, then dropped her weapon and accepted Stef's embrace. He held her tightly, mumbled something into her ear, and made eye contact with me.

Go, he mouthed.

But where to? The front door was closed, and the stairs were creaky and old. I did as he said, though, scooting myself toward the doorknob. The idea of letting go of my injured arm to try to open the thing sent cold sweat down my neck. The scene swam before me, Stef and Stonie, fusing together in a kind of wavy, dreamlike dance. My breath came in quick pants. *Shock*. I knew what it felt like because I'd been here before.

I needed to get my feet up, but my back ached. I needed to get the fuck out of there, but I couldn't move. I needed help, but no one came.

And then everything got worse because—"Maeve? Are you inside?"—Hazel showed up. She opened the door and surveyed the scene. Her eyes grew wide and angry. "What is going on?"

Stonie let a sob escape, muffled against her brother's chest. I watched as she looked at him, and his face grew serious, his eyes held a warning.

"Hazel," I squeaked, "go get help."

Instead, she knelt beside me. "Ohmygod, Maeve. You're hurt. How bad is it?" She pushed my hair back from my sweat-slicked face.

"Get. Out of here," I managed to say.

"I'm not leaving you. Can you get an arm around my shoulders?" she asked.

I shook my head.

Behind us, the twins struggled. Stonie tried to break away from Stef's grasp, but he held her tightly.

She screamed, "I have to! Stef! Let me do this! I have to

be free! No one can know! They'll tell!"

"Okay," Hazel said. "I'm going to get my arms around you from behind. Lean forward." I did as Hazel said, knowing that following her lead would be the only way she'd get out of here.

She managed to squat behind me and get her arms around my waist. "This is going to hurt," she said in my ear. I nodded. It didn't matter; everything hurt.

"Stonie! Stonie, no!" Stef yelled. She'd broken free and was already in the living room picking up the mallet.

I couldn't use my arms, but my legs were okay. And when Hazel heaved me up, I pumped them, bicycling us backward out of the house. Stonie charged at us. I screamed. Hazel fell with me on top of her, just outside the door on the little stoop I'd imagined would be the perfect setting for late-night drinking and smoking. That had never happened though. My whole fantasy had been railroaded by these fucks next door.

A new surge of rage and adrenaline pumped through my veins. And instead of trying to scoot us off the porch and out of harm's way, I kicked at Stonie, landing several. Legs, stomach, I didn't know, I just kicked and kicked and kicked.

Then, with a wild kind of yelp like a high-pitched dog whine, Stonie was up in the air. Two big muscular arms pinned her arms to her side and carried her back inside the house. I rolled to the side, pain overtaking me once more. My vision swam. The brick siding scratched against my cheek. From somewhere in the distance, I heard Hazel calling my name like a song, a pulse. Black spots appeared where her face should have been and bloomed like ink against a page until that was all there was.

Chapter Thirty-Three

September 17, 2001

IT HAD BEEN almost a week since...everything. With each passing moment, more people pulled themselves away from their TV sets and walked back into their routine lives. They kidded themselves though. Everything was different for all of us now. Normal had dissipated with the past, gone forever. The present was all new until it changed once more.

I'd woken up in the hospital, and then again later when they let me go home. Stonie had fractured my elbow, and they'd all said I was lucky I hadn't needed surgery. I stretched and flexed my fingers within the bulky, mechanical contraption of a cast, unable to shake the feeling that my whole existence might float away. My sense of object permanence had been blown to bits by the events of the last few months and days. Mama told me I just needed time, and that I could stay with them until a new plan became apparent.

But really, I think she was just worried she might have another kid run off and join the military or something. I... wouldn't be doing that.

What I would be doing was therapy. The Haven Center had an art therapy group, and Hazel was driving me to my first session later that day.

Papa told me to "Get a job too" since I'd quit school. And while Mama had smacked him for his blunt, gruff way of communicating, it wasn't like I could just sit still and do nothing.

So that was why I stood at the diner applying for a waitressing gig. At a booth in the back, I scribbled my info into the application. The waitress brought me a coffee and said the manager could meet with me as soon as I finished.

"I have time," I said, but even that sounded false. If anything, what I heard and felt most in my heart was the ticking, pulsing beat of time slipping away. Nobody had the amount of time they really wanted, and the image of Stonie appeared in the seat across from mine, nothing more than a ghost. She kept doing that, showing up and staring at me. She hadn't spoken yet, so that was probably a good sign—a single plus in the ole mental health column. Auditory hallucinations? Not yet.

But she came to me for some reason. And I could guess at what she wanted. Her gaze skewered my soul, practically a dare. One girl gone missing, and the story behind Michael's case had really been Stonie's. Just like Ryan's case had been about Shirlee, which had turned into a whole other story, connecting to Hazel's mom... A tale as old as time, with women too overshadowed by men's actions to stand alone.

I tapped my pen against the table, sipped the coffee, and tried to remember the dates of my last job, but I drew a blank. It would have ended my last year of high school, so I jotted down "2000" and hoped that was enough information. I signed my name at the bottom and headed to the counter to turn it in. The waitress took the paper and said the manager would be right out.

Soon, a lumbering, middle-aged man with a bald head and black mustache scooted into the seat across from me, dissipating Stonie's spirit. Oh, well, she'd be back.

The nametag on his shirt said "Dan," and his belly pressed against the table edge. I couldn't muster any kind of goodwill or kindness for him, and it seemed as though he felt similarly toward me. He held out his hand; we shook half-heartedly. He asked a couple of mundane questions, then offered me the job. I accepted.

"Milly, bring me the schedule, will ya?"

Milly, who leaned dramatically over the counter reading the paper, gave a sigh, yet did as asked. Appearing a minute later with a manila folder, she handed it to her, our, boss. She headed back to the counter, and the newspaper crinkled as she turned the page. That was when I caught a glimpse of a picture, the face I would never forget—Michael.

"I *said*, does that work for you?" Dan asked.

"What? Oh, yeah, put me down for whatever. Except I have a thing"—therapy—"Monday and Wednesday afternoons."

Dan pursed his lips, obviously disliking how I didn't hang on his every word. But he'd have to get over that. It did everyone good to be ignored every once in a while.

"Well, all righty then." He drew the phrase out,

attempting some lame-ass impression of Ace Ventura from the '90s. "We'll see you tomorrow morning, 8:00 a.m., for training. Introduce yourself to Milly on your way out. She'll be the one you'll be shadowing."

"Thanks." I took my coffee mug straight to Milly, who was reading the funnies. "Hey, I'm Maeve. I'll be shadowing you for a couple days."

Milly snapped the wad of gum in her mouth. "Hi," she said but didn't hold out her hand for a shake or even look up.

"I start tomorrow."

"Mm-hmm."

"Okay, then. See you," I added, then turned for the door. But Stonie blocked the exit. Her ghostly, transparent self, stood right in front of the doors. As much as I wanted to stay out of this or ignore what had happened, I couldn't, not with her following me everywhere I went. And honestly, I didn't even want to leave the mystery of her story behind. That was the self-discovery a week off had led to—I was too nosy, too curious, too desperate to leave it alone.

I turned back around and asked, "Hey, are you done with the local news section?" Michael's left eye stared up from the counter. The rest of his face buried under the paper's other sections.

"Oh, yeah. Here." Milly shuffled through, the newspaper swooshing as she filed through it. "Just take all of it," she said, giving up on finding the part I wanted.

"You sure?"

"I'm done reading those parts."

I grabbed the whole thing, a kind of jumbled mess in my arms, and walked out of the restaurant. The elementary school and a public park were across the street, next to the library. I waited at the crosswalk until the light changed. My gaze zeroed in on the closest park bench and I headed there. Nearby, school kids screamed through their morning recess.

I sat and straightened the papers, looking again for the local news. Michael's face made the second page—B1 and 5. The headline read: Police Say Case Closed on Oakley Athlete's Murder by Gayle Jackson. Gayle had helped us find the identity of the *dead_papers* internet account last year, so seeing her name in the city paper made me smile.

The article mentioned "a person of interest" closely linked to the original victim—*Stef*—had been taken into custody after a second attack near campus and subsequently confessed to the murder of Michael Gillespie. The police captain was quoted: "We'll continue to investigate if any new information arises, but for now, the death of Mr. Gillespie is considered closed." The rest of the details were hazy, just a quick rehashing of how Michael's body had been found. No mention of Stonie, and no motive listed.

He'd covered for her. And now the whole thing felt unfinished. But maybe Detective Patterson would say that was the job. There would always be unanswered questions, scenarios that didn't end as neatly or as finally as I'd like. I folded up the paper until it was small enough to fit in my bag. A bell rang at the school, and the children all lined up, their yelling withering to quiet. Birds hopped along the park's green lawn.

After a while, I headed home. A heavy kind of weariness stopped me from rushing. I turned onto my street and our split-level home, painted tan with brown accents, came into view. I stopped at the mailbox and pulled out a few letters, mostly junk.

Inside, I set the mail on the kitchen counter and hit the button on the answering machine. I grabbed a glass from the cupboard and turned on the tap while the voicemails continued, only half listening until a woman said she was the county prosecutor and she wanted to talk about the Shirlee Hensen case. She left a phone number, asked me to contact her immediately, and the message ended.

The court case. The thing with Shirlee wasn't over either. Of course, I'd be asked for testimony. So I'd have to see Shirlee again. Hazel would too. *Shit*. She probably got the same phone call. I abandoned my glass of water and headed upstairs to call the lawyer back and then Hazel.

At the top of the stairs, a flash of movement near the end of the hall caught my attention. Evan's door had been left a crack open. *Rrrrrip*. What was he doing now? Standing just outside, I pressed my palm against the wood, ready to push my way in, but thinking better of it. One didn't grow up with three brothers and *not* figure out how to knock, even if the door was slightly open already.

But just as I made to knock, I paused, fist midair. Evan stood in front of his dresser, lifting something long and flowing from a box. His wrists made a snapping motion, and the fabric flapped. Then he placed it over his shoulders. A robe? No, *a cape*. The maroon patches, the silky fabric, the shoddy stitchwork: I'd seen this particular cape before.

On Michael Gillespie.

Oh, no. No, no, no, no, no, no. Evan shouldn't have access to Michael's things. How would he have ever gotten his hands on it? Unless...unless.

"Why the fuck do you have that?" I blurted, my voice

aggressive and accusing, even to my own ears.

"Maeve?" The cape whipped as he turned toward me.

"What is this, Ev?" I stepped into his bedroom, closing the door behind me. "What did you do?"

"Nothing." He held up his hands. The string of the cape, the bow that he'd tied, sat right above his clavicle, pulling flush against his skin. "I'm not even sure what this is." He turned back toward his dresser and picked up a slip of paper.

"Take that thing off." I yanked the note from his grasp.

"What is it?" he asked.

"Something you don't want."

He pulled the string, and Michael's cape fluttered to the ground.

I read the note. Written in the same overly precise handwriting I'd noticed in the yearbook were the words: *The beast no longer hunts me*. Signed, *Stonie*.

"I thought she was—"

"Dead? Yeah, not quite," I said.

"So she's alive and just...out there?"

I nodded, reading the one line over and over.

"Why would she send me this?" he asked.

"I don't know." I shrugged. "It was Michael's."

"Fucking"—Evan wadded up the fabric and shoved it back in the box—"sick. That's what this is—just—sick."

I checked for an address but only a PO box from Kentucky had been taped to the package. She'd moved on, started over; Stef had made sure of it. And Hazel and I, well, we'd been too wrapped up in the trauma of another attack to make sure Detective Patterson knew someone else had been involved. Although, that wouldn't last—our sense of justice wasn't that skewed. The bitch did break my arm.

"What're you gonna do with it?" I asked.

"Trash it." Evan sidestepped past me and stomped downstairs.

"Might be evidence!" I called after him, but my heart wasn't in it. Stonie would have her head start because it wasn't my job to catch her. Not anymore.

Day 9

Free

None of my worries felt quite as heavy when I stood at the shoreline of the Gulf of Mexico. As I stared over the rolling turquoise waves, a warm breeze pressed against me, pushing me backward, nature's way of indicating I should go back to Ohio and face the aftermath. But Stonie's life had only ever been consequences. Siobhan, however, she was her own phenomenon. Not even a wind would sway her.

Epilogue

3 months later

THE FLOOR TO ceiling windows in the art therapy room at the Haven Center let in a huge amount of light all day long. It stayed warm and bright here, no matter what happened outside. The room faced the courtyard garden, where rows of sunflowers would grow next summer. A volunteer had been out there earlier, clearing away the dried-up stalks and huge, drooping heads. I'd missed their full bloom, when they'd been undoubtedly beautiful and carried a lot of symbolism around here, but the crunching leaves and blackened stems did, too, in a way.

At the back table, I pulled out a white oil pastel and the black piece of paper I'd been working on the last few sessions. This had been good for me. This place and this group or class or whatever. My shoulders lowered and my jaw loosened each time I sat and spent an hour working.

Rachelle, the lead therapist, had spent a lot of the first sessions encouraging us to move beyond making something pretty, saying our culture was set up to encourage those with what was viewed as traditional "talent" to move forward as artists, but really, we all could and should create. Afterward, I compared it to the drawing class I'd taken at Oakley and could see exactly how that path had been closed off to me because my work hadn't met some arbitrary standard or aesthetic. And maybe that class hadn't even been art at all; it hadn't set my brain on a low, simmering heat the way these sessions did. I craved this now, the focus and the making—the healing in a way I never considered necessary.

The rest of the group filed in, only five of us, plus Rachelle. She sat on the head table, at the front of the room. A flowing, peasant-style skirt swished around her swinging ankles. When everyone pulled out their pieces from last week, she began.

"This is one of my favorite assignments, because, for me, it always challenges my perspective. When you use black paper and white pastel, you can really only focus on the light. Where is it? What direction is it coming from? Where can it not reach? Think about those questions today while you work. I'll be your witness."

She always ended her brief talks with that last line, "I'll be your witness." And it resonated with me, a deep thrum vibrating through my chest and arms every time she said it. *Witness*. What a powerful word. Why didn't we use it more often?

I unrolled my project, and the little bird, a robin, stared up at me. A common bird. Nobody ever thought twice about them, always hopping along the grass, fluttering to the low branches if an intruder came too near, flashing their bright orange chests. When people did think of them, they were regarded as cute, sweet little birds, their image plastered on Christmas cards even. Robins have been underestimated. They were aggressive and territorial birds that wouldn't hesitate to kill. True of most wild creatures, even us.

Where did the light touch this little bird? I swiped a line on the top of its round head, then smudged it with my finger, pressing the color down toward the bird's neck and wing. I'd finished most of the body last week and even filled in some of the background. What I hadn't started were its *talons*. Every time I thought the word, I heard the sound of that bird leg hitting my drawing paper in the courtyard last fall. In the moment, it had seemed like just a weird, darkly funny story to tell people about why I'd quit art. But it had been so much more than that. I'd stopped dancing, stopped making things, stopped running even. I'd made up a story about who the leg had belonged to, picturing a small bird, a thrush, being eaten by a red-tailed hawk or some other bird of prey. I never even considered it might have survived until last week as I stared at this piece of coal-black paper. In a quick flash, this cute little puff of an aggressive one-legged robin looked up at me from the paper. They'd survived and deserved to be seen.

I imagined its one remaining talon and set out to capture the light. Everyone worked silently today. Rachelle observed. And a whole hour passed that way. When Rachelle announced the end of the session, my cheeks felt flushed, and my fingers were slick and sticky with pastel.

I rolled up my finished drawing and pulled a rubber band around it. As I fit the work into my backpack, Rachelle approached.

"Finished?"

"I think so."

"How does that make you feel?"

I considered the question. Rachelle's questions some-times made me defensive, as if I didn't explain myself well enough, she'd kick me out or deem me not worthy. Maybe even laugh. "Content," I said.

She nodded, a small smile on her face, offering no judgement or response. Just a witness.

"Thanks for today," I said and turned to leave.

"I have another question for you," Rachelle said, her hands behind her back in a stance so open it made me wince.

I looped my bag over my shoulder and crossed my arms, waiting. This close, the fine lines around Rachelle's eyes be-came more prominent. She wore her brassy blond hair loose, her natural curls suiting her hippie persona.

"I could use an assistant. My group sessions on Tues-day-Thursday are bigger than this one, and my individual sessions are scheduled back-to-back those days. Would you be interested in coming in, gathering supplies beforehand? Maybe doing some light secretarial work for me?"

"Yes!" My heart leapt forward in my chest awkwardly, like the robin in my drawing, wobbly on its one remaining leg.

"I think it would have to be volunteer to start—"

"I don't care. Yes. I wanna do it. I wanna be around more of"—I indicated the art room—"this."

Rachelle let out a laugh. "Well, okay, then. It's settled. Can you be here tomorrow? Say ten-ish?"

"Yep."

"Great. See you tomorrow." Rachelle turned to leave, then stopped. "Is this art therapy something you're interested in? Like, beyond just group participation?"

I nodded.

"How wonderful. An opportunity for learning, then." Her lips turned up at the corners, offering one of her serene smiles.

"Thank you," I said. "For thinking of me."

"The sessions affect you deeply."

"They do. Help, I mean." I couldn't decide if I wanted to expand on that, but since I'd be working more closely with her, I did. "I don't know if I'd be really functioning without them, to be honest."

Rachelle nodded, listening intently; her expression remained impassive. I'd have to learn how to do that—listen, not judge. "Everyone comes to the art with a unique perspective. We'll be lucky to have you among our volunteers, Maeve. Have a blessed day." She walked out of the room, her skirt swishing all the way.

I left the building feeling lighter than when I'd walked in, but that had been true every time I came. This was good for me; this was right for me. And I couldn't wait to tell Hazel.

I hopped in my car and drove toward ACC where she'd decided to continue the peace officer training program after TO Gillespie had been placed on administrative leave. When we finally came forward about Stonie, we didn't leave out the part about him being involved in the original investigation. It hadn't taken Detective Patterson long to find the ways in which he'd made sure to keep his nephew's name out of the reports—witness intimidation, failing to log pertinent evidence, mainly Stonie's saved voicemails and journals, where she'd left detailed notes about the abuses she'd suffered, and just general shoddy work.

I merged onto the highway thinking of that, plus all the other things that had changed in the months since Michael's murder. Our cute little row house apartment with the cozy front porch had gone back up for rent last week, too many bad memories. I stayed with my parents and still worked at the diner. Eventually, I'd start looking for something closer to campus, especially if my work at Haven Center panned out or turned into something paid, but for now, it felt safe at home and that was what I needed most.

Hazel's aunt had found a one-bedroom in a converted Victorian within walking distance of ACC campus for Hazel, and she'd moved in shortly after we decided to let the row house go. I took the next exit and turned onto her new street, all cobbled and everything. I pulled into the first available space and took a breath, taking in the beautiful rows of Victorian homes, spired and veering off into a dozen different directions at once. I counted the colors. Most had three, specifically selected to highlight the structure's unique features; Hazel's place had nine. The gradient went from a dark, almost black-green to blue-green and jade to an antique gold, including all the subtle variations in between.

I turned the car off and pulled the keys out of the ignition. As I put them in my bag, I spotted Doug, bounding down the steps of Hazel's place. They'd made up, the two of them.

Doug knocked on the hood of my car and waved. I got out.

"Hey," I said.

"Hey, yourself." He seemed mighty cheery. "Did Hazel tell you?"

"Tell me what?" My heart dipped in my chest. What had been light and airy from today's therapy session became lassoed and chained to the insecurity I felt toward Doug. I bit the inside of my cheek and tried not to hate my own vulnerability. *Go easy with yourself*, Rachelle would say. *Your trauma will speak first in your body for quite some time.* I'd wrapped way too much of last year's traumatic experience into these feelings toward Doug. I'd almost lost Hazel after Shirlee's attack, and I'd latched onto that fear of abandonment. A total misdirection, but since I'd decided not to actually *deal* with anything, Rachelle said it would pop up in weird places. This was one of them. "What's up?" I cooled my tone, tried to relax.

"I'm leaving, transferring eventually."

"What, why? Where?"

"Because I wanna be in California."

"Okayyy, that seems kinda random, Doug."

"It's not." He scratched a spot beside his nose. "California's always been the dream. I was just putting it off going to school here in Ohio, making my family happy, ya know?"

I nodded; I did know. "What're you gonna do out there?"

"Find a place, go to the beach. Job. School. The usual things." He put his hands in his pockets and raised his shoulders. "Live a life that doesn't revolve around things, people, that aren't for me."

"She's for you," I said.

"Nah, not in the way I'd hoped."

"Well, good luck," I offered.

"Don't blow it with her," he said.

I laughed awkwardly. "Okay, I won't."

"I mean it. She's special."

"She is," I agreed. "But so am I." I winked at him, and he laughed.

"You always get me with those one liners," he admitted. "I might even miss them."

"Doubtful." I cleared my throat, then straightened the strap of my bag. "Look, I know things have been kinda weird between—"

He held up his hand. "Nah, don't do that. Let's just be friends, okay? Make sure to message me every once in a while." He looked back up at the house, at what I knew to be Hazel's bedroom window, took a deep breath, then turned away from it, from her. "It's just time for me to move on, chase my own dream or some shit."

"Right," I said. "I get that."

He held out his arms, and I moved in for the most uncomfortable hug of my life.

"Bye, Maeve," he said.

"Bye, Doug."

I watched him walk away because it felt like someone had to. He really was a good person, likeable in a way I knew myself not to be. After he drove off, I walked up the sidewalk toward Hazel's house. The owner had installed a buzzer, and I pressed the little button next to her apartment number.

Her voice came over the speaker, scratchy and thick. "Hello?"

"It's me," I said.

She rang me into the building, and I climbed the maze of spiraling stairs that led to her spire. At the door, I knocked and could hear her rustling around on the other side. Finally, she answered.

"Hey," she said like a sigh, then threw her arms around my neck. Mine fit neatly around her waist, the same way they had in the ravine. I inhaled her scent, a new shampoo, something kind of beachy and coconut.

I fought the urge to kiss her neck—we were still technically in the hallway. She backed away, making room for me to come inside.

"I saw Doug outside; you okay?" I asked.

"You should know that by now," she said, and a mischievous smile played across her features, lips and eyes. "I don't want to talk about him."

"I do," I said, not even trying to stop my lopsided grin. "Know that, I mean."

As soon as the door closed, I stepped toward her and kissed her, not waiting another second, relinquishing the need to draw out any tension between us. Been there, done that; this felt even better.

Her fingers found their way up my neck and onto my cheek. I pulled her tighter against me. She moved forward, and my hip banged against the kitchen table, but it didn't stop our embrace, didn't even come close. When the mattress pressed against my calf, I thought, *Yeah, this is way, way better than being at the edge of a cliff.*

And this time, we fell together.

Acknowledgements

"Every book I write is the hardest book I've ever written." I texted that sentence to one of my critique partners the other day, who is in the thick of it with their own book. The sentiment was especially true for *Amid the Haze*. While I'd always pictured Hazel and Maeve going on more than one adventure together, and had a good chunk of book 2 written when its predecessor came out, writing a sequel is really, really hard. I went back to the drawing board on this one multiple times. Luckily, I've assembled an amazing group of writer friends who, without their help dragging me through it, I'm not sure this book would have been possible.

Sarah Armstrong-Garner, you're a Godsend. You swooped in at the eleventh hour and pushed this book and me to the finish line. Without your detailed eye and swift reading, this book would be less than.

C. Vonzale Lewis, I should've listened to you sooner! You knew early on this book needed another POV, that the whole story couldn't be told completely through Maeve alone. I just couldn't see it until I'd gotten more meat on the bones, so to speak. But I always take your notes and suggestions to heart because they are spot on, friend.

Lauren Emily Whalen, thank you for your early read and notes when this story, and especially the ending, was such a mess! I think I finally found a path for Maeve.

To Elizabetta and everyone at NineStar Press, thank you for your work and dedication to story.

To my family, thanks for knowing I can do this when I don't think I can.

And finally, readers, I'm so grateful for you. Investing money and time and brainspace for other people's stories is no small thing. I hope I did you a solid.

About Jessica Cranberry

Jessica Cranberry lives in the Sierra Nevada foothills and spends most days striking a balance between parenthood, teaching, and writing suspense novels or eclectic short stories.

Email
booksbyjessicacranberry@gmail.com

Website
www.jessicacranberry.com

Connect with NineStar Press

www.ninestarpress.com

www.facebook.com/ninestarpress

www.facebook.com/groups/NineStarNiche

www.twitter.com/ninestarpress

www.instagram.com/ninestarpress